CHAPTER

Standing on the top deck of the Cal... home disappear into the distance Andrew Edward ... tourist talking longingly about when they would be back and how much they would miss their holiday haven in the meantime. But he wasn't listening. At that moment the only certainty in Andrew's life was the fact that he would never be back – ever. Sailing away to God knows where – and crushed.

He was only 24 but his youth had not stopped him becoming something of an island celebrity. To the tourists he was Drew the piper. Drew the boyfriend of the laird's daughter. Drew the key player in an island business that had grown these past few years to become a major employer. Now he was just Drew the despondent.

His long brown unkept hair was blown by the gentle summer breeze to cover his face hiding the tears. He slumped his 6'2" frame onto one of the red plastic seats bolted in neat rows to the deck for the winter storms.

The summer visitors had an unfortunate habit of treating the locals like specimens in a zoo asking intrusive questions and wanting to know all the detail of island life – and gossip. Drew's body language and obvious distress gave a clear 'do not disturb' message that was understood and he was left alone to his thoughts. And pain. A real agony created by events over which he had very little control.

The ship's Tannoy announced that it was time for last orders for hot meals but Drew's usual monstrous appetite had left him and he had barely eaten a thing in the hours that had passed since he made the decision to go. In the event that decision had not been a difficult one to make. Circumstances had dictated he had no choice but to leave the place where he had grown up, built an exciting looking future for himself and fallen in love.

Just a few weeks ago Drew's world was full of fun, excitement and fulfilment. Now that was all gone. Shattered into pieces and beyond fixing.

Sitting there being taken into an unknown future at a steady 16 knots he went over and over the events of the past few weeks trying to work out if he could have done things differently. It was only now that his dreams had come crashing down that he realised it was always going to be this way. No matter what he might have done he had virtually no control over his own destiny. It didn't ease his pain. It merely confirmed in his own mind the taunts of some of his fellow islanders that he had got carried away. Forgotten his place and was now paying a dreadful price.

His mind went back many years to the first time he had been the victim of the serious inequalities of island life. Then he was too young to fully understand. Now he could see clearly that when the chips are down the lairds win and folk like him loose. When he was just 11 he had allowed misplaced loyalty to have a potentially devastating effect on his life. Then, he eventually got over it. He knew today's agony could never leave him.

That fateful day 13 years ago in many ways had set him off on a course that led all the way to today and the top deck of the ferry and his raw despair.

All those years ago the weather had been much the same as today. Early summer sunshine. Almost the school holidays. These are the days that make the Hebrides special and draw visitors from around the world. At the end of classes that day the three oldest boys in the school had begged the headteacher to be allowed to go across the road to the white strand of soft sand and play for a while as they waited for the minibus to take them back to their scattered homes.

The head, Alistair Morton, had not given it a second thought and told them only to keep an eye open for the bus and watched as the trio ran over the road to the beach. He turned and went into his cramped office to begin catching up on his administrative duties, duties that were so often neglected.

Less than ten minutes had elapsed before their return. Before their bloody, screaming, hysterical and terrifying return. Hearing a gut-wrenching howling, Morton had hurried to the school door to see what was up. Two of the boys had blood pouring from facial injuries and already their clothing was soaked in glutinous red. The scene was so horrific and so completely out of his experience he momentarily froze. After this brief, fear-forced

2

The Island Race

By
David Johnston

pause he shouted for his wife Flora who came running. She, as ever, brought a little calm to the situation gathering the two obviously injured boys close to her and sending the third to fetch hand towels from the toilet. Morton's role was made clear as she quietly told him to get Dr McLeod, the island GP.

It was less than five minutes before Dr McLeod was on scene, her medical bag gaping open with an arsenal of first aid essentials, and working on both boys, assisted by Flora. Young Andrew, had a single long deep wound down the left hand side of his face. The other boy Mateusz Kowalski, had multiple cuts and bruises all over his face with blood oozing from several of the wounds. The third, George Emberton appeared to be just shaken and looked confused and frightened. Flora and Dr Alison McLeod led the two obviously injured parties away on the short walk to her home come surgery.

As the youngsters disappeared off at a brisk pace, each supported by one of the women, Morton turned to George and as gently as he could, and maybe it was not gentle enough, demanded to know what the hell had happened. The boy just stared blankly, with all the colour drained from his usually rosy face and a hint of a shiver passing through that slight frame. He seemed to want to say something but his lips just trembled. The stare off lasted only a few seconds and the teacher took him gently by the shoulder and led him into the school building, past the now empty row of pegs on the corridor wall and into the larger of the two classrooms.

"Are you OK George?"

Those words were enough to unleash a well of emotion trapped inside this young mind by the events of the last few minutes. At first it was a sob but within seconds George was crying, howling uncontrollably in such a way to make Morton worry that he was suffering from unseen injuries. Stupidly this had not occurred to him. Two boys pouring with blood and a third with no visible signs of bodily damage had appeared to him as just two casualties.

"Are you OK George? Have you been hurt?" he tried again.

3

George managed a few words in the midst of the sobbing. Very quietly he was able to say that he was alright. He obviously wasn't but Morton took it to mean that he was not suffering from some feared unseen injury.

By now the younger pupils had left their classroom where they had been enjoying after school games with Flora their teacher. They crowded into the tiny hall to find out what was going on. Seeing that at last the minibus had arrived Morton hurried them out as best he could without adding to George's obvious distress.

All his training and common sense told him now was not the right time to try and find out what had happened. A distressed 11 year old with no support questioned over a very serious incident by a teacher without witnesses. Not good practice. But he felt speed was essential. Was it an accident? Unlikely. Was someone else involved other than the three pupils? Equally unlikely. Was there an aggressor and a victim? Most probably.

Andrew had been a pupil at the island school for seven years and Morton knew him well and liked him a lot. He was bright, cheerful and willing despite a very difficult home life. Mateusz had only been at the school since the start of the Easter term when his parents moved over to work for the proprietors of the island estate. He struggled with English, the teacher had virtually no interaction with his parents, but he seemed a nice enough kid and always appeared to be trying hard. The third, George Embereton, was, like Andrew, a decent enough boy, a bit more reserved than the rest of the kids in the school, a bit more difficult to engage with, but certainly a pleasant young man, and a boy heading down a very different educational route than that which had been followed by nearly all of the school's other pupils over the years. Not for him the mainland comprehensive and its attached boarding hostel for kids from far flung communities but instead a great English public school where generations of his family had been educated.

Outside in the minibus the driver, Bobby Campbell, had been doing his best to keep the others calm and distract them from the violent goings on in their hitherto exceptionally peaceful school. So after making sure George was ok Morton led him out to the bus and told Bobby to do his usual run dropping the kids off round the island and he would phone the parents of the three involved first of all and then the rest of the mums and dads and let them know the bare bones of what had happened.

Morton had a hunch and it turned out to be correct: one call to the big house at the other end of the island found the parents of all three participants in these afternoon events. Lady Telford answered the phone and was told the little Morton knew. Obviously relieved that her son George was unhurt and apparently uninvolved she undertook to send the mothers of the two injured boys down to the doctors immediately. They had both been both working in the Telford's sprawling family home.

After a second quick call, this time to his education departmental line manager on the mainland to tell her about the day's events, the teacher walked over to the surgery hoping above all else that the wounds were not as bad as they looked.

The doctor's home was one of the few remaining examples of such properties that once would have been found in small communities across Scotland. Downstairs the two front rooms were the working end of the house, the doc occupying the rest of the building as her home. No receptionist, no appointments. Attend at one of the two daily surgery times, walk through the front door and turn into the room on the left. More untidy sitting room than doctors waiting area, but comfortable and clean. In the corner the Roberts wireless was permanently tuned to Radio 2 with its banal presenters and middle of the road music taking away all risk of those waiting to see the doctor hearing the conversations of people being treated in the next room.

Flora was sitting on the huge and rather battered old sofa with her arm gently round Mateusz, his face now covered in plasters and obvious blobs of antiseptic cream. He looked calmer than when Morton had last seen him, thankfully, as he sat almost disappearing into the cushions with their bright patterns resembling autumnal leaves and staring somewhat vacantly through the sash bay windows to the harbour beyond. He would have been able to see at least a short stretch of the beach on which whatever happened to him had taken place. It took only a raised eyebrow from Morton for Flora to give a condition report.

"Nothing broken. Mateusz is sore but he's being very brave, aren't you?" The boy nodded grimacing as he did so.

"What about Andrew?" "Stitches I'm afraid. Alison thought she might have to get a medivac but the bleeding has been stemmed and she's putting a few stitches in to hold it all together. She says apart from that one deep cut he's fine."

Now that the initial panic was almost over the enormity of the challenge faced by the teacher began to sink in. Working at a remote island school doesn't give a man much experience of dealing with incidents of extreme violence involving 10 and 11 year olds. His gut feeling was that in all likelihood Andrew was most probably to blame for starting whatever happened. Not that he was a violent sort of kid – far from it he was probably one of the best behaved and most reliable pupils to go through the school. The teacher thought he had picked up from George, by implication only, that it had been Andrew's fault. Mateusz? Well he wouldn't say boo to a goose, even if he knew how to say boo in English which he most likely didn't. In his six months at the school he had hardly made any contribution at all. He lapped up Flora's extra English lessons and was progressing steadily but lacked the confidence needed to demonstrate his new language skills to a wider audience.

All the basic administration that had to be done so far in reporting details of the incident had been completed. The department knew and had made it clear they were happy for matters to be dealt with by the school, but had stressed that in normal circumstances, on the mainland, the police would have been involved straight away.

Shortly after Morton's arrival at the doctors Mateusz' parents, Darek and Dominika, rushed into the surgery- their imminent arrival being heralded by the roaring sound of their exhaustless car. Flora stood up to allow the mother to collapse onto the sofa hugging her child close to her body, being careful, it seemed, not to get into contact with his plastered and rapidly swelling face. Her questions and his answers were in Polish and the others could only guess at what was being said. Darek seemed more angry than worried and sensing his rage was nearing tipping point Morton ushered him out into the passageway and through the door into the tiny front garden. In his broken English he demanded to know what had been going on and how it had been allowed to happen. Slowly, the teacher, trying as best he could not to appear negligent but to make it clear that he had no idea how his son came by his injuries but assured him the truth would be discovered. The father started to rant, partly in Polish and partly in very hard to follow English. The sentiment, however, became clear. He was sick of this place, sick of the people, sick of his employer and his squalid accommodation and this was the final straw - he was going to take his family away as soon as possible.

The tirade shattered the peace of the late afternoon with Darek's loud deep voice echoing round the buildings and across the crystal sea startling the handful of tourists enjoying the seemingly compulsory stroll round the harbour before the midges arrived driving them to seek sanctuary, most probably in the island bar. Attempting to calm things down Morton promised Darek that he would get to the bottom of it and deal appropriately with the perpetrator, if there was one. "If you don't mind my saying so your priority must be Mateusz and making sure he is ok. Take him home, keep him warm and watch out for shock setting it. If you are at all worried give me a ring, or better still Dr McLeod."

This gentle reminder of his main responsibilities did the trick and the Polish handyman went back into the surgery and came out seconds later holding his son's hand with mum following on holding the other.

Morton told them not to send Mateusz to school the next day, see how it went and maybe take Wednesday off too. He told them he planned to speak to all the boys involved and their parents. On Thursday after lessons, once things had calmed down.

As the Polish family walked back to their car Andrew emerged from the doctor's front door with his mum and dad in tow. Jim and Caroline Edward had gone straight into the surgery whilst the rest were all in the waiting room. Andrew's appearance shocked Morton. His normal white unhealthy palour had been replaced with grey making him look even worse than usual. His face was clean, the stitches looked awful, maybe half a dozen. Worst of all his wild long brown hair was matted with blood. Dr McLeod had done her best to clean him up but there were still

7

traces of blood on his arms and hands and his tee shirt was covered. Jim and Caroline were given the same advice as the Kowalski's and they appeared to accept it: for once managing to walk past the island bar during opening hours without popping in. Flora and her husband headed back to the surgery to see what they could learn from Dr McLeod. As ever she was the discreet professional and declined to say if either boy had told her anything of substance about what had been going on.

Later that night Flora and Alistair walked down to the beach with their two black Labradors, Ralph and Daisy. In the quarter hour it took to reach the school from their house the only words spoken were admonitions to one or other of the dogs. There was no one about which was quite unusual for such a beautiful evening at the start of the holiday season.

They reached the beach and settled on a rock. The events of the day were going round and round in their minds. Finally, Flora spoke.

"What on earth are we going to do? I just can't begin to understand what might have happened. I thought even just being here might help us understand – but it doesn't."

"The one thing we must do Flora is to make sure that it is handled here, by us, by the people who know best what is involved. I do not want it to escalate any more than it has. The police, children's panel, social work heavens knows where it could end."

"That's all very well Alistair, but we have two badly injured pupils – pupils injured while in our care. If we are not careful the whole thing could turn and we will get the blame for whatever it is that happened.

"Lucinda told me she's certain it must have been Andrew that started it and it does seem the most likely explanation. I know he's a quiet sort of kid but there is a lot going on in his life that we have little understanding off."

"Flora," he said cutting her dead. "Lucinda Telford has no idea what happened, unless George has told her something that he hasn't told us, and she would do well not to speculate." As the words left his mouth he felt it was an over reaction, but the Telford's bring out the worst in him. "Sorry Flora, that was a bit over the top, but you know what I mean."

"I suppose you are right, Alistair, but George can't have been involved because he is completed uninjured, not a mark on him. I can't begin to think what could have caused Mateusz to attack anyone. He hardly interacts with the other kids, let along fights with them. It has to have been started by Andrew, but why. What on earth could Mateusz have said or done to him to spark this off. It can't have been an accident; they are too quiet for that. Something is being hidden and you had better find out exactly what it is."

Morton went back to silent mode. Flora was quite right but stating the obvious was not helpful.

Ralph and Daisy, obviously bored of this repetitive analysis had wandered off. A piercing whistle bought them charging back from the far side of the beach. As they neared Morton could see Ralph had something in his mouth – a stick. In true Labrador style he dropped it at the teacher's feet. He picked it up and turned to Flora pointing to a nail protruding from the end: " I wonder if that is the weapon?"

Flora said she thought it would well be.

They stood up together and with the dogs running ahead started back home, past the school and up the hill. Walking once more in silence, Morton was wrestling with two thoughts. One how lucky he was in having a wife like Flora, steady, sure and sensible. The other one was the question that often troubled him: how could she bear to be friends with such a ghastly person as Lucinda Telford? Ok they shared a love of dogs but Flora knew full well how appalled Alistair was by the awful way the Telford's managed their island estate and the misery caused to so many others by their greed and incompetent idleness. It was a question he had learnt to leave unasked.

By the time Thursday afternoon arrived Morton was still no further forward in discovering anything much about the incident. He had asked the parents of all three boys to see him after school. Needless to say the Telfords had said they were too busy and as George was not involved there was no point in them attending. Jim and Caroline Edward were in the head teacher's office for the first part of the investigation. The Kowalskis were sitting on old fish boxes outside the building, the warm June sunshine a

9

sharp contrast to their frosty demeanour, waiting to be called in to give their version of events.

"Andrew it is very much in your interests to tell me the truth. To say exactly what happened. How Mateusz came by his injuries. How your face ended up like that."

Andrew just stared down at the desk in silence. Head bowed and silent. His parents sat either side of him not saying a word either. Their main contribution to the meeting was to fill the room with a smell of stale cigarettes and a hint of drink. It was after all, very nearly 3pm and on their way to the school Jim and Caroline had presumably stopped at the island bar for a refreshment to fortify themselves ahead of their ordeal.

Morton's sense of frustration grew the longer the silence endured. One of these young people, maybe even two, must be guilty of a vicious assault resulting in severe injury. This was not a mere fall out amongst friends, he feared, but savagery to a degree most unusual involving children so young, let alone supposed friends on a remote island. He held Andrew firmly in sight for an age and then switched his stare first to Jim then to Caroline willing them to say something in defence of their son. The silence was deafening.

He had known Andrew and his family since the boy was in a pram and taught him these past six years. Morton tried to put his liking of Andrew to one side - personal likes and dislikes cannot be allowed to colour the professionalism needed to deal with a situation like this.

Jim and Caroline were never easy to deal with. They were rarely completely sober for afternoon meetings and they suffered from an acute sense of imprisonment – trapped in a life far removed from the dream that brought them to the island in the first place. Morton felt sorry for them. It would be easy to criticise but the teacher had an understanding of how they had ended up in the mess they were in. At first they had relished island life and the freedom of the hills and shore but years of working on low wages and living in grossly substandard accommodation had worn them down and the hope and ambition of yesteryear had been replaced with drink and cannabis in a vicious circle of misery. It was clear to him they loved Andrew, but equally certain they would have found life without him much easier. Without their son they may have upped sticks and drifted away, with him they felt the need to offer what they considered to be a good home. These were not matters for today. He had to get to the bottom of what happened on Monday afternoon.

"Were it not for Mateusz' parents' insistence not to, I think my instinct would have been to involve the police," he told them somewhat disingenuously. "However you must be aware that I have, obviously, reported this incident to the education department and it is up to the director what further action to take. It would be really very helpful to have a clear understanding of what happened and why – not least to ensure it ends here and there is no repeat of this dreadful behaviour. Andrew?" The youngster looked up at for a second before putting his head down again. "I don't know what happened Sir". The words trickled out in a voice barely audible. Caroline put her arm round her son. "Andrew if one of the others hit you then you must tell Mr Morton. He needs to find out what was going on."

Morton was taken aback by her out of character gentle tone. It made no difference to Andrew. The boy simply pulled away from his mother and refused to look up.

After quarter of an hour or so of this gentle questioning it became clear that no progress was being made and so he asked the three Edwards to go home and discuss the whole issue amongst themselves again and hopefully realise the importance of Andrew telling his side of the story. Give his version of events. He stressed that conversations with the other boys and one set of parents might end in a suggestion that Andrew was somehow to blame and it was important for his side of the story to be heard before that happened, if it did. The Kowalskis were waiting outside so time may be short, he felt obliged to warn them.

The underlying fear was that the truth would never come out fully because of the involvement, maybe only as a witness, of young George. If three sets of parents were united in pressurising their young to reveal the truth of the incident then there was hope of a breakthrough.

It was entirely typical of the Telfords to conclude that one of the most serious incidents ever to happen on their island had nothing to do with them because of their son's perceived lack of direct involvement. They cared not a jot that their son was at least a witness to the children of two of their employees sustaining serious injuries in an act of violence, the exact circumstances of which were still to be established. Flora had tried to talk about what had happened with Lucinda during the couple of walks that had been taken as usual but the countess had just brushed it away in a "boys will be boys" kind of manner.

Morton suspected Mataeus' inability to reveal what had happened had less to do with his poor English than the fact he was maybe frightened to speak out – or even reluctant to incriminate himself. He was sure the boy could have said more, but for some reason was holding back. The brutal force had also left him in a state of shock. So much so Dr McLeod had given him some sedatives as well as painkillers.

The teacher felt it appropriate not to push the Polish couple and their son too much having more or less concluded that Mateusz was the victim in this and should be treated as such. In his faltering English Darek said that try as they might they had been unable to get anything out of their son these past few days and as he had become badly upset at times during their questioning of him they had decided to leave it. Completely.

"It can't just be dropped, Mr Kowalski, two young people have been seriously injured whilst in the care of the school. My care. It is simply not possible just to leave it like this."

He just gave a shrug of the shoulders and made no attempt to reply. His wife looked at the teacher expressionless. Mateusz, the scars and scratches still prominent on his face, stared at the floor, as Andrew had done a few minutes earlier. They were told exactly the same as the Edwards. Further inquires would be made and then there would be another chance for the boys to put their sides of the story.

Chapter 2

On the island the widely help presumption was that Drew, as he was known to everyone apart from his parents, had simply lost his temper with Mateusz who in turn had lashed out with the first thing he could find – maybe the wood with a protruding nail that the dog found on the beach. Somehow, it seemed, Andrew had managed to get the weapon and attacked Mateusz with it. For Andrew it was almost a case of guilty until proven innocent. As so often in this community rumour stood proud over fact and an absence of known facts allowed a field day for the gossips of the bar and shop.

So the next day with a heavy heart and a lot of trepidation Morton asked both lots of parents once more to see him after lessons. First Jim and Caroline squeezed into the little office with Andrew once more sat between them. There was no point in attempting pleasantries. It was going to be difficult no matter how the next conversation was approached.

"I have to tell you, Andrew that it has been suggested to me that you were the one who attacked Mateusz first – for no particular reason." The youngster sat bolt upright and turned to his mother.

"Hang on Alistair," said Caroline. "Who told you that? It's not true. Andrew wouldn't hit another kid, would you son? He's not like that"

"I hear what you say Caroline – and I certainly don't have any firm evidence to suggest that was what actually happened out there. But as I have already told you we have to find out what went on and why. Two pupils in my school have ended up with serious injuries. Of course it could have been worse but even with Mr and Mrs Kowalski wanting nothing more done I cannot, and will not, leave it at that. So Andrew – for one last time will you please tell me your version of events?"

The cry of the seagulls carried on the warm summer breeze through the open school office window was the only sound to be heard as teacher stared at pupil, pupil stared at the ground and his parents looked uncomfortable shifting their gaze between their son and his teacher. After a few moments of this uncomfortable stand off, once it was clear to they were getting nowhere, Morton asked Andrew and his parents to pop outside whilst he spoke to the others.

As Jim and Caroline left with their son in tow only Darek Kowalski stood up from where he and his family were sitting on the chairs in the hallway and without exchanging words or looks with the Edwards as they squeezed past he walked towards the office and in his heavily accented English said as far as he was concerned the case was closed. He did not even move fully through the door, let alone sit down.

"Meester Morton – Ve have decided to go – to leave the island, and ve are going tomorrow on the ferry. The cases are packed, the car is loaded and we are going," adding, as if it was necessary, "and ve are not coming back." Before Morton had a chance to respond the Pole simply turned and walked off ushering his family out ahead of him. Flora had been keeping her eye on things from in the classroom. As she saw the Kowalskis leaving she went in to enquire as to the outcome.

She could see from her husband's exasperated expression that things were no further forward. "You know Flora I just have not got a clue as to what happened. George's story, sketchy as it is, suggests that Andrew attacked Mateusz. It just doesn't add up though. Andrew seems to me the least likely person that I've ever taught to do that sort of thing. If Mateusz had attacked first then George and Andrew would surely have said. They owe nothing to him. He's only been here five minutes. If George was the culprit then how is he uninjured?

"I think I am going to have to say that I think Andrew is to blame and impose a punishment if only to stop the department sticking their noses in and the whole incident getting out of hand." And that's exactly what he did, with grave reservations. The balance of probability pointed to Andrew being the aggressor and a speedy conclusion and a report back to the department may close the whole matter down and let them get on with the remaining few days of term and then, bliss, the summer holiday. After an hour or so reflecting and talking it through with Flora he called Jim and Caroline back into the office with their son. They were outside the school but too late the teacher realised he should have left things until the morning. They had, of course, repaired to the bar in the intervening time and as soon as they came back into the office it was obvious anything said incriminating their son was not going to go down well and, spotting that they were well fuelled by drink, he was instantly having second thoughts.

Choosing his words extremely carefully the guilty verdict was delivered: "Andrew – it is evident to me that for whatever reason you attacked a boy in our school who is younger and smaller than yourself and caused him serious injuries."

His voiced quietened in the face of the obvious gathering rage of Andrew's parents.

"I am extremely disappointed that your time here at the island school should have ended like this. I find it beyond comprehension that you could have done such a thing." Andrew started sobbing once more.

"Wait a fucking minute." Jim leapt to his son's defence.

"No Mr Edward. You have had your opportunity to speak. I must ask you to listen to what I have to say."

Caroline's rage was obvious as she snarled: "But Alistair, how can you blame Andrew – just on what George said? He hasn't given you a proper story about what went on. You can't prove it was Andrew. You are just blaming him because his dad doesn't own this fucking island."

"Mrs Edward – and you Mr Edward – there is no need to use foul language. I have enough evidence to satisfy myself that Andrew was the aggressor in this. George told me his version of events at the time and Andrew's silence speaks volumes.

"Because I know that this is completely out of character for Andrew I am going to do all I can to keep this low key. But I have no choice but to suspend Andrew from school with immediate effect for two weeks. That means his time here ends right now because we will have broken up before the suspension is exhausted.

"It also means, I am sad to say, that he will not be able to go to the high school for his taster sessions next week and I will have to tell them why." He fixed Andrew in a gaze but the youngster avoided it. More tears were flowing down his cheeks.

15

Jim exploded with rage half yelling: "So with no evidence you are chucking the kid out of school and telling his next school that he's a little bastard. You are not getting away with this. We're going to take this further."

With that Jim leapt to his feet, pulled Andrew up from his chair and stormed out of the office without so much as a backward glance. The sight of tears glistening on Caroline's face as she passed in her husband's wake made Morton feel deeply uneasy, but it was done.

Sitting down in the quiet of the now empty office he agonised over what had just happened. Had Andrew's disadvantaged lot in life just been dealt another unjustified blow? About to start his new school branded as a thug after seven years of exemplary endeavour in the little school. What a dramatic divergence for these two island friends.

For George it was prep school and Chevening College – the great English public school that had educated so many members of his family. For Andrew in was a boarding school too. Not, however, one of the great schools that provide generations of national leaders, soldiers and sporting heroes. His boarding school was the hostel attached to the high school building on the mainland a lengthy ferry ride away. George had his head filled with talk of his ancestors' achievements at Chevening and he would feel an increasing expectation to join them on the various rolls of honour that decorated the walls of its ancient buildings.

Andrew too had received a fulsome briefing from older friends of what he could expect at his future school, far from home and subject to a regime where the island children were looked on as almost second-class citizens, certainly by their peers. How much worse will it be for him starting with this reputation hanging over him?

For George it meant aspiring to the greatness of those who had gone before him. Playing for the 1st XV, like his father. Captaining the 1st 11 like his grandfather. The Telfords had even managed a few of their number in various Tory governments over the years keeping up the tradition and status of their founding forebear.

For Andrew the next stage in his education, he knew, would centre on his ability to survive. Survive the loneliness of the

16

school hostel with the added fear of the bullying that he may be subjected to like others from the island had endured during their time at the mainland high school.

This educational challenge ahead for Andrew was one that made many families leave the island at their children's start of secondary school. They did not view boarding away from home for young children with the ease, or indeed relish, of the Telfords. It was a fact that island children from the many communities that send their young to the mainland often find the transition tough and even if they managed to avoid the attention of the bullies there was a record of poor supervision in the hostel which meant many of these kids fail to reach their full potential preferring instead a near feral existence, once school was over for the day, in the town.

The friendship that had been enjoyed by these two young people was not a mirror of their parents' relationship. Caroline and Jim, both worked for the Telfords. Caroline as housekeeper and Jim as a labourer come handyman splitting his time between the island farming enterprise and the upkeep of the big house and a number of holiday letting cottages dotted about the place.

Once these cottages had been family homes – now they were self catering holiday lets for tourists, a week of enjoying what they took to be an idyllic community in surroundings of great beauty filling their days walking the hills and beaches, surfing and fishing, enjoying the great outdoors and the warmth of the local people.

Once fully 10 men worked just in the gardens of the big house now the entire Telford empire employed a total of just that all year round with extra seasonal workers coming across for the summer months.

Jim and Caroline had few certainties in their lives but one thing of which they were sure was that they were not going to leave their home anytime soon. The island gave them shelter from a mainland life that they would struggle to cope with and allowed them to pursue their nefarious interests unbothered by the authorities.

Jim had built a ramshackle greenhouse of sorts near their cottage at the top end of the island that he used to grow some food and plenty of the cannabis he needed to keep him going.

17

When the illegal crop was exhausted, he would rely on other island smokers to include his needs in their buying trips to the mainland.

The couple rarely ventured off the island and whilst they were not keen for Andrew to go to the school hostel, reality dictated there was no choice in the matter.

George Telford and his wife Lucinda were, in the main, desperate to get off the island as soon as possible and back to the relative anonymity of their multimillion-pound Clapham home with its spectacular views on the North side of the Common. It is fair to say that for them life on the island was far removed from their ancestors' experiences. The big house fully staffed would have been joyous but when the staff was Caroline, often hung-over and always unwilling, there was little joy to be found. The heating was inadequate, the roofs barely watertight and the windows draughty, to say the least.

The upside of the island for George and Lucinda was that they were monarchs of all they surveyed, the downside was that had grown to resent the place in equal measure to the resentment in which they were held in by most of the island population. The casual observer would think the Earl and Countess of Telford would have had a lifestyle to be envied. The reality though was that they felt trapped – they, unlike their forebears, had to live more or less on the relatively meagre income this remote part of the UK could produce. The money coming in from holiday lets, and marginal farming did not add up to a glamorous aristocratic lifestyle. George Telford was handicapped by a severe lack of imagination and a crippling idleness that stopped him developing his assets to meet his family's ever growing needs. This in turn led to resentment when he saw other people in his "kingdom" making use of the island's undoubted qualities to create successful businesses for themselves.

Nowhere was this more evident than on the shoreline. One of his fellow islanders, Kenneth Murray, had come up with the idea of harvesting and processing seaweed. The earl had heaped scorn on the project – he hadn't realised the potential of the market himself – and worse still as far as he was concerned he had little control over the enterprise. His writ ran only to the high water mark – beyond that the rich seaweed beds that surround he island are part of the Crown Estate and the Queen's representatives were much easier for Mr Murray to deal with than Telford would have been.

The innocence of youth saw young George and Andrew protected from such stresses and concerns, free to enjoy their time at school together. Even at their young age they seemed to realise, in their own way, how lucky they were to have such a special education. Morton sometimes felt like a circus juggler spinning plates catering to the needs of nine pupils working together at different levels in the same room.

Flora was his salvation. They were a team. Many of the people in the community thought them eccentric. He did not give hoot what people thought, seeing their jobs as something of a all-consuming mission. Outside of work, winter and summer, they were always happiest when walking the island they had grown to know so well and love. Work, nature and God were their Holy Trinity.

The tourists who enjoyed a craic and refreshment in the bar with Jim and Caroline would not see the other side of this unequal equation. Andrew arriving at school the next morning reeking of cigarette smoke, his clothes often less than clean, his hair a mess and his appearance sometimes that of a young person who has not had an adequate breakfast. George too was not immune from carrying such signs of neglect only in his case the smell that often exuded from him was the dampness of the big house, the stale mustiness of a neglected home.

Obviously the Mortons were well aware of the challenges faced by the families of many of their pupils and quietly went about doing what they could to make up for the deficiencies of the kids' parents. Flora taught and prepared lunch for all seven pupils. She usually had something ready to quell the hunger of those arriving at the start of the day without the benefit of breakfast at home.

The majority of youngsters that had attended the school over the years had parents working for the Telfords which was shorthand for saying they lived in substandard accommodation, parents with virtually no disposable income and who often preferred to put their wages back to the Telford's over the bar of the estate owned hotel rather than into the future of their own children.

At least once a week Andrew and George would have tea together in one of their homes. Usually it was the Edward's cottage that was the venue. Cramped as it was it felt like a family home despite the smell of stale cannabis and cigarettes that so often hung in the air and the bottles piled at the back door on their slow journey to the recycling bin. The big house was always cold, George's parents never welcoming and as Andrew had spent many hours listening to his mum and dad complain about their treatment by the Telfords the truth was he almost felt as though he was siding with the enemy when he had tea at George's. Jim and Caroline however drew satisfaction from George's obvious preference for their home; it gave them a warm sense of satisfaction that they had one over their employers.

On the occasions the boys did go to the big house after school it was a wonderful playground. They spent hours charging round the huge building, fourteen bedrooms, three grand turrets and even went out onto the roofs and hid amongst the decorative battlements, much to the horror of everyone.

In the way of children it must have seemed to Andrew and George that the other had the more exciting prospect. George was certain life would be better if he were able to stay on the island full time and not live in the smelly city. Andrew was equally certain a life in London and a posh prep school would be immensely preferable than anything his future may hold. These youngsters spoke with accents that could best be described as unusual. Rough Essex, posh English, both infused with a distinct smattering of island Scottish.

If Jim and Caroline had been capable of self analysis they might have been able to see the toll their lifestyle was having not only on themselves but their child too. They could fool most people that they were on the island because of the opportunities it offered them: Their child bought up in a place of beauty with a carefree existence far removed from the negative pressures of the mainland. The truth was, however, that they could not persuade themselves that they were there for any reason other than their inability to cope in the real world. Both Edwards and Telfords trapped in a virtual prison. At least for the Telfords parole was heading their way as George neared the end of primary education.

So it was that the dreadful events of that Monday afternoon were concluded. The Kowalskis departing, the Telfords indifferent and the Edwards fuming. Jim and Caroline nursing a deep sense of injustice – their son branded a thug and his move to the big school darkened under the black cloud of suspension for violence. They took their bitterness to the bar and inflamed it with more drink as Andrew sat outside managing his anger and trying not to cry.

Nothing before or since has caused Morton so much anxiety and distress – he had tried to protect the innocence of the island and the young people involved and just ended up blighting the future of an 11 year old who needed all the help he could get.

CHAPTER 3

Five years later George and Andrew are back on the island at Hogmanay – George with his parents and a group of friends from Chevening College – Andrew home from the hostel for the holidays relishing his time on The Island. It is December 30.

The passage of time had allowed Mr Morton to rebuild his relationship with Jim and Caroline – and most importantly Andrew to the extent that he was a frequent caller at the teacher's home on his visits back to the island from school. His many successes at school had allowed the grim nature of his departure from island education to be left forgotten in a dusty file. Morton had the utmost admiration for the way he was developing into a high achieving and thoughtful young man, a stark contrast to his parents who had given their lives over to virtual full time drinking since their son's lengthy term time absences. Flora and Alistair were only too aware that the many hours Andrew spent in their home chatting away about everything and nothing was perhaps more about avoiding having to spend too much time at his own home rather than any great love for them – but it suited both parties.

The teachers had built their island home on a site chosen more for its spectacular sea views rather than shelter and easy access to the shore. It was an ever changing vista that greatly aided conversation as there was always something going on in the dramatic seascape to help fill in the silences, not that there were many of those when Andrew came calling. They had been giving him some help with his maths, he found the subject a real struggle. The Mortons felt they had a duty to support him, which wasn't difficult such was his likeable personality, but equally felt powerless to do anything much by way of substantial assistance, other than listen. The brutal fact was that he was the only child of fairly chronic alcoholics. They couldn't intervene in any meaningful way but Flora did use her dog walking friendship with Lucinda Telford to good effect when she could, dropping into the conversation news about Andrew, what a decent young man he was turning into sort of thing in the hope this would reflect well on his parents and maybe allow the Telfords to give them a little leeway – unlikely though that might seem.

It was mid morning on December 30th when Andrew arrived at the teachers' house for the first time that holiday, shortly after Flora had got back from her walk. Alistair was in the kitchen making some coffee and heating mince pies in the Rayburn when he heard Andrew arrive, west coast style, the most casual of knocks and straight in. When he realised who it was the tray of two mince pies came out of the oven and another four laid on – they would be needed. There was no surprise to see how over the years Andrew and George had drifted apart. So Morton was surprised when Andrew told him of a big house invitation he had received.

Caroline Edward could not have been in a worse mood when she came back from the big house after an unusually long day at work. She had a lot to be angry about. The Telfords seem to put in effort in inverse proportion to the number of people staying at the house. As it was going to be virtually full that meant Caroline would almost single handed be looking after the needs of the Telfords, and preparing for the arrival of their six adult guests, along with young George and three of his school friends. Her resentment was exacerbated by the fact that despite having been on the island for over a week George had made no attempt to get in touch with her son.

Andrew had asked if George had mentioned him at all.

"No he hasn't," snapped Caroline as she reached into the cupboard above the kitchen sink, its door hanging precariously from a hinge and a half. She pulled out that rarest of things in the Edward's household, a half drunk bottle of red wine and poured most of its contents into a beer glass that had not managed to reach the sink from the previous night.

Andrew was still frightened by his parents drinking habits even though he had developed an insider's view of being plastered during his badly supervised stays at the school hostel.

"You would think that he might have wanted to. I've not seen him since the summer holidays." His years of mainland education had resulted in Andrew's accent becoming ever more Scottish, but the occasional hints of Essex were still to be heard.

23

"Well he obviously doesn't." Caroline took a long gulp from the glass. It wasn't her first of the day. One of the few bonuses of working for the Telfords was that in the mornings there were nearly always half finished drinks left lying round to clear up, and it seemed such a waste to pour them down the sink.

"You had better face facts, Andrew," she couldn't bear to use the abbreviation Drew that was favoured by his friends and nearly everyone else on the island, "you and George have gone your separate ways. It's ok when you are kids together in the island school, but now you are heading in different directions. If you ever spend time with him in future it will most probably be because he'll be your boss, not your friend."

At that very moment the phone rang. Andrew answered it with a gruff 'hello', and was left near speechless when he recognised the voice of his somewhat detached friend on the other end.

"Drew its George. We are having a Hogmanay party tomorrow night and my mother has asked me to invite you."

The initial excitement of contact after all this time was killed stone dead as the significance of the wording of the question sank in. "My mother has asked me to invite you"

"That's a shame," Andrew had lied, "'cause I'm already going to a party with those folk from Birmingham we used to hang round with – the Thompsons."

"That'll be crap Drew. Tell them you've changed your mind and come up here. It will be great."

Drew felt his principles falling away as quickly as his mother could get her way through that half pint glass. He suspected the invitation was at best lukewarm He had reconciled himself to his mother's view that their ways had parted, but at the same time the glamour of the big house, though faded, still held an allure and the thought of meeting George's, no doubt, posh, school friends was too much to turn down. It would have to be fun.

"OK, thanks, I'll tell the Thompsons something. What time shall I come up to yours?"

"Come as early as you like 6 or 7 – we're having a big dinner then God knows what. But listen. I need you to do me a couple of favours."

The reason behind the surprise invitation was becoming clear as Drew realised it wasn't just the pleasure of his company that was required.

"Can you bring your pipes, and is there any chance some of your dad's dope could come with you too?"

So that's it, thought Drew, they wanted some entertainment and he was their best chance.

"Fine for the pipes but I doubt I'll be able to get any of dad's dope – I looked in the shed the other day and there did not seem to be much going on. I'll have another look though."

"Ok – do your best – see you later" – and George was gone as abruptly as he arrived. No chat, no catch up – just a couple of commands.

Andrew Edward's life at the high school had not been blighted by the feared isolation or bullying that so many island children suffer. In his first weeks away from home he had, quite randomly, taken up learning the pipes. The Great Highland Bagpipe had served him well. A natural aptitude for the instrument had seen him progress quickly from the starting point, the practice chanter, like a recorder but less tuneful, if that is possible, and onto the full instrument.

By the end of his second year he was playing with the high school's second pipe band and working hard to progress into the competing band.

Now at the age of 16 he played with the main band and had spent much of the previous summer taking part in various championships and some solo competitions as well, not without success.

Fully 6 feet tall and good looking with island wild long brown hair Andrew knew that he could be something of the star of the show tomorrow at the big house – the centre of attention come the bells of midnight and so he was not at all intimidated at the thought of being an island guest amongst a sea of privilege. He and his pipes could conquer anything.

"That was George, Mum"

"Really. What did he want?"

"His mother asked him to invite me to their Hogmanay party. With my pipes," said Andrew not mentioning the other matter that had been discussed.

"Are you going? I'd have told him to get lost."

Andrew recognised that his mother's suggestion was probably the one he should have gone with. He felt slightly sheepish in confirming that he was, in fact, going to go to the party. With his pipes. On the face of it Andrew's relationship with the great highland bagpipe was incongruous. Here he was English born and still with distinct Essex undertones in his accent and yet was one of the stars of the school mainly because of his ability to get the best out of this most challenging of instruments.

The pipe band had been a relatively new activity for the school, predating Andrew's time there by only a few years. However fired up by their inspirational tutor Patrick Young the band had quickly become a force to be reckoned with in competitions across Scotland.

Schools' piping is dominated by the private sector and Young's war cry of: "Come on – lets stick it up these posh kids" had hit a resonance with his players and their competitive outings had become something of grudge matches.

For Andrew, and the other players, it meant a status within the school once reserved for the best of the football team. Certainly, the school had enjoyed much more success of late in pipe band competitions than on the soccer pitch. As one of the better players Andrew had the respect of his peers and his teachers. All down to the pipes. Combined with his good looks and the aura of mystery created by his island existence he was also a big hit with the girls.

"You do realise they are just using you," said his mother unhelpfully.

"They just want the quaint wee island kid with his funny bagpipes to amuse their friends."

"It'll be more fun than staying here watching you and dad get getting off your faces, again."

Caroline ignored the insult but prompted by that assertion asked Andrew when he had last seen his father.

"Not since breakfast. He said he wouldn't be home until tonight."

At this festive time of year that most likely meant a day in the pub. The island hotel bar was dead out of the tourist season save for a two week burst of life at Christmas and New Year. Jim was a character. That is a shorthand way of saying that Jim was happy to spend hours on end standing at the bar entertaining visitors with tales of the island of yesteryear and giving them the low down on some of today's personalities.

This flow of information and entertainment did not come cheaply for the tourists though. It had to be kept moving along with a steady stream of half and halfs. For all his English upbringing and retained national pride Jim had been very happy to adopt the old-fashioned Scots working class habit of drinking half and halfs. A half pint of beer to wash down a measure of whisky. Bell's in his case. Bought by someone else, of course.

It suited Andrew and his mother best if Jim did come home completely off his face. That would mean a quick collapse into a chair, sofa or even bed and nothing more heard until the morning. If the process of inebriation had not been fully completed Jim could be an obnoxious drunk. Best to face the consequences of his drinking in the morning when he would just be hungover and unpleasant, not the unreasonable and frightening Jim that might be seen the night before.

"What are you doing tonight?" asked Caroline as though the island offered a multiplicity of activity choice for a teenager. She knew her son's options were, stay home watching telly, stay home playing a computer game, or go out to nowhere much.

For Drew, most of the time, staying home was best avoided. He had seen too many nights of drunken argument between his parents to hang about if he didn't need to. Computer games could have been more attractive but his parents had long since given up with the worldwide web – it cost too much and everywhere on the island it was slow. In their particular corner it was virtually non-existent.

"The Thompsons asked me over tonight as well. They said to come for tea so I'll probably head there quite shortly."

Caroline sounded relieved as she gave her permission, as if it were needed. The truth was she and Jim had rather grown used to Andrew being away at school for weeks at a time and whilst they did not actually resent his return to their rather run-down nest they did find it a little inconvenient. Not least because feeding the visiting 16 year old knocked a considerable hole in their strained budget. Basically keeping the wolf from Andrew's door cost his parents the equivalent of maybe eight bottles of wine a week – a substantial part of their usual intake.

"I'm going to go over to Sandy and Jean's for tea. They're having a wee night before party but I don't suppose your father will make it. He'll be in the bar until he runs out of folk to buy him drink," She might have meant to sound disparaging of such an arrangement but was actually only too happy to be a beneficiary of her husband's garrulous tale telling. Many the night she too had sat in the bar enjoying the generosity of the visitors maybe prompting the odd tale or two from her if, unlikely though it seemed, Jim was running out of stories.

She poured the rest of the wine into the half pint glass, it only came quarter of the way up, gulped it down in one and put the tins that would have formed the basis for Andrew's tea back onto the shelf and paused for a second.

Much as she loved the island and most of its people, Caroline often thought of what might have been. Her polytechnic degree might have been a starting point for a proper career. Where that could have taken her was a matter for speculation. One thing was certain. It would have led to employment more rewarding and better paid that being housekeeper for the ungrateful Telfords. But life is a series of compromises, she kept telling herself, and you had to look at the upside of life on the island as well.

The one thing she hated above all else about living in this remote community was the state of her home. She was not house proud, a matter obvious to even the briefest of visitors to the cottage, and a matter of great annoyance to her employers. There is though a difference between being relaxed about your surroundings and living in squalor.

Her habits and surroundings had impacted on her appearance and the years had not been kind. Her long straggly hair was usually in need of brushing or washing. Cheap ill-fitting jeans and tee shirts covered with holey jumpers were her usual attire. Occasionally Jim would catch a glimpse of her that reminded him of the girl he fell in love with twenty or more years before. But usually her tired face did not demand a second look from him or anyone else. She was 39, but even on a good day, easily looked ten years older.

Had Andrew not been away at school for most of the last five years she might have tried to do something about the state of their home. The fact that his visits back were increasingly infrequent as piping commitments and band friends kept him away from the island gave her the excuse, in her own mind, that she need not put much effort into the house.

It belonged to the Telfords, of course, had been a family home in the grandfather's day but had been a letting holiday cottage for twenty years before the Edwards moved in. The only reason it had been taken off the holiday letting market was that two decades of minimal maintenance had left it – a dump.

The basic fabric of the house was past repair. It had not been well built in the first place, no insulation, ill-fitting and now rotten windows, inadequate heating. She had worried when Andrew was little and living there full time that the ever present damp would get to him, leave him with a weak chest or compromised immune system. In fact the constant draught and poor heating seemed to have created a good foundation for a piper. His tutor at school was always amazed how from the earliest days that his stamina to keep playing was far in excess of most of the other kids.

The heating at Lighthouse View Cottage was provided, if that is the correct word, by a boiler behind the open fire in the sitting room. In the winter the non stop gales seemed not to pause on their journey through the house and no matter how much expensive coal was poured onto the grate the system never seemed to get up enough heat to do its job properly. The kitchen was immediately behind the fireplace wall and so benefitted a little from its heat and also had an expensive to run single bar electric fire in the space left where the old cast iron range had been taken out, probably in the 50's. It was only used on the coldest of nights and then for as short a time as possible.

The bathroom was an after thought; a lean too added on many years after the original house was constructed. It was one of those bathrooms that once the bather was immersed in the warm water it became a battle of will to get out again. As soon as the submerged parts of the body were exposed to the frigid air one could feel the cold biting deep into the bones. The towel would feel damp after even just a short time in the room.

At the other side of the house the two bedrooms were little better. Many was the morning that Andrew woke up to find a layer of ice on the inside of his window.

It wasn't until years later that Andrew actually thought about the difference in conditions between his permanently occupied home, giving, as it did, limited shelter to people working full time for the landlord, and the rather better equipped holiday cottages that had had considerable sums spent on them to ensure that the paying guests suffered none of the deprivations of the full time tenants.

Caroline pushed herself away from the sink and told Andrew that she may as well go now too. There was an understanding between the pair that this was the end of their day together. The mother would be at Sandy and Jean's house a couple of miles down the road until the chat, song or drink ran out.

Andrew grabbed his heavy tweed shooting jacket, wrapped himself in it, opened the back door and headed off into the wet and windy night. He was immensely proud of this incongruous jacket. It must have cost a fortune, fitted him well and just wasn't the sort of thing he would have been expected to wear. There was a story to it, a simple one. A stalker, a paying guest who had come to the island to shoot deer, had left it on a wall on warm autumn afternoon and after it had lain there a couple of days Andrew decided it was his. To have taken it on the first time of noticing would have been theft – however by leaving it for a few nights meant that he had found a discarded article. He knew the stalking party had left the island and so it was for him. And grateful for it he was as he fought his way through the icy wind to the old farmhouse where the Thompsons were staying. Lighting the way with the torch kept in his pocket - the total number of streetlights on the island – zero.

Chapter 4

Brian Thompson and his wife Linda loved the island. They had enjoyed holidays there for the previous 10 summers in a row and had in the past few years made it their festive season destination too. For them it was more about the place than the people. Brian was uncomfortable with the hard drinking culture of the locals – as a trauma consultant at one of the main hospitals in the English midlands he had seen far too much of the downside of alcohol and was anxious to set an example to his three children, Ben, a week older that Andrew, Mollie, 13 and 10 year old Tom.

The routine of holiday life on the island varied little between winter and summer for the Thompson family – December saw them doing exactly the same sort of thing as they did in the summer, only with more coats on. When the westerly gales were sending huge rollers crashing onto the beaches on that side of the island you would see them out with their strange cross breed little dog fighting the gusts to throw it a ball. While most on the island lit their fires and hit the whisky the Thompsons would be on the pathways and trails that they had got to know like the back of their hands.

As Andrew knocked gently on the farmhouse door and walked into the kitchen he knew he would be warm, welcome and well fed. Linda was a great cook and delighted in foraging as much as she could from the land and sea. Mussels gathered from the rocks were always a hit but Andrew had not dared try the fried seaweed that Linda worked so hard to convince him was delicious.

"Hi Andrew – great you could join us tonight – Ben's bored, he says, so you have the task of entertaining him," said the father.

"That's ok," smiled Andrew, "I'm sure Fifa and I will manage."

Brian Thompson wasn't the sort of man who liked his children sitting round playing computer games but, in the circumstances, tonight was fine.

Andrew heard a shout from the kitchen "Dinner in an hour" as he passed through the sitting room barely acknowledging Ben's siblings, and headed out into the front hall and the little room - pretentiously described as the library on the Telford's holiday website - where Ben was well into his, heaven knows how many, game of Fifa. Andrew sat down, picked up the second controller which obliged his friend to end the current match and start a new game, for two players, which he was only too happy to do. Human company was a bonus.

If he was the sort of man given over to reflection Brian Thompson may well have allowed himself a moment of contentment at the scene around him. Children all happily enjoying their island festive season, wife at home in the kitchen rustling up another great family meal. The evening stretching out ahead offering familiar and very real quality time together.

Mr Thompson radiated his medical persona. He was quiet, deliberate in all he did, and always smartly turned out. Boden. Bright cords, shirts and jumpers. His wife Mrs Boden, blond and thin, almost elegant in a laid back sort of way. The children too would not have looked out of place in a clothing catalogue – their smart clothes and groomed appearances quite at odds with Andrew's scruffy and dishevelled look. But he didn't notice and would not have cared if he had.

Despite their frequent visits to the island the Thompson family had not established many friendships locally, except with Andrew and to a lesser extent his parents, So it was something of a surprise to hear to hear a car pulling up outside, its headlights shining brightly through the sitting room curtains, thin as they were.

The engine didn't stop and no car door slammed shut – the back door of the farmhouse was flung open without so much as a tap and into the sitting room burst the familiar figure of the shopkeeper, Peter McGilvary. It soon became apparent he wasn't there in a shop capacity but in his role as leader of the local volunteer fire service.

"We need help Brian," he said. He looked frozen, his hair and face were soaked and water was dripping off his waxed jacket.

"There's been an accident. Jim Edward's been found in a ditch and he seems to be in a bad way. We've asked for a medivac and the chopper was on its way but it's been diverted to something more important and they say it will be at least an hour before it gets here – probably longer.

"He's been lying in the ditch for some time, we've got him out onto the road but don't want to move him any more. He's pissed, really really pissed and we can't make sense of what's happened or how he is. Can you come?"

Drawn by the racket Andrew and Ben had joined the group in the sitting room. Andrew half thought he had heard it was his dad who was in trouble.

"Is it dad you're talking about?"

"I'm afraid it is Drew," said Peter. "We're not sure what's happened but Brian's going to come down and see if there is anything he can do to help."

"I'm coming with you," said the now very worried teenager. "Do you think you should?" said Ben's mother, but Andrew didn't bother to reply and was already heading for his jacket and the back door.

He sat in the middle of the back seat leaning forward to listen to what he could of the conversation between the shopkeeper and doctor, but the roar of the elderly engine and a battering by the gale blown rain made it hard to hear.

"He was in the bar from dinner time, as far as I can work out," said Peter, "and he must have started walking home or on to someone's house.

"He's been incredibly lucky. He was only found because its such a shit awful night and a group of visitors left the bar to walk back to their accommodation and heard him moaning in the ditch. They'd been planning on staying longer in the bar but thought they'd be better off at home.

"If he'd been there much longer the stupid bastard would have been dead." Peter half forgot Jim's son was in the back seat but mainly didn't care.

Everyone knew what Jim was like, there was no point in even trying to pretend he had suffered some chance accident.

"So where is he now?" asked the doc.

"As I said, they've lifted him out of the ditch and he's lying on the road covered with as many coats as we could rustle up. God knows if he's moaning because of his injuries on just because he's so pissed."

This wasn't the first time a trip to the island had turned into a busman's holiday for Brian Thompson. Usually though it was children with fishhooks in their finger, or someone falling off a bike.

Alison McLeod had not been replaced when she retired a few years ago and now medical emergencies were dealt with by the first aid trained fire volunteers and the island nurse. They are always quick to call for a medivac in emergencies. The chopper crews seemed to like a flight out to the island – one of the most distant parts of their patch.

In less than five minutes Peter pulled up just short of the rear of a car with its warning lights flashing. As he jumped out Brian could see people huddled in the headlights and a figure he knew to be Jim lying across the road under what seemed to be a vast pile of various items of clothing.

Some of those crouched round the casualty looked as they were almost medical cases themselves. Stripped of their outer clothing for Jim's benefit they were soaked and shivering as the wind and wet combined to create a deep chill.

"Let the dog see the rabbit" said Brian reverting from carefree holidaymaker to concerned doctor in those few steps from Peter's car to the patient.

"Can you hear me Jim – It's Brian – Brian Thompson. You've had an accident. Can you hear me?"

Brian took a torch from one of the earlier arrivals and shone it directly into Jim's face. It was filthy and had what appeared to be superficial scratches mixed in with the mud. He must have gone down head first.

"You're bloody lucky Jim – you could have lain there all night and you wouldn't have been here in the morning."

The complexity of that contention passed them all by.

For Brian Thompson it was far too close to his normal working day for comfort. Even with the gale and the rain the smell of drink from the casualty, his helpers and the shopkeeper was all too real a reminder of the worst of his hospital life. At least here there was an air of cooperation not the open conflict so often found in A and E departments these days. He lifted Jim's arms, gently and one at a time, then shuffled down a little and did the same with his legs. There was no discernible reaction from the patient. Brian did his best to lift the pile of clothes off Jim's torso and slid his hands underneath and pressed firmly around his stomach and chest area. Again no reaction.

"I think there doesn't seem to be anything too much wrong – other than far too much to drink. But it's a deep ditch and I'd be keen to keep going with the medivac in case there are some internal injuries – has anyone heard how long the chopper's going to be?"

As the last of the question left his lips Jim turned his head to one side and threw up. Powerfully. One of the visitor helpers was caught by a bit of the shower of vomit and all were repulsed by the sight and the smell.

Andrew's concern changed to embarrassment.

"They reckon about half an hour or so," said a voice from behind the doctor. Brian turned to see who was speaking and how much credibility to give to the claim. He recognised another of the volunteer firemen.

"But they say the weather's too bad to try landing anywhere other than the airstrip so we will have to move him up there quickly."

"Right. Ok. We need to keep him as flat as we can in case something is broken." Shouting to the wider audience that had been deafened by the wind the doctor asked if anyone had a vehicle that could accommodate the casualty and keep him flat on what was obviously going to have to be a slow drive round to the airstrip.

"I can put him in the back of my van", said another islander who turned and starting running back towards the bar where his soon to be makeshift ambulance was parked.

The lack of officialdom and assistance on the island brought benefits and challenges in equal measure. The loss of the doctor had been felt strongly by the community. The fact there had never been a police presence on the island bought immense benefits especially to those who chose to ignore some of the more demanding aspects of mainland law and the firemen were able to turn their hands to assist in most emergencies.

The opportunity for young and old alike to drive whilst over the limit, or indeed dead drunk, was near universally regarded as a boon for island life. It was commonplace the morning after major social events to see a car or two being pulled out of ditches, fences hurriedly repaired – new dents on the vehicles of locals – even the odd wall knocked down.

Usually there was no serious injury. Now here they were dealing with a potentially very bad situation and there was no car involved. Just an inability to walk in a straight line.

The van drew up and Brian took two of the bigger jackets off Jim, laid them on the ground. He detailed six people to form a stretcher party. As carefully as possible they lifted Jim, supporting his head, onto the coats and in a seamless continuation with three men each side lifted the injured party towards the open back of the van. Jim was silent save for erratic shivering and chattering teeth as Brian jumped into the back beside him. The doors were shut and, rather slower than usual, the van set off for the airstrip.

The Land Rover fire appliance was waiting for them with its blue lights flashing and headlights on full beam. It was usual practice for guiding the chopper in at night.

Barely five minutes passed before the beating of the engine signalled the approach of help. The pilots of these machines knew the islands well and despite the ferocious wind the helicopter settled hardly fifty metres from the van. The paramedic ran across, Brian made a quick introduction and explained his diagnosis – the patient was drunk, hypothermic but otherwise probably not too badly hurt.

"It's been hard to examine him to be honest but I don't think he's suffered any terribly serious injury."

Transferred to a proper stretcher Jim was loaded into the helicopter casualty bay and in an operation lasting less than five minutes he was airborne and off to the mainland hospital.

The chopper had no room for passengers so Andrew was left on the ground staring up into the darkness as the light of the aircraft disappeared from view. He felt slightly guilty that he was not more concerned for his father's welfare. But he wasn't and so that was that.

"Thanks very much Brian," said Peter. "It was much better that you were here. We would have been okay but to have an expert in charge makes the whole exercise that much safer.

"I'll give you a lift back to your house. What about you Drew? Where are you going?"

Before the youngster had a chance to give the question proper consideration Brian said Drew would have to find his mother urgently and tell her what had happened. So the three of them climbed back into Peter's car. Andrew asked to be dropped off at Sandy and Jean's house confident that once she had arrived at the party his mother would not have been planning on leaving until well into the early hours.

As Peter drove away Andrew ran to the cottage backdoor his torch lighting up the pathway. He didn't feel the need to knock. It was an emergency and anyway this was the house of his parents' best friends. Once inside the tiny porch he could hear music and laughter. It was the festive season and Sandy and Jean liked a party. He walked into the kitchen and screwed up his eyes as he was hit by the light and a huge cloud of cigarette smoke. It was still quite early, barely 9pm but it was clear to Andrew that the party was well underway.

"Come in Drew and get yourself a drink," enjoined one of the guests. Andrew ignored him, saw his mother wasn't in the kitchen and slowly edged his way through the revellers into the front room where he found her sitting in a high backed wooden chair deep in conversation with the host. She was not expecting to see Andrew for some hours and expressed her surprise in terms she reserved for evenings of alcoholic excess.

"What the fuck are you doing here? I thought you'd gone to your posh friends for tea."

Andrew put his head as near to his mother's ear as he could, Sandy was standing pretty close by, and told her his Dad had been injured in an accident and flown off in a helicopter. It was hard to determine exactly what emotion this engendered in his mother.

"What the fuck happened?"

"We're not sure but he was found in the deep ditch up from the bar. No one's sure how long he was there. He was pissed Mum – really pissed according to the folk who found him.

"Ben's dad doesn't think he has anything seriously wrong with him but he was really cold and had a few cuts round his face so they thought they'd better get him to hospital."

Sandy heard bits of what Andrew was telling his mother. "Caroline do you want to use our phone – which hospital has he gone to Andrew?"

Caroline asked Andrew to repeat Brian Thomson's verdict on the state of her husband.

"Mum, he's not certain but reckons Dad's just got a few cuts and bruises, he's really cold, hypothermic, but otherwise ok."

"Nothing to worry about then," she said raising her glass of red wine first to her son and then to her host. "No need to break up the party then – is there any more wine Sandy, my bloody glass is empty." Andrew wanted to challenge that claim because it clearly wasn't but before he could say anything Caroline caught sight of the bottle at Sandy's feet and helped herself.

Andrew was beginning to feel really uncomfortable. Enough of what he had told his mother had been overheard to send a flutter of concern round the room. In true island tradition by the time news of Jim's mishap reached the kitchen it was most likely being described in terms of a major drama with severe medical implications.

"Mum – I think we should go home. Dad will be in the hospital quite shortly – we can phone and check he's ok."

"Listen Andrew – if your pal's dad reckons he's fine then he's fine. Your father has spoilt too many nights out for me with his antics – there's no need for him to ruin this one."

Andrew's discomfort turned to severe embarrassment. What woman would be so uncaring as not to want to leave the party as her son's father was being medivacked away. But the teenager knew his mother well enough to realise that at this stage of the evening there was no point in arguing with her. She often complained of his father's difficult behaviour when he was drunk. She never managed to realise that she could be every bit as bad.

"Whatever – I'm going home – I'll phone the hospital later and come back and tell you if he's dead"

"Don't be such a drama queen Andrew. Anyway, if he is dead there's fuck all I can do about it."

That last sentiment was delivered in such a loud voice as to leave no one in the room, and maybe even the next room, in doubt as to exactly how Caroline felt about her husband's plight. Andrew turned his back to her and walked straight out of the room ignoring neighbours and friends as they asked what was going on.

He squeezed once more through the crowded kitchen and as he neared the back door paused for a second in front of the makeshift bar groaning with its array of supermarket whisky and cheap wine. He took a plastic cup and lifted the sole bottle of vodka and made to pour himself one. Then stopped, thought for a second, put it down again and, at speed, exited out of the back door into the porch and back into the night of gales and rain.

The torch once more lit the road ahead as Andrew mulled over the events of the last hour or two. It has hard walking into the wind but he confirmed to himself he had been right not to ask for a lift. He wanted the weather to help clear his head. Whilst he was perhaps, at that age, not able to articulate the sentiment as well as he might like to, he couldn't help but reflect over and over on the evening he had just had and its wider context.

There could be lots of social, political, economic and even genetic forces at play – but put all that aside and for Andrew it came down to one simple question:

"Why can't I have a family like Ben's?"

Chapter 5

Lucinda Telford had not been happy about the guest list for the Hogmany house party. She'd told Flora that she didn't like having people she didn't know all that well to stay at anytime of year – in winter when weather often disrupted the ferry service and people could be stuck much longer than their intended stay it was worse.

The added complication of having her teenage son's first real girlfriend, Claudia Williams, and her parents to stay was proving to be too much.

Claudia had become a fairly frequent visitor to their homes both in the Hebrides and in London but they had never met the parents. When she did stay with the Telfords separate bedrooms were enough to satisfy Lucinda and her husband that nothing untoward was going on – though his lordship wouldn't have cared if it was.

The parents actually quite liked the girl but they had long harboured a belief that she was not "one of us".

That belief was confirmed when they had met Claudia's mum and dad for the first time as they came off the ferry. The three Telfords had been standing at the ferry terminal watching through the rain as their son's love of the moment hurried down the pier with her mum and dad stooped against the downpour behind her, all three of them dragging wheeled suitcases that looked for too big for the length of time they had been invited to stay - just five days.

The young girl took the social lead air kissing first Lucinda and then Lord T, as she liked to call him.

"These are my parents" she said without bothering to supply further information preferring instead to walk into the arms of young George for a lengthy embrace.

"Hello I'm George and you've spoken to Lucinda on the phone I think"

"Pleased to meet you at last George – I'm Jack and this is Sally. What a bloody awful day. Claudia's told us a lot about your island but to be honest as the ferry was coming in I couldn't help asking what on earth we are doing here. No offence I'm sure it's a lovely place but this is the first new year since Claudia was tiny that we haven't been skiing." If no offence was intended by Jack's remarks the lack of intention was lost on their recipients and the Telfords took it as confirmation that Claudia, Jack and Sally Williams were indeed not "one of us"

The four adults laughed, perhaps a little too nervously for comfort, and Lord T told them to jump into his Land Rover.

The two teenagers that had followed the Williams from the ferry were quiet and largely ignored, rather rudely. They were George's school friends over for a Hogmanay bash. Tom Scott and Orlando Russell. After a graceless welcome George told them to wait at the ferry terminal, there was no room in the vehicle and someone would come back to collect them.

George had asked the two boys who shared his boarding house at school to come up to the island for a party before he discovered the Williams family were giving up their luxury new year break for a taste of island life. How he wished he had been brave enough to uninvite them. A cosy five days with his girlfriend now compromised by the need to look after and entertain his school friends, not ideal but they were here now and he was just going to have to make the best of it.

It was these boys' first ever visit to Scotland, let alone an island, and they were excited to have been invited. They stood at the little terminal as the bustle of the ferry coming and going died away eventually leaving just the two of them sheltering against the weather behind the now closed building

A few of the locals had enjoyed a wry smile at the pair dressed as they were head to foot in Jack Wills and carrying JW holdalls. Very English. Very Public school.

It was a good 20 minutes drive from the ferry terminal to the big house. The Land Rover's age and state of repair did not help conversation flow between the Telfords and Williams, shouting to be heard over the roaring exhaust.

Gorge and Claudia had squeezed into the back with the giant cases and took no part in the chat preferring to exchange whispers and kisses as they bumped along the single track road

"Claudia says your family has owned this place for a long time George."

"They have Jack – we certainly have. My great grandfather bought it in 1885. He loved deer stalking and apparently just adored the island, as did my father and grandfather. Now I'm stuck with it." Jack and Sally speculated later in the privacy of their bedroom in the big house whether Lord Telford's sentiment had been one of resignation or if he was just trying to be funny.

Lucinda tried to offer reassurance. "It's a shame you've arrived on such an awful day – it really is a beautiful place – I do hope Claudia has told you of how spectacular the island is when the weather is kind to us."

Sally jumped in to try and rescue what she recognised as a bad start with some glowing praise. "She most certainly has Lucinda. She said the week she spent her in August was one of the best of her life. I'm sure you and George's generosity was a big part of that but she told us all about your beautiful boat and picnics on various beaches and fishing and catching lobsters and all that sort of stuff. It just sounds idyllic."

"Yes we do love it, especially in the summer," said Lord Telford, "it's just as well because we are stuck with it. No hope of getting rid of the place as things stand. Politics, bloody politics. It's the nats. Politics of envy."

Lucinda moved quickly to spare her guests from one of her husband's rants. "George worries about the politics of the country and their effect on us as a family – but I prefer to concentrate on the family and our home and our island and let the politicians get on with it."

His lordship had put in place a plan to impress Claudia's family which swung into action as the Land Rover stopped at his front door. One of the estate staff emerged and opened an umbrella to shelter the first of their Hogmanay guests as they dashed through the driving rain to the house. A Gaelic welcome would have topped things off perfectly – but Frederic was Polish and didn't speak English all that well let alone the ancient language of the Gaels.

In the imposing hall the first time visitor would find their eyes being drawn to the huge log fire sending shadows dancing round the space as it crackled its welcome and also to the stags heads hanging on all four walls. It took a couple more visits to the hall for folk to see the threadbare carpets, rather rickety furniture and peeling paint.

"This is Caroline: Jack and Sally if you find you need anything Caroline will sort it out for you, won't you my dear?"

Caroline nodded and managed only a faint smile her head echoing round and round with the words "Oh I will, will I? I bloody well will, will I?"

"Claudia you are in your usual room," words uttered by Lucinda to offer direction to the girlfriend and comfort to the parents that two bedrooms were involved. "Caroline will you show Mr and Mrs Williams to their room please?"

"Please – Jack and Sally, Caroline" said Mr Williams trying to show his credentials as Jack the lad.

"Please follow me Mr and Mrs Williams," said Caroline wanting to demonstrate to all concerned that she knew the way a relationship between staff and guests should work, even if the guests did not.

Caroline led the couple up the main staircase and round the galleried landing to the left from where they got another good view of the log fire and on into one of the large bedrooms at the front of the house. Even on a day like this with the light starting to fade, it was after all nearly three o'clock, Jack and Sally Williams could see what an amazing setting the house enjoyed. Caroline told them to use the bathroom immediately next door. She assured them no one else would be requiring it so make themselves comfortable. "If you need anything I'm about until 6 after that just ask Lady Telford"

As she left the room the Williams were drawn to the window. The scene wasn't exactly their cup of tea, they preferred city life or the Alps, but the view was nevertheless pretty stunning.

The land immediately to the front of the house was given over to grass – the windswept location meant there were few trees but an army of bushes stood guard in front of the dry stone wall which separated the lawns and the Hebridean machair which in turn led down to the beach. In the summer months the machair was a brightly coloured carpet of wild flowers. The beach was one of the most photographed and painted stretches of sand in all the islands. It was always hard to determine which was the nicest view – looking from the house to the sea or the shoreline to the house. Probably the latter as long as you were far enough away from the house not to see the many blemishes that now covered the fabric of this near 150 year old building.

Lord Telford used to joke that the number of bedrooms in the house was dependent on how hard it was raining. The joke lost its effect when the ceiling of one of the worst affected bedrooms actually collapsed under the weight of water that had poured through the roof during a particularly bad storm. That was more than two years ago and it still had not been repaired. But bedroom space wasn't in short supply at the big house.

As Caroline headed back to the kitchen she passed George and Claudia in the hall. He was sitting in one of two great, grand chairs built out of stag's antlers and covered in rich red velvet that stood on either side of the fire. Claudia was on his knee.

"You two ok?"

"Yes fine thanks Caroline," said Claudia Is there any chance of a cup of tea? – I know mummy and daddy would love one too."

"I'll see what I can do – I've not time to go running round the house mind so I'll just put a tray in the drawing room. George – the fire is set – it would be a good idea to light it now – you'll have matches I'm sure". A reference to George's smoking habit that caused his mother so much concern – had let to many scrapes at school but was another area of indifference to his father.

Claudia gave him a peck on the cheek, grabbed his hand and led him off to his fire lighting duties.

As Caroline prepared a tea tray in the kitchen her mind turned to her usual thought. What did a beautiful and seemingly intelligent girl like Claudia see in George? George to her mind was average. Average everything. Height, intelligence, manners. The only point at which he deviated from average, in Caroline's mind, was acne. The island joke was that young George had more spots than his father had sheep. Whilst not true by any account it was a good indication of the magnitude of the problem.

Claudia seemed oblivious, which could only be a puzzle to any observer. She was always immaculate. She had a real public school girl figure, long blond hair that alternated between free flowing and tied back depending on her mood. Beautiful facial features and a soft smooth skin, usually slightly tanned and always made up. She had endured insults and jokes from her friends when she first started going out with George. Her popularity amongst the girls meant that the insults were never too harsh and the jokes never too cruel.

In their bedroom Jack and Sally unpacked their giant cases into the various draws and wardrobes that lined the walls. Every so often one of them would look out of the window and peer into the fast disappearing view. The white horses of the raging sea the last aspect of the scene to fade into the darkness.

"You know Jack, when Claudia first told us about George I used to think how it would be the almost crowning of our success if one day they were to get married and Claudia became the Countess of Telford.

"I've only been here a couple of hours and I just could not think of anything worse. We've worked bloody hard and created great opportunities for her. Imagine if that all went for nothing and our hard earned cash ended up being used to patch up this dump."

"I know – and George's mum and dad just look plain miserable. I told you we should have ducked out of this and gone skiing. Just think we would be back at the Cheval Blanc by now – enjoying a cup of tea and some cake as a warm up to yet another fantastic dinner with real friends drinking the best France has to offer. Instead we are here on some stupid island about to be force fed haggis and shit whisky I imagine."

"I know but we are going to have to make the best of it. Claudia is desperate for us all to have a nice time. Hopefully her fling with George won't last much longer - but when it goes tits up I don't want us to get the blame for it,"

Just then there was a gentle tap on the door. Claudia opened it and invited her parents to join her and George in the drawing room for tea and shortbread.

"Come in a minute darling, your mother and I want to ask you a few things."

Claudia walked into the bedroom, by now nothing short of gloomy as it was fully dark outside and the occupants had a choice between two or three inadequate lamps or the overpowering glare of the antler chandelier in the centre of the ceiling.

"You warned us that George's parents weren't the life and soul but mum and I are a little fearful that they may be about the dullest people ever."

"That's not very nice dad. Everyone doesn't have to be a loud mouth like you, you know. They've been perfectly sweet to me. I really hope you are not going to muck up me and George. You are only here for a few days they really are not at all difficult – just shy. I'm sure once you've all had a couple of drinks it will be fine."

"Well I hope so darling. You know your dad doesn't have a lot of patience and I certainly can't see him enjoying bracing walks on windswept beaches. But you are right. We know how important this is to you so I'll make sure dad behaves."

The truth was it had been compromises all round, except for the teenagers. George had manipulated his mother into inviting Claudia's parents there in the first place. Lucinda Telford would not budge on her plans for Christmas and New Year. It was family time, for the family to be together. She had been horrified when George had told her he was invited to go skiing at the end of December with the Williams and would probably spend Christmas with them too in case he was stuck on the island by bad weather. Lucinda's real sorrow was that their daughter Alice would not be with them for the festive season. Her gap year had started off with a ski season and she was having far too good a time to keep in touch regularly let alone endure another island festive season.

There had been a battle in Clapham between the two conflicting sides. "I'm not filling the house with strangers for New Year" on the father's side and "I'm not having Christmas and New Year without George" on the mother's.

Lord Telford's grandfather's grandfather clock struck 5 as Jack and Sally entered the drawing room to find young George and his parents already there with their daughter and the two school friends.

"Come in and get a seat near the fire I'll get you some tea and you must try Caroline's home made shortbread." Lucinda was careful not to go into detail as to why Caroline's shortbread must

46

be tried, In truth it was a variable commodity, sometimes it worked and was almost as nice as the stuff you bought in the Co-op – other times it just fell to pieces managing to do the seemingly impossible and be brittle and soggy at the same time.

"I expect you'd rather have a drink after your journey" tempted Lord Telford. Jack could hardly believe his ears as he heard himself turning down the offer. Every part of him wanted to say yes – a bloody big gin and tonic thanks, but instead the words "Tea's just fine thanks" came out much to his horror and Sally's puzzlement.

Lord Telford hid his disappointment.

As the adults struggled to find common ground and make conversation young George was noticeably reticent to make much of an effort. Later he would tell Claudia it was just because he knew what an arse his father could be and didn't want to seem as though he had much in common with his old man. The tea interlude did end up with Lord Telford on one of his usual hobby horses. He hated the island. The island hated him. He hated the Scottish government and they were out to get him. Jack and Sally may have found the tirade interesting coming as they did from the south of England and on only their second ever visit north of the border. Young George thought it somewhere between boring and offensive. Whilst he had allowed his friendship with the person he knew best on the island to drift he still felt a real connection to the place which had seeped into his soul during the first 11 years of his life spent mainly on the place that he still thought of as home.

Caroline tapped at the drawing room door, peered round without opening it far and announced her departure for the day. Lucinda Telford couldn't stop herself looking at her watch. 5.30 – another early finish. Noticing the unspoken reprimand Caroline assured all that Fiona was in the kitchen and everything was on course for dinner at 8.30.

Fiona Grant was the cook at the big house on special occasions. She would cook dinner for the eight of them tonight and for tomorrow, Hogmanay, she would pull out all the stops and produce a wonderful celebration dinner for 15 people when the party was joined by Lord Telford's brother and sister and their spouses and children. Mrs Grant was unusual on the island.

She liked the earl and countess and in turn was highly regarded by them. She also enjoyed working at the big house and her efforts were appreciated. Other employees suspected her wages were rather more than most of the rest of the estate staff. She didn't know or care.

By the time the main course was served that night the combination of pre-dinner drinks and a delightful white Burgundy had broken the ice and conversation was flowing. The main topic was the challenge of living in such a remote place and the difficulty of creating any profitable business. To Jack it was obvious this was a family going nowhere fast. He gleaned that apart from the rent from a smallish property portfolio in Shropshire the Telfords were trying to finance something of an aristocratic lifestyle from the paucity of an island income.

The reality was, Jack thought, that the entire value of the Telford's island assets would have added up to rather less than the value of a couple of houses in the Clapham Street where they lived for a lot of the year these days.

Young George, Claudia and the school friends kept to themselves as much as they could at the end of the table, the parents oblivious to the considerable quantities of wine they were consuming. Whilst this soiree was going on at the big house Jim's drama was being acted out on the roadside.

Chapter 6

When Andrew finally got home from Sandy and Jean's house he couldn't make up his mind what to do. He half thought about going back to the Thompson's but concluded that he should be on hand should his mother turn up. He even considered phoning the hospital to check on his dad but was too nervous to try that. So after an hour of mindless TV watching he went to bed. An hour of television had been about all that could be managed. The fire had gone out and he couldn't be bothered to relight it and so his bed was really the only place of warm refuge. At some point in the night he was aware of a car stopping for a couple of minutes by the cottage and he heard what he presumed to be his mother coming in and then went back to sleep again.

The first thing that Andrew noticed the following morning when he woke to his phone alarm at 8am was the silence. The wind had finally died down and all that he could hear as he lay in bed were sheep and geese. This for Andrew, and all the Edward family, was the hardest part of the day. Getting out of bed on a winter's morning. Leaving the warm cocoon of woollen blankets and an old fashioned eiderdown to brave the freezing damp air and get dressed as quickly as any human could. As he opened the bedroom door he could see his mother was already up. Caroline had an admirable ability to throw off the excesses of the night before and function to quite a high level despite the undoubted hangover that would stay with her until she found herself at the big house "tidying up" the glasses from the night before.

"Have you phoned the hospital to see how dad is?"

"Not yet" but to be honest such had been the party at Sandy and Jean's she had rather forgotten about her husband's accident.

"Do you know what hospital they took him to?"

"It will have been the Infirmary – that's where they always take folk from here isn't it mum?"

She agreed and went to find the phone. The base was there but no sign of the handset.

"Where's the bloody phone Andrew? – you'll have had it last?"

Without speaking he reached across behind his mother and passed her the handset from where it was resting on the back of the sofa.

Their lack of internet access forced them to rely on that most unusual of publications these days – the telephone directory.

Andrew watched as she slowly dialled a number. "Hello – I am trying to find out about my husband. He was airlifted in there last night after an accident.

"My name or his.

"Sorry he is called Jim Edward, James Edward, but no one calls him James. I'm his wife Caroline, Caroline Edward" she added unnecessarily.

A couple of minutes passed in silence and Caroline started all over again with Andrew listening and trying to catch some of what his mother was being told. From her questions he worked out his dad was due for more tests.

She concluded the call rather oddly by wishing the person on the other end a happy new year.

She turned to where Andrew was sitting on the hearth trying to blow life into the fire she had started earlier. It had teetered on the brink of death but Andrew's piper lungs seemed to be reviving it.

"They say he's fine but they want to do a scan or X-ray or something just to make sure there are no internal injuries and we can phone at lunchtime.

"Will you call them Andrew – I'll be up at the big house and they are apparently all wanting lunch. I'll have to help Fiona – she's doing lunch and a massive dinner tonight for them all and you – mug" she couldn't resist adding.

"I'm not phoning mum – they probably wouldn't even talk to me – you'll just have to do it. I'm sure George's parents won't mind if you disappear for a couple of minutes."

Without reply she went off into the kitchen to make some strong coffee for herself. Part out of need and part out of a desire to annoy his mother Andrew decided it was time for a tune or two on his pipes to make sure they were going ok for tonight's party.

They were kept on the top shelf of the airing cupboard next to the fire which was virtually the only place in the house where the damp could not get to the temperamental instrument.

He assembled the pipes without testing the individual parts so as not to deny himself the element of surprise for a brutal attack on his mother's hangover. A few quick breaths, and away he went – straight into one of his favourite marches. The pipes are not a great way to start the day for a hungover person – in the untuned state of Andrew's they were a criminal offence. He had his back to the kitchen door and pretended not to hear as Caroline screamed at him to "shut the fuck up". He turned and let the blow pipe drop from his mouth for long enough to give his mother a big broad grin before scooping it up again and continuing. She retreated back into the kitchen and by the time Andrew had finished playing she was gone – off to work, a little worried about her husband and very cross with her son. The pipes were Andrew's pride and joy. They were a special set, owned and lent to him by his tutor Mr Young. The instrument's rich tone and his skilled steady playing combined to make quite a name for Andrew on the under 18's solo's circuit. He worried if he ever had to give them back there was no way his parents could afford any sort of bagpipe for him, let along an instrument of this quality.

Lucinda Telford was already in the kitchen by the time Caroline arrived. When they had guests staying she was meant to be there early to help with breakfast but Caroline had decided long before going off to the party the night before that she wasn't busting a gut to get to work, not least because she knew it was going to be a late night for everyone.

"Morning" said Lady Telford not stopping as she walked past Caroline carrying a tray of cups in an over dramatic way to emphasise her displeasure at the late arrival.

"Morning" said Caroline back to the figure disappearing down the long corridor that led from the kitchen to the dining room.

She turned and saw the usual: A huge pile of unwashed dishes, pans and glasses covering most of the available space. The deal was for Fiona to cook and serve up until the main course – after that it was up to others. Caroline thought her employers must have been on their best behaviour – usually the dirty dishes were just left in the dining room – they must have been wanting to show Claudia's parents how egalitarian and caring they were - despite their aristocratic lineage – and had carried them back to the kitchen.

Caroline followed along to the dining room to check that all the debris from the night before had been removed. It was more or less, save, to her delight, the empty wine bottles. Some still had a bit in the bottom and so she quickly gathered them up – 8 in total - must have been a good night – and walked quickly back to the kitchen. There she swigged down the remains of the three bottles of red, spitting out some of the residue from the bottom of the bottles. She could never work out why the Telford's wine usually had stuff in the bottom – yet the cheap wine she bought from the island shop was clear to the last drop. Common sense, she thought, told you it should be the other way round.

Upstairs Jack and Sally were getting dressed. They had opened the curtains onto rather a different scene from the one that greeted them when they arrived in the room the previous afternoon. The sea looked calm, the bushes were no longer at risk from being torn from the ground and it wasn't raining. It even looked as though the sun may shine once it had reached these far-flung parts but for now it was still fairly dark outside.

Young George and Claudia lay in bed together wondering when the adults would have all gone downstairs and it would be safe for him to creep back to his own room. They whispered as quietly as they could and held each other listening for Sally and Jack to go down stairs. George really didn't want to bump into them in a naked dash along the corridor that would take him right past their bedroom. Sure enough they heard Jack and Sally coming out of their room and footsteps approaching along the corridor. There was a tap on the door that caused the young lovers to freeze. Neither said anything but they stared at each other holding their breath. In the next second they heard the footsteps start up again and Claudia's parents headed downstairs to start their first full day of island "fun".

George knew he didn't need to worry about bumping into his father. The dark winter days saw him follow a familiar routine for so many people, rich and poor alike, in the islands. After dinner, when the guests had gone to bed he would retreat to his library, probably the nicest room in the house, and sit in the battered old chair in front of the wood burning stove and drink whisky. Bruichladdich from Islay was his first choice. It had the character of Hebridean whisky but less of the peat and more of a floral bouquet.

The library had at one time contained a vast collection of rare and valuable books gathered by his forebears. A decade ago a conservation expert had warned him the damp state of the house would lead to a quickening and irreversible deterioration in the fabric of the collection which was all the cue he needed to consign the best of them to an auction house and donate the worthless ones to various institutions the family had enjoyed connections with over the years. The book sale cash had been a welcome fillip to paying the school fees for George and Alice preventing the need to sell something more useful.

Now as he sat drinking his Islay drams a rather lesser collection of reading material lined the walls, but they looked good enough on the shelves and that was what counted. Whisky was one of the few things that Lord Telford liked about Scotland. Despite his ownership of the island estate he did not consider himself Scottish and made no concessions to the culture or history of this part of the United Kingdom. His family's Earldom pre-dated the union of the parliaments of Scotland and England and he thought of himself as English. Very English actually. He just happened to own a grown-ups playground in Scotland. The only problem was that now he had to largely rely on the income generated by that playground to keep his family going, and it wasn't easy. Anyway the net result of all this was that Lord Telford was not an early riser. The 1st Earl received the title from Charles II in 1661 for his role in the restoration of the monarchy after Cromwell's Commonwealth. With it had come thousands of acres of rich farmland in Shropshire. The great Telford estate had kept the first few in the long line of earls in some splendour but later generations had gradually frittered away their inheritance.

The current Earl still owned some properties near their historic heartland but these, and young George's courtesy title of Lord Emberton were the only remaining connection to the once great landholding. Telford Hall had long been sold and was now a hotel, the last of the farms were disposed of by the current earl's father. Income these days came from the relatively few Shropshire houses and cottages they had managed to hang onto which together with their island estate made them asset rich but cash poor, like so many landowners.

Back in the bedroom young George reckoned it was safe. He gave Claudia a lingering kiss and climbed out of the ancient bed across the room and out of the door. As he ran as quietly as he could back to his own room he wished he had worn a dressing gown when he left his bed the night before but he had wanted to make a dramatic entrance to Claudia's presence and wow her with his naked form. The young couple could not hide their smirks when a short time later Claudia came into the dining room where George was already tucking into his breakfast and said good morning to him as though they had not just spent the night together.

Jack and Sally didn't notice – they were listening to Lucinda as she outlined what she thought would be a good plan for the day. It involved a whole lot of stuff that neither Jack or Sally thought would be a good idea for the last day of the year, or indeed any other day for that matter. As they laughed to themselves through their cereal George and Claudia heard Lady Telford's plans unfold. All walk together across the beach, climb up the hill at the end and head overland onto the main island road and back to the house in time for lunch. Then she would get her husband to take them all on a Land Rover tour of the whole island and point out some of the places of interest and characters of note before getting back to the house for afternoon tea.

Cocktails at 7 when they would be joined by her husband's brother and sister and their respective spouses who were arriving on today's ferry. Lucinda added, as a distinct afterthought, "and a boy from the island that George used to go to school with here who is going to pipe in the New Year for us."

"That's all sounding great to me," said Jack making little attempt to disguise his horror at the prospect of a day tramping round what he could think of only as a bleak wilderness. "Yes I'm really looking forward to seeing the place," said Sally enthusiastically, trying to repair the damage caused by Jack's obvious distain at the day's plan, but failing.

A little while later back in the privacy of their bedroom Sally put Jack on a final warning. "It's a couple of days – for your daughter – at least you can bloody well smile. It won't kill you." Her tone left Jack in no doubt he needed to try and make the best of a very bad job.

"I don't know what you mean," he said certain that his wife did not believe that claim any more than he did.

Lady Telford took a pile of breakfast dishes through to the kitchen and was about to chide Caroline for her late arrival but was silenced by the bad news.

"Jim had an accident last night and was airlifted off. He's in hospital. Dr Thomson – you know the Birmingham doctor or whatever – treated him before the helicopter arrived and has told Andrew that he thinks he is fine. But when I phoned first thing and they told me to call back about 12 – they are going to x-ray him. Maybe things are not as fine as Dr Thompson thought. Is it ok if I phone from here?"

Ignoring the question Lady T unhelpfully observed: "I suppose he was drunk."

There was no doubt in Caroline's mind that drunk may be an inadequate way of describing the state of intoxication her husband would have achieved after a day in the bar but as no one had told her definitively she conjured up a tone of outrage to partially counter the suggestion. "I really don't know".

Her ladyship managed only a "hhmm" in reply.

"Of course phone from here, and let me know how he is when you find out."

Lucinda immediately spotted a potential problem with her planned star turn of the Hogmanay party – the piper. If Jim was in a bad way she could hardly expect Andrew to entertain the guests, not that he would have understood his invitation to have been issued in those terms. She thought it insensitive to enquire as to Andrew's continuing availability just yet.

His lordship eventually surfaced and then immediately appeared indignant that his wife and guests weren't ready to start their day's activities. Eventually boots were found for the visitors and out they went to the front of the house. Jack and Sally had both thought they needed appropriate island outerwear and were sporting their brand new Barbour jackets as they headed across the lawns towards the beach. Inside the big house young George and Claudia, along with their friends Tom and Orlando had made it plain they were excluding themselves from the day's adult activities.

Caroline looked genuinely worried as she walked back into the kitchen after speaking once more to the hospital. Fiona Grant was busy prepping the dinner ingredients having already created a substantial lunch of homemade soup and a plateful of sandwiches. The rest of the big house Hogmanay party would be arriving from the ferry shortly.

"How is he?"

"I'm not sure. They say something has turned up in the x ray and they need to do some more tests. To be honest they weren't saying much. I suppose they can't really on the phone. They did say I should come down as soon as I can and speak to the doctors.

"The nurse said that they were going to give Jim a full scan tomorrow – that's an indication of how serious they think it might be because they only have a skeleton staff on over the holiday. What do you suppose it could be?"

"I'm sure there won't be anything to worry about Caroline, Jim's made of strong stuff. Listen if you end up having to go away I can cover for you. I think everyone's away on the first ferry after new year so it'll just be the three Telfords and I can manage them, she said with a meaningful smile."

Caroline starting taking the food through to the dining room to await the walkers' return. The sun was actually shining and the four of them would be hungry.

She looked out of the front door to see if there was any sign yet of the next lot of guests arriving and sure enough she could hear the Land Rover in the distance bringing the rest of the relatives "home".

If the view of the family on the island was that Lord Telford was a throwback to a bygone age, most were certain his younger brother Lord Henry was basically a total waste of space. However nearly everyone in the small community had time for the girl of the family, Lady Virginia, or Ginny as she was known by all.

56

Henry and Ginny had left their home on the island straight after university many years before only returning for the odd holiday. Their visits these days usually meant arriving with their children for a summer break. It was rumoured Lord Telford didn't much welcome his relatives staying and he even made them pay towards the extra expense created by their sojourns. Henry's wife Sarah and Ginny's husband Tom were virtually unknown to the locals. In keeping with the way the whole Telford family was these days they did not mix with the ordinary folk on the island. The personalities of George's siblings were remembered from the far off time when they did join in with things. The same was true of young George. Since leaving the island school he hadn't been seen much in the community and each year his contact with his former local schoolmates grew less until reaching the position of today-virtually non existent.

The Land Rover and the walking party arrived at the front door at more or less the same time. Lord Telford lingered long enough to give his sister a welcoming kiss, shake hands with his brother, rather coldly it was observed, and then turned to Claudia's parents – "come in we will do proper introductions in the drawing room over a drink. It's time we got Hogmanay started." Using such a particularly Scottish word when there was a perfectly good English alternative was unusual for him. He was immensely proud of his English heritage and despite the years he had spent in Scotland he didn't want anyone thinking he was by any measure even a little bit Scottish. God help anyone who called him the Laird.

"Let's have some Champagne before lunch" He disappeared from the room for a moment and returned carrying three bottles of what he referred to as Champagne but was in fact Australian sparkling wine. Despite the deception Jack's mood lightened further. He and Sally had actually enjoyed the walk. It was longer than they would usually have attempted – fully three hours had past – but the sun had shone for most of the time they were out and they were genuinely moved by the island's beauty.

Caroline came in with a tray of Champagne flutes and put them down on the table nearest the great window which looked out over the lawns and down to the sea. Pop – the first bottle was underway – pop –then the second and by the time it was drained all the glasses were filled and the hosts were handing them round. Caroline had stayed in the room awaiting further instruction. Lady Telford came up close to her and half whispered: "What news of Jim" Realising her employer probably didn't care all that much she abbreviated her concerns to say simply "more tests tomorrow."

"I'm sure he'll be fine," said her ladyship without giving a hint as to what she had based this supposition on.

"Thanks. I hope so. I may have to go down to the hospital on the third, but if I do Fiona says she'll cover for me here." At this Caroline turned and walked from the room to make sure her employers realised this was a statement and not a request.

"Caroline – before you go" She half re-entered the room. "Is Andrew still coming for dinner with us tonight?" She received the affirmative and offered more instruction. "Tell him it's black tie".

As Caroline walked back to the kitchen, in no particular rush, she could not stop the anger welling up inside her. The words kept going over in her mind. "Tell him its black tie." That just underlined how stupid and out of touch the Telfords were. "Tell him it's black tie". Because of course he would have a dinner jacket hanging in the wardrobe of their cottage. Their damp cottage. Their damp and cold poorly maintained cottage. Of course all sixteen year old's in the Hebrides kept a dinner suit handy for that out of the blue special invitation.

At least, she thought, he would have his pipe band kilt and jacket and they would have to do.

It was nearly three pm before lunch ended. Lord Telford had opened a few bottles of red to wash down the soup and sandwiches and by the time they were finished no one was much in the mood for a sight seeing trip round the island and so the afternoon plan was modified to having a nap, in preparation for the night ahead. The adults all drifted off towards their bedrooms. Young George and Claudia announced they were going for a walk with the two other teenagers.

"6.30 in the drawing room and let battle commence" Lord Telford had sunk sufficient champagne and red wine at lunch to lift his mood from its default morose to somewhere near mildly

58

happy. About as good as it ever got for a few glasses more would have induced melancholy – his lordship's personal favourite disposition.

It was nearly half past five before Caroline got home to find Andrew playing his pipes in their living room. She heard them as soon as she turned off the engine of their exhaustless old Peugeot. Another benefit of a police free island: no great need for car maintenance. She walked into the room where Andrew was still playing, red in the face with the effort he had obviously been going for some time, and signalled for him to stop. He got to the end of the part and cut the pipes dead.

"Your big house pals say its black tie tonight."

"How do you mean black tie – I've only got my school tie."

"No that means bow tie and dinner suit. You'll just have to wear your pipe band kilt and jacket.

"That's not going to be easy mum, they are at school."

"Well that's your problem. I don't care. I'm going to the bar and there'll be no black tie crap there."

"Seriously – what can I wear?"

"Please yourself. You are only there was the novelty – they won't mind as long as you play your funny wee instrument for their English pals." The growled emphasis on the word English seemed to suggest that she had forgotten that she too came from South of the border.

Andrew put down his pipes and ran to his room to see what he could find. The best he could turn up were the new jeans he'd just got for Christmas, more Co-op than designer – and his school white shirt and blue jersey.

Either confidence or indifference meant that he was not fussed what he turned up at the big house wearing. George was his supposed friend – the others – well who cares.

So it was that pipe box in hand on the stroke of 6.30 Andrew knocked on the front door. The weather was better than at any time during the holidays. His mother had dropped him off at the end of the drive rather thn driving up to the front door – she did not want to take any longer than necessary for her journey to the bar but he didn't mind. The air was still, there was a near full moon and it was dry and mild.

Mrs Grant opened the door and invited him in. "Dump your jacket in the hall here."

"You know where to go – they're gathering in the drawing room." Carrying his pipe box for comfort he walked into the room hoping the first person he met would be his old school buddy. Sadly it was the buddy's dad that he saw first.

"Oh Andrew – come in. Everyone. Everyone. A minute please. This is our piper Andrew who lives on the island. He's going to play for us later."

That left no doubt in Andrew's mind He was there as the piper. Not the friend of young George. Just the piper.

"Now go easy on him. His dad was airlifted to hospital last night and I imagine he's a worried lad. How is your father, Andrew? Before the teenager could answer Lord Telford helpfully filled in the background for the benefit of those who did not know already. "Fell into a ditch walking home from the bar. Pissed. Paralytic in fact I've been told. Is that right Andrew?"

Andrew could only manage a nod and strained smile. His earlier confidence drained and he felt humiliated. "Fuck". He thought, "fuck fuck fuck I wish I'd gone to the fucking bar." Even though he knew that would have meant yet another night of watching his mother slowly sink into a drunken stupor or even, perhaps, the arms of one of her cronies.

Young George realised the crassness of his father's introduction and went over with Claudia hand in hand, to offer comfort.

"Don't mind him, he doesn't get any better does he?"

Andrew smiled at George and held out his hand to Claudia. "Hello"

"Hello" returned Claudia. "Claudia isn't it?" She nodded. "I went to school here with George but now he's too grand to bother with the likes of me." Andrew thought he may as well be straight and say things as they were.

"I'm sure he isn't – he's actually told me a lot about you and the things you used to do when he lived here all the time."

It was a slight exaggeration. George had mentioned Andrew a couple of times, not it a good way, but the gesture had its desired effect and Andrew felt a bit better.

Andrew was then introduced to Tom and Orlando and seemed to get on fine in the way teenagers do, oblivious to many of the social challenges that older guests might have been concerned by.

About 200 people live on the island and the fact only one of them was considered worthy of an invitation to the Telford table told the whole story.

By the time they were ready for dinner it was nearly 9 o'clock. Andrew piped them into the dining room giving him a sense of purpose to be there.

Once all the guests were seated Andrew put his pipes down in the hall on a chair out of the way and returned to see the only empty seat was at the bottom of the table with Lord Telford at the other end and Andrew facing him directly. The young were largely around Andrew's end of the table with Claudia on one side of him and Aunty Ginny on the other. George was on Ginny's right hand side so Andrew reckoned if the worst came to the worst he'd be able to talk to him.

Two and a half hours of drinking before dinner, on top of a boozy lunch, meant that most of the people in the room that night were well on the way by the time the first course arrived. Lord Telford and brother Henry comfortably out in front. Jack Wiliams turned to Lucinda Telford made a couple of small talk remarks and then asked what he thought was an innocent enough question.

"Do you have any sort of party for the people who live on the island at this time of year Lucinda?"

Overhearing the question Lord Telford obviously thought it better for him to provide the answer to that one.

"Good God no. They'd drink the place dry and if there was anything left half of them would bugger off with it. My father used to have a New Year party but I stopped it after he died.

"The fact is, Jack, they don't like me and I don't much like them. Of course there's a few good folk here who are fine to pass the time of day with. But to be honest in the last few years we've been taken over by a pretty low bunch – and the rest of the island are either retired people or second homeowners.

"You would not believe how some of the people here live. Its worse than bloody Africa. Drunk half the time and bone idle all of the time.

"I mean look at young Andrew there. Nice enough kid but his father's a waste of space and his mother isn't that much better."

If Lord Telford was trying to be discreet in offering his opinions to Jack he was failing because like the rest of the guests Andrew heard almost every word. Instead of trying the impossible and taking on Lord Telford directly he turned to Claudia to offer her his own commentary on the island and what they thought of his lordship, and exactly why.

"People here aren't as bad as he makes out. It's just that after years of the older generation tugging the forlock to the Telfords there are now people here like my mum and dad who really don't care.

"He's an idiot. He tries to screw every penny he can out of the island and does nothing in return, ask anyone."

Andrew was emboldened by wine and Claudia seemed genuinely interested. He continued in his assessment of things and did not seem to care that Lady Ginny was listening, though pretending not to be.

As the evening wore on young George couldn't help noticing his girlfriend and his old school buddy seemed to be getting on well. Perhaps too well. By the time the soup was finished, the lobster plates cleared away and the beef, from the island, rare and tender, was over Claudia was at the stage of emphasising the points she was making by reaching over and covering Andrew's hand with hers. They seemed engrossed in each other's company and, from the laughter, pretty amused by it too.

None of the adults noticed much, they were spending most of their time discussing schools, politics and listening to Lord Telford lay bare another raft of his prejudices.

George left the table and came back a short time later standing behind Andrew and suggesting swapping seats because he was fed up with talking to the aunties on either side of him.

"You can't do that George," whispered Claudia. "It'll seem rude. Go back your seat – its not long until midnight and we are going outside for fireworks so I'll see you then."

You can put a teenager in a dinner suit and make them look like an adult but it doesn't mean they will behave like one.

"It's funny to think Andrew that one day we will be just like our fathers. You'll be working for me. You'll be saying what a twat I am and I will be enjoying a life you could only dream off." If George meant to be clever it didn't work. He sounded like a prat. George gave his girlfriend a menacing look and rather grumpily went back to his seat and some more auntie chat.

Not long before the bells of midnight Lord Telford half shouted down the table. "Ok Andrew – time to sing for your supper. I'm sure our guests would love to hear you pipe in the New Year".

The clear implication was that Lord Telford would not be so keen. Offend his English ears no doubt. Andrew stood up and headed to the door wondering if he would be able to play after the bucket full of booze he'd had. He'd been knocking back champagne, he knew no better, and red wine for over five hours. Of course he could. It wasn't the first time. Tune the instrument out in the hall, and back to the dining room, pipe in the bells and lead the guests out for the fireworks. Easy.

He went to the chair when he'd left his pipes and there they were. It wasn't until he picked them up that he realised something was wrong. The hall was gloomy and his eyesight compromised but he could clearly feel and then see the chanter and one of the three drones were broken. The African blackwood shattered. It looked as though the drone had just been snapped in two but the chanter was so badly damaged someone must have stamped on it. His thought processes were too weakened by the booze to work out anything very quickly. So he went back to the dining room carrying his now useless pipes. As he walked in he saw George next to his girlfriend and pointing right at him. George was laughing. Claudia was not.

He twigged. His pipes were shattered. George was laughing heartily to himself. No one else was paying any attention. He came to a rapid conclusion. He put his damaged pipe down on the sideboard and half walked half staggered at George who was still chuckling away. Andrew towered over him and screamed "Why did you smash my pipes?" The room fell silent.

"It was an accident man, I was going to bring them in for you but they got a bit damaged somehow."

"Bit damaged – they are smashed. Totally fucking smashed. You fud," he said employing a good Scots swear word. "You complete cunt," he added offering a translation in case the Scots was lost on George.

George made to stand up and when he was almost completely on his feet he turned to face Andrew. "Why did you do it? Jealous your girlfriend was talking to the common kid?"

No one spoke but they looked on with varying degrees of comprehension as to what was happening with most of the adults impaired by drink

Before an answer was forthcoming Andrew leant right back and then smashed his forehead as hard as he could into George's spotty face. As he pulled back blood began pouring from his nose and George was swaying as if he was about to fall over. Just for good measure Andrew smashed his head into George's nose once more and kneed him as hard as he could, right in the groin. George collapsed on top of Claudia and slid towards the floor leaving her, no doubt rather expensive, blue and white dress covered in his blood.

The shocked silence in the room was broken by Lord Telford shouting as hard as he could: "What on earth do you think you are doing." He got up as quickly as his drunken state would allow, his chair falling back smashing the front of a glass china display case behind him, and lumbered towards Andrew who was unscathed so far by his handiwork.

The 11th Earl of Telford didn't look like he was planning on stopping as he staggered quickly towards his son's assailant. His face was contorted by fury and drink. Andrew must have reckoned it was every man for himself and so the father got the same treatment as the son as he smashed his forehead hard into Lord Telford's face. He was not as resilient as his son and fell straight to the floor with blood pouring from his nose and mouth.

Lady Telford screamed. Nearly everyone screamed or shouted. At Andrew, at Lord Telford. At anything. Claudia screamed at Andrew too. In a different way. "Get out, quickly get out." If anyone had been capable of analysis they may have

64

concluded that Claudia was showing more concern for Andrew than his victims.

"Yes – get out – now" screamed Lord Henry. His lordship and his heir being indisposed the spare obviously thought he should jump in but it was noticeable Henry appeared reluctant to become physically involved preferring to remain in his seat.

Andrew seemed as dazed as his victims as he staggered towards the door along the other side of the table from where Lord Telford was lying

As Andrew passed the stunned guests he leaned over towards Henry and slurred: "That was for the Polish kid." Henry, of course had no idea what was meant or its significance. Andrew grabbed the smashed pipes from the sideboard and bumped heavily into the dining room doorframe as he made his unsteady way out into the hall. Lucinda screamed at Andrew as he headed to the front door: "Don't you ever come near my home or my family again. And that goes for your useless mother too. Tell her she's fired. She's not to set foot on our property again. Go. Get out before there's any more trouble."

Lucinda had not known whether to go to the aid of her son or husband. Even in her drunk state she could see young George was now sitting on a chair stemming the flow of blood with a napkin. Her husband lay prone on the floor and so it was to him she rushed.

The teenager put his sad looking pipes back into their case and walked straight out of the front door up the drive and into the night.

Andrew did not notice Frederic the Polish handyman hiding in the bushes waiting to set off the Hogmanay fireworks, Federic thought Andrew was the first of the guests to come out to watch and prepared to start the display. He had no way of knowing the pyrotechnics had already happened – inside – and for the Telford family Hogmanay was over.

Chapter 7

Even for a teenager used to the delights of cheap, strong cider consumed in unhealthy quantities in parks and bus shelters this Hogmanay hangover was hard to bear for Andrew. By the time he woke in his bed it was getting light outside, so it was at least 9am. Today the challenge of leaving the warmth of his bed to face the biting damp and cold of his draughty bedroom was compounded by the nausea and headache that signifies a good night had been had.

Only as his level of consciousness raised did he begin, slowly, to recall that it had not been a good night – certainly not towards the end. He remembered Claudia, her soft hand touching his, meaningfully he thought. Then with a wave of seething rage he remembered his smashed pipes. He could clearly see the chanter lying by the chair in the hall of the big house in splinters. Rage quickly turned to horror as he recalled head-butting George. Oh my God, he thought. "I nutted Lord Telford."

Surely not.

As he lay trying to make sense of patchy recollections of the previous evening it slowly sank in: he had smashed Lord Telford and his son smack in the face. A Glasgow kiss some might call it. The lack of desire to leave his bed became a firm resolution to stay put. Never to put his head above the blankets again. Reflecting on the events of the previous night took some time. It was time well spent though as Andrew was able to talk himself into believing that George deserved it and Lord Telford? Well with him it was just sort of self defence. He suddenly felt his whole body shudder as he heard once more Lady Telford screaming at him. "Tell your useless mother she's fired."

His attempts at self-justification crumbled into sheer panic. What if his mother was fired? What if George or his father had been seriously injured. They couldn't be. He'd never nutted anyone before surely he couldn't have done that much harm. As the sense of panic intensified he leapt from his bed and pulled on last night's clothes pausing only to look in the mirror where he caught the sight of a big bruise on his forehead and smatterings of blood on his shirt.

The panic turned to terror as the vast implications of what had gone on at the big house the night before dawned upon him in ever greater detail. It was a lot for a teenager to assimilate. There was no one to speak to about it. His father was in hospital. His mother would, no doubt, be lying in her bed dead to the world, and anyway she was pretty useless at the best of times.

He made enough space amongst the dishes piled up in the kitchen sink to allow him to stick his head under the cold tap. Shaking off the excess, like a spaniel coming out of the sea, Andrew gulped down a glass of water, then another and then a third. Instinctively he set about lighting the living room fire as the horrors of last night kept going through his mind. As the kindling began its work lighting the coal he resolved he would have to wake his mother and tell her all, or at least as much as he could remember.

Events as monumental as this quickly became common currency on the island. Soon everyone would know what had gone on in the big house. The stories would grow and take on a new life with each telling. By the time it had been round the island and back God knows what people would be saying, and believing. Get your defence in first, he concluded.

He hesitated momentarily outside his parents' bedroom door, tapped as loud as he dared, enough, hopefully, to wake her but not as hard as to annoy her - though he knew her fuse would be short after Hogmanay. He pushed the door open to find the bed empty. Whether it had been slept in was hard to say – he hadn't seen it made all that often. His mother liked it to "air" which he took for shorthand that she couldn't be bothered to make it properly.

New year first footing is the way of the isles with the population moving in little groups along no predetermined route from house to house with whisky, good wishes and a drink fuelled optimism for the future not seen at other times of the year. Lighthouse View Cottage was always on the circuit. People tended to go there later on new year's day because they knew the cupboard would most likely be bare and callers could not expect to be offered too much hospitality. Best to go to more certain watering holes first.

However first footing here suddenly appeared to have started early. Just as Andrew was trying to work out where his mother might be there was a knock on the door and rather unexpectedly into the kitchen walked Ben Thompson. It became clear he wasn't there for refreshment. Information and explanation were his goal.

Ben got straight to the point: "What the hell were you doing last night?" his wide smile that indicated he obviously knew a fair bit already and did not think whatever happened the previous evening at the big house was anything to be overly concerned about.

"What do you mean?" said Andrew, though why he bothered trying to feign ignorance of what had gone on was beyond his or Ben's comprehension.

"What do I mean – well how about flattening George for a start – let alone sticking the head on his father"

"Oh that" There was no point pretending to be anything other than quite pleased with some of the outcomes. Andrew smiled back. "They deserved it – and more. George used to be my friend – but he's just a twat, a fucking stuck up pleased with himself little twat.

"Anyway who told you?"

"We were just in the house watching the telly after the bells when George's uncle, Henry is it? came hammering on the door saying there had been an accident and asking my dad to go up to the house because people were hurt."

"Did he go"

"Yeah, of course – he kind of has to. It's his job."

"So what did he say?"

He didn't say much really, doctor and patient and all that kind of stuff. But he did say that George's nose is basically fucked. You must have given him some smash and he thinks Lord Telford may have a broken cheek bone.

"Apparently when he left to come home they were both lying on sofas with packs of frozen vegetables on their faces."

For Andrew the seriousness of the situation was greatly eased by the thought of his two victims lying stretched out feeling sorry for themselves and balancing packets of Birds Eye on their damaged faces. He felt good. And worried. And frightened. All at the same time.

"What are you going to do?" asked Ben.

"What can I do?" He paused for a few seconds before offering a conclusion. "They both asked for it. George smashed my pipes for no reason. No reason at all and his father looked as though he was going to hit me. So fuck them." He knew in his heart that this level of bravado would not carry through to explaining what had happened to his mother, or indeed to his father when he eventually saw him.

"I don't know where my mother is – you didn't see her on your way here did you?"

A shake of the head.

"But my mum and dad are up already – why don't you come over and have some breakfast?"

Andrew accepted the invitation saying he would have to put something else on to wear – the bloodied look wasn't a good one.

He left Ben in front of the fire for a couple of minutes to go and change. There was no point in putting coal on the fire as they left, he concluded, it wasn't going to be a day for sitting round the house.

"Andrew – happy new year" smiled Mrs Thompson. She was standing at the farmhouse kitchen stove frying bacon. It smelt good. The smile didn't last long. "Are you ok? You seem to have had," she struggled to find the right word, "an interesting new year, I think it's fair to say".

He tried, not entirely successfully, not to smile and nodded assent to the suggestion. Mrs Thompson offered a bacon roll which was accepted with less enthusiasm than might have been evident on other occasions.

As Andrew took a bite she walked to the door through to the passageway and shouted for her husband.

The doctor walked into the kitchen and straight up to Andrew and held out his hand. "Happy New Year young man", he said adding: "Though to be honest the way things have started out I think this year may not be the happiest twelve months of your life."

"What was it like after I left last night?"

"I can't say too much, you know. I was there was a doctor and they were my patients but I am sure you realise you got them both a good belt in the face."

"I'm not sure. George was howling a bit and his father fell down. But he was pretty pissed. To be honest so was I. It was all over in a few seconds."

"I was there for rather longer than that. I thought we were going to have to medivac Lord Telford off the island. I thought his injury was pretty bad at first.

"Needless to say the air ambulance was busy and by the time they thought there was a slot to get out here I reckoned it wasn't worth it.

Dr Thompon felt conflicted between maintaining his professional discretion and trying to help the young man he had come to know quite well and like over their many visits to the island.

"What do you think I should do?

"Should I go and apologise? I don't want to. I don't need to. I remember Lady Telford saying something horrible about my mother and telling me she was fired. Mum needs the money. She'll kill me if she has been. They can't do that anyway can they?"

"I'm a doctor, not a lawyer. But to be honest I don't think there is much point in you going up there at the moment. I think you have done rather more that stick the head on them. I think they are seeing it more in terms of the start of an attempt at revolution." His chuckle spoke volumes.

The meaning, let along implications, of that sentence was not immediately apparent to Andrew as he finished off his bacon roll and tried to make up his mind between seeking more advice or more food.

The bacon roll won and seeing his eyes staring at the breakfast pile Mrs Thompson offered the plate again and it was gratefully, if silently, received.

Just then Dr Thompson's phone started to ring. Not for a serious man like him the frivolity of a novel ringtone but a solid, old fashion bell sounding out. The farmhouse was one of the few places on that side of the island that received a mobile phone signal.

"Good morning Lucinda." The doctoring of the night before had obviously moved him onto a less formal relationship with the island's proprietors.

"Yes. I'll come up shortly. I tell you though – I'm expecting a big discount on our next booking." He wasn't kidding.

Mr Thompson left his family a short while later saying he hoped not to be long. Andrew stood in the kitchen with not a clue what to do next. Then Mrs Thompson gave him the prompt he needed. "What's your mum saying about all this?"

There was nothing else for it. He had to find his mother and tell her all about the night of high drama, before someone else did. Sandy and Jean's. That would be the best bet. If she wasn't there they would probably know where she was.

"Thanks for the rolls." He rushed out of the back door in the wake of Ben's dad. "Will you drop me off at Sandy and Jean's if you are going up to the big house?"

He jumped into the Thomson's rather plush Land Rover Discovery. Far too smart for an island vehicle.

The curtains were all closed at Sandy's house, but he knew the door would be open. Andrew went round the back and stepped into the stale darkness of the kitchen. He found a light switch and illuminated the remnants of what must have been another good party. There were far too many half drunk bottles for it to have been a sophisticated event, not that the teenager took any notice of that. Plates, food, ashtrays scattered all about. No sign of life.

Through to the living room - again devastation but no people. He didn't want to go upstairs. Was it an emergency. Did he have the courage, need, or standing to shout. Of course he did. He had to find his mother. What to shout. Could it be just mum, she mightn't be there. Other mums could. As he plucked up courage to shatter the sleep of the not so innocent he took far too long to decide what to shout. In the event it was the rather unimaginative

"Hello. Hello" then a longer pause and as loud as he could "Hello"

"Fuck off. It's too early for first footing" came the response, it sounded like Jean.

"Is mum there? Its urgent. I need to speak to her."

"What's the problem? Have you run out of food? There's plenty here."

He didn't want to shout details of his predicament to just anyone who may be in the gloom of the upper floor. To announce that he was there to discuss his violent assault on the island's proprietor and his heir. So he just repeated his original request to speak to his mother. After a few minutes Caroline half walked, half fell down the stairs and into the room. Andrew had opened the curtains in preparation for her arrival. Time and lifestyle had not been kind to Caroline Edward. This New Year's day she looked about as bad as a human can outside of a mortuary.

"My God, what a night," she said giving the impression she thought her son had just popped round to talk about their respective New Year celebrations.

"Mum." That was the easy bit. He agonised over how to pitch the rest. Choice of words were going to be important. "I....I...I got into a bit of bother last night. A lot of bother I think."

He could think of no clever way of saying it, no way of mitigating the enormity of his actions. For Caroline it was too much. She felt like death. She was still half drunk. If she was a different person she might have been overcome with concern for her son's obvious distress, however that was the least of her worries at that moment.

"Make me a cup of tea, Andrew."

He didn't. He went on to slowly tell his mother as best as he could remember the full horror of the events of last night. He even told her that Lady Telford had said his mum wasn't to set foot on their property again, though charitably left out her ladyships appraisal of his mother's work ethic. Seemingly not overly concerned Caroline said she was sure it would all blow over. Events get out of hand on the island at Hogmanay.

She had obviously, and sadly, failed to grasp the devastating certainty that her new year had got off to a bad start and would probably get a whole lot worse.

Chapter 8

Lord Telford had felt the blood running into his mouth before he the pain hit him. He'd falllen flat out directly behind his sister Ginny, his brain fuzzy with drink, struggling to make sense of the situation. Within seconds Lucinda was kneeling over him staring at his bloodied face. It's the question most often asked after an incident like this and certainly the least necessary. "Are you alright George?"

He tried to say he was far from alright but such was the shock he had just suffered the words didn't come out. Ginny, probably the most sober of the company that evening, ran off towards the kitchen saying she would get the first aid box that always sat on the top shelf in the big house's cavernous pantry. By the time she returned her brother was sitting up pressing a napkin onto his damaged nose,

Her nephew was slumped forward onto the dining table, his face buried in a napkin as well. Lucinda was trying to help her husband to his feet, her sister in law was attending to young George who appeared unconscious. Lady T helped her husband into the seat beside their stricken son and sat next to him her hand steadying his shoulder. Ginny said they needed to get help. "Who can we call on now the doctor's no more?" she asked.

Lucinda replied: "I can't think. How's George. Can someone see if he's awake. I can't let go of George," aptly illustrating the confusion caused by naming the son after the father.

Henry went over to his nephew and gently lifted him up from the table by his shoulders. The napkin stayed on the table causing the blood from George's nose to cascade off his chin. Henry grabbed another clean one and pressed it tight in an attempt to stem the flow. George yelped in pain. Too tight. Lucinda suddenly remembered the doctor staying at home farm. She turned to Jack Williams and told him to go urgently and ask for help. The keys will be in the Land Rover. Having been at the other end of the noisy dinner party Jack had no firm gasp on what had happened. He had picked up that somehow Andrew's pipes had been damaged. He must have blamed young George and hit him, he thought.

"What on earth happened there Lucinda?"

"There's no time for that – please just go and get Dr Thompson from the home farmhouse as quickly as you can – Claudia you go with your father and show him the way will you." Henry said he'd go with Jack.

At this point in the minutes after the fracas and Andrew's dramatic exit the attention of the gathering turned to the teenage girl in their midst. Her face was pressed into her hands. Tears were flowing out from underneath and she was shaking and sobbing. Without speaking Claudia half stood up and ran for the door still with her face in her hands her body stooped forward, her father following on closely.

It seemed an age before the rescue party returned with the holidaying medic. Not much had happened other than Lucinda was gently dabbing the faces of her husband and son in turn from a bowl of hot water as she sat between them.

"Good heavens what on earth has happened here?" asked the doctor of no one in particular.

Lucinda was quick to provide her view of events. "One of the locals repaid our hospitality by getting drunk and viscously assaulting first my son and then my husband as he tried to calm things down,"

Neither Jack nor Sally had felt it was their place to challenge that account of what had been going on but both felt it was somewhat removed from their own understanding of how the old year had finished. Dr Thompson looked first at the father then the son. They had suffered remarkably similar injuries. Though perhaps not all that remarkable as they had both been assaulted by the same person in the same way in the same period of time.

"I can't be sure of course but it looks to me as though both of them have suffered a broken nose. Also, I'm afraid Lord Telford, I think there is a good possibility you have a broken cheekbone.

"If we weren't here on the island I would suggest going in to A and E but we are. I don't think it is bad enough to ask for a medivac. Especially tonight. Everyone will be run off their feet.

"I've got painkillers which I'm happy to leave with you. I'll check back tomorrow, but not too early if you don't mind. May I suggest everyone has a cup of tea and sits quietly for a while to let things calm down – on all fronts.

"You do need to be examined properly as soon as possible, X-rayed most likely, so if I were you I would make sure you're on the first ferry off the island and straight to casualty."

As he turned to go Dr Thompson couldn't resist half turning back to the now quiet room and wishing everyone a Happy New Year. Ginny came in with a tray of cups followed by her sister in law with the giant teapot that was usually used only on deer stalking days when folk came in from the hills. Lucinda satisfied herself that the patients were able to be interviewed and asked her son: "What the hell was all that about?"

"I've no idea," said young George trying to sound indignant. "Andrew just went for me. I was sitting chatting away to him and Ginny – he went to get his bagpipes and came back and without warning went for me. I didn't have a chance. It just came out of the blue. He's a fucking nutter."

Claudia felt she had enough invested in the situation to shine a little light onto the truth of the recent events. She felt any loyalty she had to her boyfriend had been exhausted by his behaviour. Anyway, she was certain, he was no longer her boyfriend. She'd seen it coming for a time. This confirmed it. She and George were no more.

"Lady T that's only half the story."

George glowered at her.

"What George didn't tell you is that he had smashed Andrew's pipes. You must know how much they mean to him. George just smashed them and seemed to think it was really funny." Her voice was quiet. He words deliberate.

"I didn't smash them. I stood on one bit of them by mistake. I didn't see them. Whatever, it certainly didn't mean he should break my nose, and beat up my old man."

"You were being a pain. You didn't like me talking to Andrew. I was watching you giving me evils all night. If you were a proper friend you would have been pleased for me to have someone to talk to other than your boring relatives."

Whoops. The gloves were off, thought Claudia. George was a prat and his family were all he deserved.

"Do you mind – that's my family you are talking about," warned her now ex-boyfriend.

"Of course it's your family I'm talking about you half wit." Indignant and semi slurring she continued: " There's no one else in the room apart from my family and they are not like yours at all thank God."

Lucinda jumped in: "I think everyone should calm down. Whatever happened there was no need for that thug to assault one of his oldest friends and then viciously attack a man who had shown him nothing but kindness over many years."

Sally Williams could see it all going down hill quickly. Her relatively sober senses told her a speedy withdrawal was required. She calmly stood up, walked round the table to Claudia, gently took her hand and said the party's over. Time to go to bed. The protest Sally anticipated failed to arrive. Claudia obediently stood up and still holding her mother's hand walked past the causalities and their carers and out of the room, and out of the Telford's lives she hoped.

Lord Telford's shock faded and the pain of his injury set in causing his general cantankerous personality to exhibit deeper than usual depths of distain towards his island and its inhabitants. In a slow almost menacing tone he told the gathering in no uncertain terms that this new year was going to be the start of something very different in his relationship with the island. "What we have seen tonight is a powerful demonstration as to why we need to part company with this place.

"For nearly 150 years the Telfords have treated the people here as extended family. We have been the constant in the lives of countless people. We have invested huge amounts of money is this place and thrown away a whole lot more.

"But tonight. Tonight it all changes. There is a thoroughly ghastly bunch of people that have ended up here and they have destroyed it for the rest of us.

"No family typifies what's wrong with this place more than the Edwards. Father and mother useless. Drunkards. And we have learnt tonight that their sweet little boy is a violent thug who repays friendship with a punch in the face. It's not just them. It's all jealously at the end of the day. These scum don't like working for us. Working – that's a joke. The better people are having their heads turned by politics. By the nationalists who want to take our possessions from us for no reason other than envy. I'd like to see them make a living here. Put in the work we have to make this place pay. Our family has given their all for the future of this island. This is how we are repaid."

Buoyed by Burgundy Jack tried to interject. "Surely it can't be that bad?" he began but his Lordship was not in listening mode.

Missing the irony of his drunken rant against the island drunks he kept up his assessment of the state of play in his domain and continued to outline how things were going to have to change for the betterment primarily of his own family.

"It bloody well is Jack. Most of the decent folk here have died and some moved away. The respect for my family built up over generations of coexistence on this island died with that old generation."

Jack wanted to say that he thought respect was a commodity to be earned, not inherited, but he knew old George wouldn't listen, or even be interested, and, Jack reckoned, he couldn't care much either. All he wanted to do was go to bed.

Lord Telford droned on pausing every few moments to sniff the dripping blood back into his nose and wipe up the bits that escaped with his napkin.

"Listen Ginny," he said fixing his sister with a squinted stare. "I want you to be at their cottage at 9 o'clock tomorrow morning and tell them they are evicted. I am not going to give shelter to people who abuse my kindly nature, let alone assault me and my son."

Ginny was going to protest but stopped herself considering it to be entirely pointless at this stage in proceedings and she no doubt suspected her brother would have little recollection of his instructions by the time morning came. So it went on. The remnants of the Hogmanay dinner party were fixed to their seats, wanting to leave but afraid of shattering the appearance of support for the injured. George's young school friends had no such qualms and disappeared off at their first opportunity into the vastness of the house. Of those remaining Jack was keenest of all to get out of the room. And off the island come to that.

Looking down on the unhappy scene were some of the previous Earls. The ones painted by artists of little distinction. The Gainsborough of the 5th Earl had long gone for auction. Earls seven and eight watched over the rantings of their descendent. Their little known artists had saved them from being sold but as a result they were condemned to a cold and damp existence on the miserable walls of an island house far from their ancestral home in Shropshire and the luxurious surroundings they had hung amongst in better times for the Telford family.

"Lucinda – phone the police" demanded Lord Telford suddenly.

"Why, they are not going to come out here tonight. What's the point?"

"The point, Lucinda, is that I want this crime recorded. That little bastard is going to pay for what he's done tonight. He's not getting away with it. There's no excuse."

"Do you honestly think that's sensible George? Can't we deal with it ourselves. Caroline's not coming back. I'm sure we can get rid of Jim easily enough once he's out of hospital. It won't take long to give him a couple of written warnings. And if you are serious about kicking them out of Lighthouse View Cottage they'll have to leave won't they. There's nowhere else I can think of for them to stay."

"Phone the police. Phone them now and tell them exactly what has gone on here tonight. Unprovoked assault. Violence of the worst order."

Ginny tried to talk him out of it. "George if they investigate this won't they just say he was provoked by George smashing his bloody bagpipe. If it ever got to court we would look pretty stupid."

Her brother appeared not to have heard her plea for clemency, but after a longish pause muttered that on reflection he would sleep on it, if he could with a throbbing nose and face, and make up his mind in the morning.

By the time Jack reached the haven of his room Sally was already in bed but sitting up with the bedside light on. Even blurred by an evening's heavy island drinking he could see she looked shocked. "Why have you been so long coming to bed? Is that throwback of a human being still ranting on? Claudia's really upset. She's only just gone to her own bed a few minutes ago. I've calmed her down but she is devastated. She's blaming herself for talking to that boy for most of the night but I've told her she's done nothing wrong and there's no excuse for what George did. On good thing, though: she says she's over him. She's gone to her room and locked the door. Apparently, they've been sleeping together."

Jack was past caring. He wanted to go to sleep. He wanted to go home. He wanted to be in a ski resort with real friends drinking good wine. He wanted to be anywhere but the big house on this bloody island.

Chapter 9

Andrew managed to persuade his mother to leave Sandy's and head home for the tea she had asked him for. He didn't want everyone still at Sandy's house joining in the discussion of the events of the previous night. Once home he put the kettle on and set about getting the fire going. Caroline needed both hands to steady her teacup. Her son crouched in front of the struggling fire trying to bring it to life. The driftwood his father had gathered and stacked had not had time to dry out properly before the torrents of the old year. The flame was producing more steam than smoke and the logs hissed. Like a pantomime audience giving their opinion of the villain.

"What are you going to do mum?"

"I'm going to go to work as though nothing has happened. If they ask I'll just say I haven't seen you. They'll just have been pissed as usual," said in such a manner to suggest such a state would never befall her "and I bet they're not as badly hurt as you think."

"Ben Thompson reckoned his dad thinks they've both got broken noses and Telford may have a broken cheek bone." He had spoken the words in a deliberately measured fashion trying not to give them impression of someone who was pleased with their handiwork. He failed.

"Well that's got bugger all to do with me. If George hadn't smashed your pipes none of this would have happened. It's me that should be on the warpath, not those arses."

The flames gathered some force in the fireplace and gave every indication that before long they might manage to generate a bit of heat. Andrew made to go outside to try and find some drier logs but as he walked into the kitchen there was a knock at the door and the visitor walked in.

"Andrew," greeted Lady Ginny. They looked at each other for what seemed like an age, neither knowing what to say.

"I'm sort of sorry for last night Ginny" mumbled the now embarrassed teenager faced with the acceptable face of the Telford family.

"Sort of?"

"Yes sort of. I shouldn't have hit your brother, is he ok? George got what he deserved – he deliberately smashed my pipes. God knows what I'm going to say at school. They'll cost a fortune to repair."

"My brother is quite badly injured thanks to you. The doctor staying at home farm thinks you may have broken his cheek bone as well as his nose. I've never seem him so cross before and I've seen him in some pretty foul tempers."

Caroline had recognised Lady Ginny's voice and went through to the kitchen. "What on earth was going on last night – and do you know why George smashed up Andrew's bagpipes?'"

"Caroline I'm afraid the bagpipes are the least of the problems. Your son carried out a vicious and unprovoked attack on my nephew, and then my brother. Both of them have serious injuries that are going to require hospital treatment."

"It wasn't unprovoked – your bloody nephew has smashed Andrew's pipes. Where am I going to get the money to pay for that. He'll have to pay. You lot have plenty cash – you can bloody well pay." Caroline's anger was fuelled by her hangover and she wasn't for dwelling on niceties this morning.

"When I get to work this morning I'm going to sort it out, but someone's going to have to pay for those pipes, and it's not me"

"I'm afraid you won't be going to work this morning, or indeed any other morning at our house. That's why I'm here. Lord and Lady Telford have asked me to tell you your services are no longer required, with immediate effect."

Caroline didn't know what shocked her more. Getting the sack in such a peremptory manner or hearing her employers referred to as Lord and Lady Telford, as though they were important. Ginny must have been doing that to underline their status and maybe even warn against trying to fight dismissal.

"They can't blame my mother for what I did. That isn't fair. It's nothing to do with her. It's between me and George. My mum needs that job. They need her."

"I don't need the bloody job Andrew. I was going to quit anyway. I'm sick of those arseholes. I'm sorry Ginny nothing against you – but the rest of your family..........."She stopped at that point. Mainly because she was lost as to what to say next.

She needed the job. Without it, well God knows what would happen. Jim, unreliable, Andrew, a drain. Hungover as she was, her brain at half speed. She hadn't thought it through. It was a gut reaction. Fuck off. Fuck off to all of you. Telfords, Andrew. Everyone. Fuck off. That's what her brain as saying. Fortunately her mouth was more measured,

Caroline then did something her son had never seen before. She cried, Quietly. But he could see the tears in her eyes. Ginny could too. Tears of self pity. Of anger. Of hungover pain. Tears. Real tears. Caroline was nearly as shocked as the other two. She walked out of the kitchen and perched on the edge of the chair nearest the fire. It was, by now, the only bright thing in the house. The wood was blazing and throwing out real heat. Caroline was blazing too. She couldn't think straight. There was still enough alcohol flowing round her body from the night before to embolden her resistance to the emissary from the Telfords. There was thankfully enough common sense to rein it in.

Ginny walked up to the other side of the fire. "Caroline I don't know what's gone on before last night but George is adamant he doesn't want you back in the house. I should also warn you that he wants you out of this house. I did try to get him to see sense but he won't have it.

"He wasn't up when I left this morning but I'll try and speak to him when I get back."

"If he wasn't up how do you know he still wants rid of me. He might have changed his mind, or forgotten."

"I know. I also know he won't forget. He wants to involve the police and have Andrew prosecuted for assault."

"I can do without all this. I feel like shit and Jim's lying in hospital. They're doing tests on him today. Do you lot know that. I don't suppose you care. They say there may be something seriously wrong with him. Its New Year's Day and they said yesterday they were going to get people in today specially to look at him. I've got to phone shortly. Surely even his lordship will be able to see how upset Andrew is. How worried he is bound to be about his father. Surely he must have some understanding of what we are going through."

Andrew was quite impressed by the speed at which his mother appeared to be building the case for his defence. As he listened to her plea he began to feel quite guilty. In truth he hadn't given his father much of a thought. Jim Edward was usually in some sort of trouble. Self inflicted most often, as it was this time, and he hadn't thought his father's latest escapade worthy of too much worry despite the drama of the medivac.

Ginny took her leave trying as best she could to make sure that Caroline understood it would not be in her interests to go to the big house today. She told Caroline if things changed she would come back, but made it quite clear it would be foolish to hold out any hope at all.

Nursing their hangovers Andrew and his mother sat in silence staring at each other and then the fire in turn and reflecting on where they were. For Caroline, it was a tussle as to what to worry about most. Her husband's health, her imminent unemployed or her son's potential prosecution for assault. Slowly she concluded that prosecution and unemployment were matters over which she could have no influence and so she decided to concentrate on Jim. She had better phone the hospital.

The next visitors to Lighthouse View Cottage were more friendly and better motivated than the last.

Brian and Ben Thompson, uncomfortable with the island ways, waited for their knock at the door to be answered before walking into the house. It was Brian's first time inside the cottage and he tried not to show his disapproval at the sight that met him, the dishes and bottles lying about, the battered furniture and dirty walls, the peeling paintwork, thin and frayed curtains. Brian had wanted Andrew to know that during his morning visit to the big house Lord Telford had made in perfectly clear that he wanted Andrew prosecuted for assault. He was equally clear that Andrew should not under any circumstances attempt to go to the big house to apologise.

Before that conversation could go any further Caroline came back into the sitting room from the kitchen where she had gone for privacy to speak to her husband's doctor. She was pleased that Brian Thompson was still there because there had been bits she didn't understand. The main diagnosis she did understand. All too well.

"Dr Thompson," she said. "Jim's doctor has just told me that blood tests have revealed sclerosis of the liver and they are going to do a CT scan shortly." Her tears returned. She sat on the arm of the chair nearest the fire and asked: "That's bad, isn't it?"

The doctor confirmed that it was indeed bad, but on its own treatable and not necessarily life threatening. "Whatever stage it is at Caroline the one thing for sure is that if Jim wants to try and get better then his drinking days are over."

Mother and son both realised the implications of that sentence and doubted the likelihood of sobriety being embraced by such a committed drinker. Brian Thompson concluded in was neither his place nor the time to expand on that diagnosis. He also felt it inappropriate to speculate further on why the doctors had thought it necessary to give Jim a full CT scan and what that might throw up. However, he could not help thinking to himself how things were going to change in the Edwards' lives. That change could be for the better, but a long career in trauma medicine had severely dented his ability to believe in happy endings.

"Caroline, would you and Drew like to join us for lunch? Linda is planning roast beef and Yorkshire puddings to start the New Year – maybe about 4 by the time we've been out for a walk."

"That's very kid of you Dr Thompson but after I've spoken to the hospital again I'm going over to Kenny Kelp's. He's always got a good spread on New Year's day. What about you, Drew? Are you coming to Kenny's?"

Drew shook his head and asked if it was ok for him to go to Ben's instead. Assured that it was he said he'd be joining them at the farmhouse later in the day. He didn't want to go for a walk, even though it might do him some good, and he knew the Thompson's wouldn't countenance him and Ben staying behind if he arrived in time for the exercise. Added to that he was beginning to feel really concerned about his father. He felt he ought to stay with his mother at least until the latest news had been gathered from the hospital. Then, no doubt, she would be off to Kenny's and another party.

Strange but neither mother or son seemed to feel any need to attempt to do anything about the Telfords. Perhaps they had concluded matters were out of their hands and there was little point in trying to influence outcomes. What will be will be. Caroline felt too angry, too worried, too hungover and, to be honest, too thirsty to care much about her predicament. Unemployment and homelessness could wait.

Brian and Ben took their leave and Caroline silently went about breakfast. For all the morning was nearing it's end she hadn't eaten. Cereal and the last of the milk. It would do for now. They'd be plenty later at Kenny's.

After a while Andrew broke the silence. "What happens if they mean it? What will we do if you are out of job, dad is ill and we are out of this house?"

The questions were too big to be considered from behind a befuddled brain and so Caroline just met them with a half shrug as she continued to eat her Weetabix.

"Seriously mum. What are we going to do?"

Again, a mere shrug in reply. What else could her response have been. Events over which she had no control were unfolding round her. There were too many imponderables, too many big questions springing out from that one little inquiry.

Brian and Ben didn't go straight back to the farmhouse. Brian thought he really ought to do his rounds fully and make a final check on his big house patients. No one walked uninvited into the Telford's home, but that morning Brian Thompson felt his position was rather different than most. So after telling Ben to stay in the car he walked straight in through the front door into the hall. There was an unkempt air to add to the usual image of decay presented by the entrance. One table lamp was on, the fire in the huge hall grate was long since out, and a few empty glasses were dotted about the furniture waiting to be picked up. Normally by now Caroline would have attended to them, and their left over contents, but this was day one of life after Caroline – and no one in the big house cared.

Dr Thompson announced his presence with a loud hello, repeated up the stairs, down he rear corridor. After a while he heard movement from the back of the house and Lady Ginny appeared at the door next to the stairs that led to the kitchen. "Hello doctor, have you come to check on your patients?"

"I have indeed, how are they?"

"Both up and both in foul moods to be honest. Neither had much sleep, both look ghastly, both are hungover and we are arguing over what to do."

"Do about what?"

"About last night. My brother and sister in law want to involve the police. George just won't have it that my nephew provoked the whole thing. He keeps saying Andrew Edward is a thug and coming up with ever more bizarre things to do about it.

"He wants Caroline out of this house and then all three of them out of their home . I keep telling him he can't evict a worker because of their child's actions but you know what he's like. Well perhaps you don't know what he's like. Let me tell you that this has just fired up his dislike of the island and most of the people here and he's not for listening to Mrs Nicey Nicey, as he calls me. Between you and me doctor Lucinda is worse. She can be very hard and insensitive. She sees black and white and she is out for revenge. It may be they would listen to someone like you but I rather doubt it.

"What George has never been able to understand is why people here don't like us. He keeps going on about what my father and grandfather did for the island and the people here, but that was a long time ago now and folk have forgotten daddy and grampa and just see my brother as a grasping and resentful, largely absentee landlord."

Lady Ginny's assessment of the situation was stopped by approaching footsteps and her brother emerged from his bedroom and walked slowly down the stairs. Brian could see his face was badly bruised and his nose well out of alignment. Then as he got closer the doctor could see swelling round the bottom of the eyes and blood caked round the nostrils.

For the doctor there was no need for sensitivity. He told it as it was. "That looks pretty bad Lord Telford – You need to have it looked at properly as soon as possible. It looks to me as though your nose will need reset a bit and there may be other damage. Andrew obviously packs a mighty punch."

"It wasn't a punch. I might have seen that coming. It was the thug's weapon. The forehead. I wasn't expecting that. To be honest I wasn't expecting any violence from that young man despite what he had just done to my son.

"I would have thought he might have had the brains not to assault the person who has kept his useless parents in work and shelter for most of his life but sadly he obviously has not. Ginny has been at their house this morning already and made it clear they are not welcome here ever again. I'm also going to take immediate steps to get them out of Lighthouse View Cottage. It's about time that cottage was done up but I wasn't going to spend money for scum like that. Renovated it will make a good home for people prepared to do an honest days work for an honest day's pay."

"Don't you think you are being a little hasty, Lord Telford?" asked the doctor. "I mean this is basically a drunken fight between two teenagers that you seem to have got in the way of"

Before he could press his case any further Lord Telford shot him down in flames. "Thank you for your wise words doctor. But to be frank you don't know what you are talking about. It's all very well for holidaymakers like you with your romanticised image of this place and the people here. I have to live with the reality and as far as this family is concerned that is simply they are useless drunks who have benefitted for too long from my generosity. But no more. They are out and their thug of a son will go with them. We don't need people like them here and you should stick to what you know and let me get on with running my business."

The words spoken by Lord Telford made the doctor angry by both their tone and content. Here was a man born to privilege who was seemingly unable to behave in any other manner than like a bully. OK so the doctor knew he did not have a grip on the whole background of the relationship between this master and his servant but he could see a man in front of him who was a stranger to decency. He had gone to the big house for medical reasons but suddenly felt no obligation to volunteer his services any more.

As he turned to leave he made a final plea for clemency: "I might not know the ins and outs of the position but I can see a family struggling with the challenges of our modern world and living in accommodation provided by you that could best be described as squalid." He took Lord Telford's shocked silence as a cue to continue. "Do you ever stop to think that respect is earned and not given as a right. You may be an Earl and descended from all sorts of famous people but at the end of the day it seems to me that you are a bad employer that cares nothing for those who work for you and I rather think you are now reaping what you have sown over the years.

"On each visit to your island it becomes increasingly clear to me that the challenges of remoteness and physical isolation from the mainland are nothing compared to the challenges of having an incompetent bully like you as a landlord. One only has to look at the decaying buildings, collapsed walls and toppled fences to see what your tenure adds up to here.

"I take it you have no further need of my medical skills and so I'm off to spend the first day of the new year with people who mean something to me."

With that blistering attack he turned and walked to the front door and out to where Ben was waiting for him in the car.

"You were quite a while dad, are they ok?"

"Yes fine" said the doctor as he pulled away down the muddy puddled track and out onto the island road.

Fine is not a word Lord Telford would have used to describe his demeanour. Apoplectic would have been closer to the truth. Not only had he been violently assaulted in his own home, as had his son, but he had now been verbally assaulted by some jumped up holidaymaker who felt he had the right to lay down the law despite the fact he could have no real knowledge of what he was talking about. He walked over to where he telephone was sitting on top of a rather nice but under polished sideboard. He hesitated for a second and then poked 999 into the buttons. "Police." Pause. "Hello, I want to report two vicious assaults. Yes. My name is Lord Telford."

Attention was focussed on the phone across at Lighthouse View Cottage as well. There the news was incoming. Caroline had been told by Jim's doctor that they had found what could only be cancerous growths which seemed to be coming from his liver. Whilst, they had explained, they did not want to say too much over the telephone and without more tests, it would be a good idea for Caroline to get to her husband's bedside as quickly as she could. She had explained that there had not been a ferry since his condition had become a matter of concern and the next boat to the mainland was fully two days away. She would come then, but there was no chance of an earlier escape from the island.

Caroline deliberately avoided using the C word when telling Andrew about what the doctors had found preferring instead to say they had discovered a couple of growths that needed further exploration. She said she was leaving the island on the first ferry, the ferry Andrew had been expecting to take back to school, and he should go with her to the hospital. School wasn't back until the seventh so he had plenty of time.

The phone was also playing a large part in the lives of another little group on the island that morning. Jack Williams was desperately phoning round trying to get an aircraft of some sort to pick him, Sally and Claudia up as soon as possible. The couple had woken early, talked over the events of the night before and concluded they had to get out. They could not bear the thought of having to spend two more days with the Telfords. Claudia wasn't even upset that she and George were finished. She was angry. Angry with him for his behaviour at Hogmanay and angry with herself for taking so long to realise what a prat he was. She now understood why her Chevening College friends were so puzzled by their relationship and how it could have gone on for so long. They all said she was far too good, far too nice and far too intelligent to be going out with George Emberton, for that was his Chevening College name – using the courtesy title that had been avoided on the island. Lord Emberton might be good at rugby, heir to an earldom and in line to inherit a Scottish island and much reduced estate in England but it took more than that to impress his school friends who were able to see through the gloss to the real person behind.

As Jack and Sally went over and over their options and searched for air taxis their uncomfortable predicament was solved, sort of. They had been dreading going downstairs and facing the Telfords, injuries and all. Dreading their daughter meting her now ex-boyfriend. It was going to be bad enough for her going back to school but here, in his own home, beyond difficult. The solution came heralded by a firm knock at the bedroom door. Sally opened it to find a stony faced Lucinda standing there. She made to smile and was about to wish her hostess a happy new year but didn't get the chance.

"I think in the circumstances it would be a good idea for you and your family to leave our home." There was not a hint of friendliness, Sally realised civility was not going to have to be a necessary part of her response.

"That's exactly what we are trying to do. Jack has called umpteen air taxi companies and can't find one willing or able to come out here before the ferry on Thursday and so I fear we are stuck".

Lucinda was ahead of her. "Not stuck here. I have spoken to the hotel and they are making up a couple of rooms for you. It's usually closed for the whole winter but I'm sure you will be quite comfortable. The bar's open and there will be food available. Henry is waiting outside to take you down and I think you should leave as soon as possible.

"I have to say my son is very upset by your daughter's behaviour last night and his father and I are saddened that she has chosen to repay our hospitality in this manner."

As Sally tried to gauge how her response should be, least said soonest mended, or fight fire with fire, Jack jumped in.

"Lucinda, Claudia has done nothing wrong and I deeply resent you trying to say that she has. Your son showed himself to be spiteful and a bully last night and got what he deserved. You can't believe how happy we will be to get out of this dump and away from you people. We should have been having a nice new year holiday with folk we like and value not stuck in this place with a bunch of throw backs. You and your husband need to get yourselves into this century and take a long hard look at yourselves. You wouldn't survive in the real world and as far as I can see you are in danger of dragging down this whole island with you. Not that I care. I'll never be back here, that's for sure."

Before Lucinda had a chance to respond the bedroom door was slammed in her face leaving her to turn on her heels and disappear into the depths of the house and wait for her guests to pack up and go. A short time later from the safety of her husband's library she heard the Land Rover driving off.

So it was that by six in the evening Jack, Sally and Claudia were in much more agreeable company in the bar of the island hotel. They felt no sense of loyalty and were happy to tell anyone wanting to hear just how ghastly their new year had been and how relieved they were that in future they need having nothing to do with the Telfords. The locals lapped it up.

Caroline was well refreshed at Kenny Kelps and rather beginning to enjoy the sympathy that her husband's accident and illness had engendered amongst the wider island community. There were many fault lines and fueds on the island but when the chips were down the population retained an ability to come together and look after their own.

At the farmhouse the Thompson family and Andrew were doing their best to put troublesome matters to one side. Andrew had naturally been seeking the doctors views on what his father's newly discovered illness might mean. Dr Thompson for his part was cautious not to say too much. From what he had heard and what he knew if Jim's lifestyle the outlook may well be bleak, but he couldn't be expected to know and he certainly wasn't going to speculate. In the circumstances, he was quite happy for Ben and Drew to share wine with the food, but in a measured medical sort of way. Not the sort of way things were going at Kenny Kelp's or indeed at the big house. There Lord Telford was sitting in the drawing room, all the family mustered for their council of war. Punctuated by sniffs and long sips of whisky he went on, and on, about what had happened and what he was going to do about it.

He dismissed the pleas of first his sister Ginny and later brother Henry to be reasonable. He had been reasonable and this is where it had got him.

There were new enemies to take on too – not just the usual island scum and layabouts. The Williams. What on earth was Chevening thinking about taking in girls like Claudia Williams. "The whole point of paying for education is to ensure you don't end up mixing with people like the bloody Williams," was a concise summation of his Lordship's view of independent schooling in general and Chevening College in particular.

"When I was there it was people like us. Now…….."His voice trailed away as his glance settled on the near empty glass of Bruichladdich.

Young George had seemingly got over whatever distress he may have suffered by the ending of his relationship. He didn't feel the need to jump to the defence of his former girlfriend preferring instead to concentrate on feeling sorry for himself. His sore face. His tiredness – its very hard to sleep with a broken nose – and his disenchantment with his friends Tom and Orlando. He had spent a good part of the day remonstrating with them for not jumping to his defence and giving Andrew a good doing. As the evening wore on the patience of the house party wore out and one by one they made their excuses to wander off into the kitchen where Mrs Grant had left enough food to keep them going for a week and disappear off to other parts of the house for an evening away from the egregious earl.

At the farmhouse things were pretty quiet too. The dramas of the previous evening had cast an air of gloom over New Year and no one could really be bothered. So it was by 11pm the father suggested giving Andrew a lift home. They were all tired and the forecast for tomorrow suggested it would be a good day for walking – their last chance to spend the day outdoors on the island before heading off on the first ferry of the new year.

Andrew declined the offer of a lift saying he would prefer to walk. It was a still and cold night but he would enjoy the fresh air. At the back of his mind there was also an embryonic plan that he did not want to reveal to his hosts that he might perhaps make a slight detour to the bar, or to Kenny Kelp's. There would be fun to be had at either. He rather imagined the goings on of the previous night might well have earned him something of a celebrity status amongst the locals. Anyway a wee party would be better that going home to a damp cold cottage and waiting for his mother to stagger in – which could be anytime between now and the weekend, he thought.

So with expressions of gratitude and assurances that he would be fine Andrew set off, nominally, home but actually in search of fun.

He was especially glad of his expensive shooting jacket that night. The heavy cloud cover had done little to stop the temperature plummeting and Andrew maintained a fast pace to keep warm, save for the hand holding the torch. It was pitch black. A couple of times he turned off the torch to see what he could see. Nothing. That's what could be seen that night. Visitors to the island from the mainland were quick to notice just how dark it was on moonless nights like this. A complete darkness most had not encountered before.

After about twenty minutes, and by now on course for the bar, he could first hear and then see the headlights of an approaching vehicle. Experience had taught him to be cautious. At night on the island it was very likely anyone driving would, to put it nicely, not be at their most alert for a darkly dressed pedestrian. So Andrew stepped right back onto the verge to give plenty room to the fast approaching Land Rover, by the sound of it, to pass.

However the Defender stopped just short of Andrew, his eyes blinded by its full headlights shining right into his face. "Thanks" he thought. He stood for a second trying to make up his mind whether to continue or if the vehicle would take off again. Suddenly he saw two silhouettes running towards him through the main beam.

They didn't pause. Not a word was said. The figures didn't hesitate. A fist smashed right into Andrew's mouth. Simultaneously he was being kicked and then there was another fist to the face. The pain was instant and intense. His lanky frame couldn't cope with the brutal onslaught. He lurched forward completely unable to defend himself. Smash. Smash. Smash. Three more blows to the face. He was losing vision. He tried to push away the person that seemed to be taking the lead in the attack but he was by now completely unable to focus. He could feel his mouth filling up with blood. The pain was unbearable. He simply didn't stand a chance and fell to the ground trying his best to protect himself. He half screamed, half groaned. "Fuck off. Get off me." Other than that his words were lost to shock.

Two onto one. The element of surprise. The savagery of the attack. A particularly brutal kick to the head was enough to end Andrew's immediate suffering. He slipped into unconsciousness. One of the attackers put his foot on Andrew's body and rolled it over better to inspect their handiwork. His face was covered in blood. His arm assumed a most unusual position.

The savagery was over in probably less than a minute. The silhouettes walked back to the Land Rover, climbed in, reversed quickly up to a passing place and turned round before speeding off the way they came. The engine noise faded into the distance leaving the night still and silent once more. Andrew's breathing was irregular and quiet. Then a shiver set in. A shiver of cold and of shock. Many minutes passed and slowly he began to come round. An attempt to open his eyes found him blinded by a powerful light. He managed to move his head slightly without taking it off the road. It was his torch. It had fallen shining straight at him. He tried to sit up but his whole body was screaming with pain. His chest seemed to be stabbed by each breath he took. His legs were throbbing. His arm was dead. He tried to rest on it but it just collapsed leaving him crashing back down onto the road with pain searing all over.

Lying there on the road he could only think of survival. He rolled over onto his other side grimacing as new areas of pain revealed themselves. This time he managed to sit up. He wiped his eyes with the sleeve of his jacket and gingerly leant over to pick up the torch. He could see the rich tweed covered in his blood.

There was nothing else for it – he would have to get up and walk. It could be hours before anyone drove past. What if his attackers came back? He half rolled into a kneeling position supported by the arm that was still working and pushed himself up. He couldn't straighten his body. The pain from his guts and chest was too bad. He paused for a second for orientation and crouching at a near right angle shuffled off once more towards the bar which was over a mile away but the nearest habitation. He stopped for a second to throw up and was terrified to see blood red vomit. He prayed for someone to pass. A friendly face. There was none. He kept shuffling, stumbling over the grass verge a couple of times as he went. It was near impossible to see with his eyes caked in blood. And cold too. Freezing and shivering. Teeth chattering and his shoes scraping along the road. He was having terrible trouble working out what had just happened let alone why it had happened and who could have been responsible. It took an age but Andrew eventually saw the lights of the bar shining through the darkness. They were faint but at least it gave hope that he was going to reach people and help.

The entrance to the public bar was protected by a porch which also gave shelter to the smokers. As he neared, he saw no one outside. Reaching the door he could hear music and lots of voices inside. His hand was shaking so much he couldn't turn the handle. It was always a bit stiff. Someone inside must have realised a latecomer was trying to get into the party and, perhaps presuming the new guest was a little worse for wear, opened the door from within.

Andrew could just make out the shape of a woman as his eyes screwed up against the light. The woman screamed. He recognised the voice. It was Jean, his mother's friend.

Still stooped with pain he half staggered half fell into the bar.

"My God – what's happened to you?" a male voice asked. Someone tried to help him by grabbing an arm for support. It was more than Andrew could bear. The simple helpful gesture caused a bolt of acute pain to run right up his arm and neck into his head and explode somewhere behind his eyes. He screamed. That cry of pain left no one in any doubt as to the seriousness of the situation.

More gently this time hands came to help and he was led carefully to the bench seat at the back of the bar next to the fireplace where a pile of peat was smouldering away.

The bar was packed and most of the clientele were drunk. Once more it fell to shopkeeper Peter McGilvary to come to the aid of the Edward family. Two days ago it was the father. Now the son needed help. The son, Peter thought, looked as though he was in a much worse state than the father had been. As usual Peter had been at the party but in keeping with his belief that new year was a dangerous time he'd not been drinking as long or as hard as some in the bar that night.

He shouted to no one in particularly: "Keep and eye on him. Try and warm him up – I'm going to the farmhouse for the doctor."

No one seemed sure what to do. Blood was continuing to ooze from his wounds. The ceilidh music coming from the CD player behind the bar leant an unreal dimension to the shocking situation. It had taken a little while for the seriousness of what was going on to become apparent to everyone in the bar. Some of the revellers were so far gone they struggled to comprehend anything very much, one even complaining that someone had stopped the party.

Another one of the drinkers was confused as to who the visiting doctor was and staggered off into the hotel part of the building to find the family that "had been thrown out of the big house" as the rumours had put it thinking they must be the medics.

Jack and Sally Williams had deliberately kept out of the bar once the party had started. They felt their dismissal from the big house had made them of too much interest and had spent the evening watching television in the resident's lounge where another peat fire had eventually taken the damp feel off the room. Claudia was looking at the TV without taking any of it in. She would have been hard pressed to say exactly what she was watching even if anyone had bothered to ask.

The "helpful" man walked in and in a voice reduced to near incomprehension by a combination of accent and drink asked Jack if he was the doctor.

"I'm not – why, who needs a doctor?" he said thinking half the bloody island would probably need a doctor by this time on New Year's night.

"One of the island kids, Andrew Edward, has had an accident and he looks in a bad way."

Claudia leapt from her seat, demanded to know where he was and rushed off to the bar on being told. She pushed through the people huddled round the injured party and sat next to him. She put her head close to his blood spattered face. She was revolted by what she saw and gagged.

Quietly she spoke: "What the hell has happened to you? You look awful."

Andrew wasn't able to respond very much able only to mutter that he had been given a doing by some people.

One of the less drunk of the adults picked up on what he had just said.

"Who's done this to you son? Who was it?"

97

Andrew sat in silence.

Claudia helped. "Was it George?"

The simple act of shrugging his shoulders caused Andrew so much pain he winced again and fell forward. Someone reached out and grabbed him to stop him tumbling right off the bench. Jack and Sally had by now joined their daughter. He might not have been a doctor but he was sober which put him in a better position to help that anyone else in the bar.

"Listen folks just leave him quiet. He's in no shape to speak. Has anyone gone for help? Can we phone someone?"

Sally said she would phone. In the naïve way of a mainlander she thought a 999 call would bring instant assistance. She went back to the lounge for quiet and dialled.

When details of the call were passed to the duty inspector in the mainland police control room it set alarm bells ringing.

The inspector turned to his sergeant and asked: "Wasn't there a couple of assaults on the island the other day?"

The other officer scrolled back through the reports on his computer terminal and confirmed that was the case.

"It says here that the guy who owns the island and his son were attacked in their house. It looks as though it wasn't considered serious enough to attend and we had an arrangement to see the victims on Thursday when the ferry gets in. They are meant to be coming here."

Questioned further the sergeant said there was a name for the attacker. A 16 year old local youth.

"It's not Andrew Edward is it?"

"It is indeed."

"He appears to be the victim of an assault this time. It looks as though it's serious. They've sent the air ambulance for him – priority."

Back in the bar Brian Thompson had arrived and was much more concerned about the state of this patient than he had been about his father Jim two nights before or indeed the Telfords last night. Some holiday he was having.

He had managed to get Andrew's jacket off him. Someone had made a cup of tea. The doctor was doing his best to make Andrew as comfortable as he could. He had given him a shot of painkiller which was working but he was certain the teenager had suffered internal injuries and had pleaded with the ambulance controllers to make this medivac a priority. He was obviously losing a lot of blood.

A quilt and blankets had been brought from one of the bedrooms which worked with the tea, peat and painkiller to calm the patient down. He was drowsy but Claudia and Brian kept talking to him.

Peter McGilvary went back out of the bar and moved his car as close to the door as he could. The helicopter was on its way with an eta just 20 minutes away.

Chapter 10

The young trauma doctor waiting amongst the welcoming party next to the hospital helipad was seen to grimace at Andrew's face which was the first part of his body to emerge as the stretcher was slid out of the chopper. He looked awful. The medical team quickly loaded him onto a trolley and rushed off towards the A and E department. Two uniformed police officers followed them in.

The helicopter paramedic recited as much as he knew of the circumstances as they sped to the main hospital building. "16 year old, name of Andrew Edward – apparently the victim of an assault and may have been left lying in the open for some time. He's had doctor administered morphine before leaving the island and we've given him oxygen on the way over."

Once inside a cubicle and transferred onto a bed and a detailed examination was underway. Andrew was by now barely conscious and was unable to understand much of what was happening. Transfusion, scan, next of kin were the main words to catch his attention.

As the doctors worked on Andrew news of what had befallen him was spreading round the island. Bad news always had better wings. As is the way in many small communities good news did not seem to garner the interest of the population in the same way as a nice juicy bit of bad luck or ill fortune. So it was that tales of Andrew's plight went from house to house.

Caroline had the good fortune to hear direct from Peter McGilvaray who had only to call a couple of houses from the bar telephone to track her down at Kenny Kelp's party. To say she was confused by drink was to be charitable beyond need. It took several tellings for the enormity of what had befallen her son to sink in. He ended the call by telling Caroline to wait where she was – he would come and pick her up. It took several moments after the call ended for Peter to question that plan, Pick her up. For what purpose? There was no where she needed to be other than at her son's bedside and that was impossible now. It seemed wrong though to leave her boozing at the party while her son lay in such a perilous predicament in hospital. The remoteness of the island community dictated that in fact there was not much else to do.

She could phone, but it was too early – she could go home, but why? He was about to call her back and change the plan when someone suggested the right thing to do would be to get her and Dr Thompson in contact. He was really the only one that would be able to give her the reassurance she might require, drunk as she was.

So once again Peter set off for the Farmhouse and another disturbance of the Thompson family holiday. They were of course far from holiday mood as they sat in the living room of the farmhouse with the wood fire crackling in the grate. Their speculation as to the cause of Andrew's injuries was punctuated by the sparking of the driftwood sending glowing embers far into the room to be dealt with by a Thompson child fielding with the small shovel that was one of the few implements provided for hearth management.

"You know Brian it can only have been George, and his two, did you say two, friends that attacked Drew. It is disgusting," said the mother.

They had been agonising over what they should do about the attack. Their only connection was Brian's professional intervention and he thought that relationship stopped him getting too involved. But he was involved and also sober, which on the island on January 1 counted for a lot. Few of the population were capable of rational thought that night. Eventually they resolved to speak to the police in the morning; it was bound to be a police matter by then if it was not already.

News of the attack reached the big house by a different route. It came direct from the attackers. Young George had been feeling pretty grim and had gone to bed to try and get some sleep despite his still throbbing face and the intense pain when his nose came into contact with – well, with anything.

He had been lying half asleep with much going through his teenage mind when his school friend Tom Morris opened the door slightly: "Are you awake George --- we've some great news."

101

George lay still deciding whether to respond. He had thought it would be good fun to bring his friends to the island for new year – to impress them with his family's estate. Reality had turned out differently and he had regretted inviting them almost from the moment they arrived to play gooseberry, as he thought. Tom was OK but he was finding Orlando Russell really tedious. Far from being impressed with the Telford's island playground he had several times asked George how he could bear to spend time in such a God forsaken place. They were also rather annoyed that their host's promise of some deer stalking and even some cannabis had failed to materialise, for no good reason they could spot.

"George- wake up – its important," said Tom turning on the light and waking into the bedroom followed by Orlando.

"Something's happened and we need to do something about it."

George screwed up his eyes and peered to where the outlines were standing in the vastness of his bedroom. He pulled himself up into an upright position looking for all the world like a hospital patient with his face still marked and bloodied and the plaster holding his broken nose in place. "What?"

Tom's voice fell to a whisper. "We found that kid Andrew on the road a couple of hours ago and gave him a bit of a doing."

Those edited highlights demanded so many questions George struggled to know where to begin. After a few seconds the first request for more information centred on perhaps the least relevant aspect of the event.

"Why were you out? What were you doing?"

Orlando took up the story: "We borrowed your dad's Land Rover and went for a drive round. We weren't looking for him but when we saw him it was too good an opportunity."

George couldn't see from which of them the snigger had come from.

"He was on the road, by himself and so we thought we'd teach him a bit of a lesson. Scum like that need to understand they can't have a go at us without paying the price."

"Exactly" said Tom. "We just stopped, jumped out and gave him a doing. He wouldn't have known what hit him."

102

"Or who" interjected Orlando with a big smile spreading over his face.

"What the fuck have you done?" demanded George beginning to get worried and cross and concerned in equal measure. Yes concerned for all he was furious at the way Andrew had behaved at Hogmanay he was coming to realise that he was equally to blame, perhaps even more so. He had spent quite a lot of the last few hours thinking about Andrew. They had been such good friends. It had also begun to dawn on him that life had dealt his playmate of all those years ago a pretty dud hand.

"So how is he? How did you leave him? Where did you leave him?"

"Put it this way," said Tom with the sort of teenage snigger that would send most adults into a rage, "he'll be fucking sore tomorrow. We did a good job on the little bastard. He'll have learnt a lesson."

"So where is he now?"

"How would we know George. We just left him where he was. He'll have got up and continued on his way."

"A bit slower than before" chuckled one of the assailants.

George was speechless. He did not have a clue what to do. He did know one thing. The attack had nothing to do with him and if he had known of the plan he would have stopped it. Long experience of the island had taught George that few things remain secret for long. Many the time he had hoped his minor misdemeanours would remain undiscovered only to find out his parents knew about some act of mischief and knew occasionally before he had even got home.

"I'll have to tell my father. He will find out, if he doesn't know already," said George getting out of bed and putting on the dressing gown that lay across the old sofa which occupied the huge bay window of the room. George emerged onto the landing to be greeted by the sounds of doors being banged. The knocking at the front seemed urgent – the crash at the back of the house was like an Atlantic storm hitting.

Downstairs his mother rushed across the hall to the front door. There was no need to attend to the back door for Caroline and Kenny had just burst in on finding it unlocked and were emerging from the kitchen corridor as Lucinda Telford opened the front door to find the doctor there, again. Before Lucinda had a chance to ask why the late night visit she turned quickly to see what was causing the commotion behind. She saw Caroline lurching across the hall towards her. She was bright red in the face and seemingly unable to walk without Kenny's steadying arm round her. "What the fuck have you done to my Andrew? Where's your cunt of a son. You'll all be in jail for this." The target of Caroline's last utterance was unclear but Lucinda and Dr Thompson both felt it could not have been directed at them.

Lucinda struggled to make sense of what was happening in her home in the middle of the night. Whatever it was that woman had no right to be in her hall and needed to get out. An uncontrollable rage took hold and she half screamed, half shouted: "Caroline – you are drunk and need to get out of my house now. What do you think you are doing bursting in here in the middle of the night. Get out. Get out right now – and you too Kenny – you are not welcome here."

With that she started shouting for reinforcement from her husband. "George – George come quickly I need help. Quickly"

Her husband was already on his way. His evening's entertainment had been mainly aimed at emptying the bottle of Bruichladdich so as he stumbled into the hall confusion was written all over his face. He stood still looking first at the raging Caroline, then his wife and Dr Thompson. "What the hell is going on? Why are you here?" he said looking directly at Caroline who by now was standing directly in front of Lady Telford who tried to back away but found herself up against the sideboard.

Brian Thompson attempted to bring some order: "Look everyone – may I suggest we all go and sit down somewhere – a lot has gone on tonight and you all need to sober up pretty quickly."

Lucinda took exception claiming she'd hardly had a drink. The doctor didn't bother apologising but watched her bump into the doorway as she made her unsteady way compliantly into the drawing room. Caroline lurched in directly behind her and started up again this time addressing the doctor. "These bastards have put my son in hospital – do you know that? They left him lying in the road. A boy. He's just a fucking boy and they have put him into hospital." She span round almost falling over in the process

104

and staggered towards Lord Telford. "Was it you? – you stuck up bastard. You got what you deserved." For a moment it looked as though she might attempt to hit him.

"I haven't got a clue what you are talking about but if you and Kenny don't leave here immediately I'm going to have you thrown out." Quite how that threat would be carried out was far from clear but reasoned analysis wasn't in great supply. Without raising his voice Brian Thompson tried again to inject some calm: "I want you all to be quiet." He paused waiting for obedience and repeated the request even more quietly. "Please. Very serious events have taken place tonight that I think concern everyone here. It would be helpful if you all listened for a minute." The calm bedside manner had the desired effect and Caroline and Kenny fell into one of the enormous sofas and the earl and countess settled slightly more seemingly onto chairs on the other side of the fireplace.

"I think it would be helpful if young George and his friends were able to join us. Are they about Lady Telford?" asked the doc.

Just at this point young George and the other two walked into the room. Brian saw three young men with very different expressions between them.

George looked shocked, genuinely worried. As for the other two – they looked rather pleased with themselves. Smirking despite the seriousness of the situation and slow to spot the volatile drunken atmosphere they had walked into the midst of. He also noticed one of the friends appeared to trying to conceal a rather grazed hand. The other one had his hand in his pocket. The three teenagers knew exactly what had been going on and the doctor knew the detail of the outcome if not the input. Only Lord and Lady Telford had genuinely not a clue as to what had occured earlier that night. Caroline and Kenny fuelled with drink and informed by rumour were struggling to make sense of the events but their ability to understand was overwhelmed by worry and outrage and, of course, booze.

Tears rolled down Caroline's face. Whether they were tears of sorrow or tears of anger was not clear. Slurring her words she wanted to know how badly hurt her son was. "Did you see him Brian? They say he is in a bad way."

"I can't really say too much Caroline. I didn't get much of a chance to examine Andrew – I just wanted to get him off to hospital as quickly as possible. By the time I saw him he had lost a lot of blood. He may well have some internal injuries and has a lot of superficial bruising. I also think his arm was broken. He needed more than I could do and I know he is in A and E right now and they will be doing everything they can for him"

Brian was hoping he was the only one to see the two friends smirk as though they were being given a score out of ten for their efforts – and reached near full points.

"He was stable when he left in the helicopter and I had given him some strong painkiller so he probably won't remember much about his flight.

"I really don't think his life is in danger, but to be honest he wasn't a pretty sight. Whoever did this to him didn't hold back."

He paused. The words slowly sank into Caroline's confused brain. The doctor took the opportunity to give the three teenagers a long, firm stare. Each in turn avoided his gaze. Caroline buried her face in Kenny's chest and her muffled howl shocked everyone in the room. Kenny patted her back and all remained silent for a moment.

Then the doctor took the lead once more. "I don't think it would be helpful for me to try and work out exactly what happened tonight it really has very little to do with me.

"But I will tell you that it is my opinion that we could well have been dealing with the death of a young man - a young man I have come to know quite well during our visits here and a young man my family like very much.

"Whatever happened to him, and whoever did it, will become clear but I say to you all I am disgusted by the events of the last two days.

"I am not going to try and apportion blame – its not my job – but for people like you, people of your standing, to be involved in something like this appals me."

Lord Telford took exception. "Doctor – in case you have forgotten my son and I were victims of a viscous and unprovoked assault by a young thug who repaid my hospitality with violence."

Caroline was oblivious to his lordship's views being expressed as she continually sobbed pressed hard into Kenny, her head spinning and an element of shock entering into her torrid emotional mix.

"That may be the case George," the doctor felt no need for continuing formality, "but someone on this island, or even some people, have decided to attack Andrew and done so in a most brutal manner. Perhaps you could shed some light on what's happened George."

Young George did not have a clue how to react or what to say. He was so conflicted his head was spinning and his emotions on the point of being uncontrollable. In the past few hours he had lost his girlfriend and been beaten up by someone he had regarded as a friend. He felt betrayed by his school mates but, at the same time, protective of them. He stood looking at the doctor desperately trying to come up with words to make clear his innocence in the attack on Andrew but yet not implicate the real culprits. Thoughts flashed through his mind.

His father intervened: "Are you trying to say my son was responsible for this latest savagery?"

"George I'm not trying to say anything. But everyone in this room needs to understand what has gone on tonight and what the implications are. I know the police met the air ambulance and so inevitably questions will be asked, and rightly so, and I for one will be happy to answer any questions asked of me. I just hope everyone else here will be so cooperative."

Young George found his voice at last: "Brian I can tell you honestly this has nothing to do with me. I had nothing to do with this. I was not involved in any way with whatever happened to Andrew."

"As I said I really do not want to get involved in that side of things. I have played my part as a doctor. I have no intention of trying to be a detective. Caroline, I think it would be a good idea if you were to go home now. I'll come with you and we can phone the hospital and find out what's happening."

The smirks had long gone from the two assailants who had tried to slip back into the relative darkness of the far end of the drawing room as the enormity of their actions slowly sank in.

Brian walked forward and offered his hand to help Caroline who by now was more crumpled than slumped. Overpowered by events she slowly allowed herself to be pulled and pushed to her feet and silently walked slowly and unsteadily out of the room with Kenny and Brian acting as supporters.

The rest stayed silent until they heard the front door shut and privacy return to their home. Lord Telford was first to speak.

"George – you need to tell me exactly what has gone on tonight. Were you involved in this horrific attack on Andrew?" Sensing a hesitation from his son he carried on. "If you were there is no point in denying it because you will be found out," with a heavy emphasis on the will.

Lord Telford's dislike of most of the people on the island was born largely out of circumstance more than prejudice. He resented them primarily because of their threat to his financial stability but deep down he did have some traces of human decency and inevitably was shocked by what appeared to have gone on. He also had a nagging doubt that his son may know more about the assault than he was admitting to.

"Dad I am telling you this has nothing to do with me. I was not involved in anything. I've not left the house all night." He did not feel it necessary to carry on and impart the knowledge that he did have, second hand.

"That may be the case – you had better be telling the truth. This is serious George and if you and your friends had nothing to do with it then fine – but you may have trouble convincing other people, like the police."

Young George was surprised his friends had been so easily exculpated but wasn't going to defer.

Lucinda took control: "George I think it would be a good idea for you and me to have a talk in private, now."

He could tell from his mother's slow delivery and strident tone it was an order rather than a suggestion. Lucinda stood up and walked towards the door glancing back to make sure her son was following, which he was like an obedient puppy, tail between legs.

She led her son through to the library, usually her husband's domain but a suitably serious room for an important discussion. Closing the door behind George she told him to sit down. There was a pause as Lucinda re-corked the bottle of Bruichladdich and put it to one side.

She turned and looked straight at her son trying as best she could to read his face but struggled to conclude anything in particular with the emotion that might have been discernible obscured by the grazes and plaster, a reminder of a Hogmanay that was like no other.

"I want the truth George and I want it now. What has been going on tonight?"

"Mum this has nothing to do with me at all," said George doing his best to achieve a tone of indignation.

"I am prepared to accept that for now, but I am not prepared to accept that you know nothing about the attack on Andrew. I hope for your sake that you have had nothing to do with it. No part in encouraging, planning or anything at all. I am going to make sure your father phones the police to report the incident," that seemed a strange word to use in the circumstances – rather underplaying a violent, sustained and vicious assault, "and I want to make sure that our story is right from the start and if you had no involvement then that needs to be made plain.

"But George you have to understand that if it subsequently becomes evident that you were involved, or even knew what was going to happen and did nothing to stop it lying now will only make things worse. So, tell me exactly what you know of what went on tonight."

Mother and son stared at each other for a while. George slowly came to the conclusion there was little point in trying to protect his friends. It was obvious they would be identified as the attackers easily enough. But, he thought, there was a chance, maybe, if the pair of them were able to keep to a story they could just deny everything. What if there had been a witness? He hadn't had time to talk things through with them. Finally he decided there was no real choice other than to tell the truth as he knew it, the whole truth. Not least it occured to him that Andrew was his oldest friend and whilst bad things had gone on between them remnants of that friendship remained, as far as he was concerned.

Slowly George began to recount the happenings of the night, as far as he knew them.

"I had gone to bed mum. My face is still sore and I had had enough. That was it. I was in bed asleep and the next thing I knew was Tom and Orlando came into my bedroom and told me they had taught Andrew a lesson." If he thought that rather abridged version of the story was going to suffice George was mistaken.

"Ok George I'm going to ask your father to join us. This is serious. Stay right there."

George found his reluctance in implicating his friends draining away quite quickly. His mother's tone reinforced what he was coming round to understanding anyway. This was serious.

The shock of the evening had gone some way to sobering up Lord Telford and he appeared to his son to be pretty switched on when he came into the library a short time later followed by his mother.

"Your mother tells me that Tom and Orlando have admitted to you that they attacked Andrew Edward, is that right?" George nodded.

"I want you to give me your absolute assurance, absolute assurance, that you had nothing to do with this. I want to be certain that you didn't put them up to it, help them in any way or have any knowledge that his was going to happen."

"You must believe me dad. I knew nothing about this until after it happened and they came into my bedroom to tell me."

"Certain?"

"Certain".

"Ok – we need to think what to do for the best. I imagine the police will be involved by now. I think it would be in your interests, in all our interests, if we went to them now before they come looking for us. God what a mess. What is your school going to think of this? Am I going to have to phone up the headmaster and tell him three of his pupils have been arrested?"

"Dad if anyone is arrested it will be two. You have to believe me I had nothing to do with this, nothing. Nothing at all."

"Ok. On that basis I think I should phone the police and tell them all we know. George tell your friends to get themselves here now, please."

As the teenager went off to find the attackers Lucinda turned to her husband. "George are you sure that we need to call the police. Aren't we just going to make trouble for the boys? I'm sure that Andrew can't be as badly hurt as they are claiming. It could just all blow over as a bit of teenage exuberance."

"Lucinda if we are to believe George, and I have no reason not to, he looks to me as though he's telling the truth, then we have nothing to fear. If nothing comes of it fine at least we can be seen to have acted properly. If on the other hand Andrew is seriously injured and charges result, a court case and then heaven knows what, it is important for George that we are honest and straightforward from the outset."

Before that discussion could go any further the library door opened and the three boys entered in single file. They formed up in front of the stove, by now long burnt out, and turned to face Lord Telford.

The older man had not taken sufficient interest in his young house guests over the past few days to be absolutely certain which one was which. He took the easy way and looking at none of them in particular asking for an explanation of events and attaching the name Tom to his request.

Yes that's the one he thought it was. Tom took on the role as spokesman.

"Sir we owe you an apology."

"Go on"

"Earlier tonight, after George had gone to bed, we were a bit bored and I suppose because we had all had a few glasses of wine we thought it would be a laugh to go for a drive round your island."

"So we just went out, got into your Land Rover and went for a drive."

Lord Telford was going to interject a few observations but just managed to stop himself.

"We were not out for long and Orlando changed his mind. He said he wanted to go back. I was driving and was ok but Orlando said we would get into trouble and he was worried about abusing your hospitality, Sir."

"So he should have been. Let me get this straight. You are 16, I take it you don't have a driving licence, have been drinking and thought it would be fun to take my Land Rover without asking. That's theft. Go on"

"I told Orlando not to be a wimp and said we would go back – the long way round. Do a complete trip round the whole island. It was then we saw that kid Andrew walking towards us.

"When I stopped things just kind of happened. We kind of slapped him about a bit and left him."

Lucinda took some comfort from the fact that the two friends looked suitably appalled at their actions.

"Slapped him about a bit, Tom. Are you sure that is all you did? Do you know this boy has been airlifted to hospital and according to his mother is having an emergency operation right now? I must have been some slap."

"Honestly Sir," interjected Tom "I don't think either of us really hit him hard. We were just trying to teach him a lesson."

"And what lesson was that?" asked Lucinda. Her question went unanswered.

"George tells me he had nothing to do with this. No knowledge of it before, didn't ask you to do it or help plan. Is that right?" Telford's stare never left his son as he asked the question.

"That's right Sir," said Tom. "It wasn't planned. We were bored, went for a drive and that's that, Sir. The kid can't be that bad, we hardly touched him."

"I hope he's not bad: for your sakes," chided Lucinda.

"Right – I think it is in everyone's interests for me to phone the police right now. I know quite a few of them and I think it will be helpful if they realise they are dealing with some decent people who may have made a bit of a mistake. No doubt, if she has spoken to them, Caroline will have painted a very different picture." And with that Lord Telford left the Library, then returned sticking his head briefly round the door and adding "I think the pair of you should telephone your parents and let them know what is happening." He looked at his watch. "It is nearly 2 am but I am sure they would want to know directly from you rather than anyone else who may have a different version of events." With that he disappeared off into the house.

CHAPTER 11

Near the top of Lord Telford's complaints about the island, and there are an awful lot of them, are his winter season travel arrangements. Summers are great. He has the powerful cabin RIB, kept at a mainland harbour, that he uses all the time to go back and forth. It is a big beast and arrives at his harbour loaded up with people, dogs and provisions. Winter? Winter is a different matter. Winter means travel by public transport. With the public.

So it was that the Earl and Countess of Telford found themselves queuing up to board the first ferry of the new year with the rest of the travelling public. The public for this service was not engaging in the sort of merry chat that would normally have been the case milling round as the festive season draws to a close. Distinct groups had formed round the ferry terminal waiting room not communicating with each other and not talking much within these groups.

The Telfords, a party of six crammed into the Land Rover. The Thompsons and Williams together and Caroline and Kenny huddled up with island friends, and not looking their best.

Once onboard the separation of travellers continued. The Telford party sat in the bar area of the ferry, but did not avail themselves of the facilities. They kept very much to themselves.

Towards the bow of the boat, in the ship's restaurant, sat Caroline. She had been joined by Claudia and her family in something of a show of support. Kenny was travelling over with Caroline. The Thompson family too had allied themselves with Andrew's anguished mother and were sitting at the next table.

As the ferry reached the mainland and manoeuvred alongside the pier the usual announcement about going back to cars and making sure all the luggage was taken with you was replaced by one that they had not heard before.

"This is the captain speaking. There is going to be a short delay in disembarking the ferry today whilst the police come on board to deal with a matter. We apologise for this delay but assure you it will be kept as short as possible."

Lord Telford looked shocked. When he had finished telling the local police about what had happened to Andrew he had undertaken to report to the station with the teenagers as soon as the ferry docked.

He expressed his surprise to the rest of his party. They sat in silence waiting to see what happened next.

Within quarter an hour of that announcement a group of four uniformed policemen and what looked like two plain clothes officers strode into the bar area. They went straight up to the Telford family group which by now had risen as one to their feet.

One of the plain clothes officers reached into his pocket and pulled out a warrant card.

"Lord Telford?" He continued on the nod. "My name is Detective Inspector Bell. I am investigating a serious assault on a young man on the evening of January 1"

Telford's patience was never his strong suit. "I know of course, it was me that told you about it. I thought I was going to come to the police station. Why are you here holding everyone up – did you think we were going to run away or something?"

"In the light of the serious nature of the allegations I was told to meet the ferry, it's normal police practice.

"I take it these are the three teenagers you told us about." Another nod.

Turning to them he asked them to identify themselves when their names were called out.

"George Emberton – Tom Morris – Orlando Russell."

As each of the boys in turn responded to their name one of the uniformed officers stepped forward and held them by the upper arm.

DI Bell flicked through his notebook.

"George Emberton, Tom Morris and Orlando Russell I am arresting you on suspicion of the attempted murder of Andrew Edward on the night of January 1. In addition Tom Morris I am arresting you on suspicion of the theft of a Land Rover motor vehicle on the same evening and driving without a licence, insurance and over the alcohol limit.

114

"I must warn you that none of you are obliged to say anything but anything you do say will be noted and may be given in evidence."

The detective turned to George's parents and told them the three were being taken to the police station for interview.

"Because they are all under 17, I understand, they will be interviewed in the presence of what is termed an appropriate adult. For the purposes of this investigation I believe as you have both been involved in the events that have led to this arrest, that neither of you can qualify as an appropriate adult and so I will seek to find a social worker or one of our panel of volunteers to stand in."

Lord Telford looked close to exploding. Aware of the seriousness of the situation, and equally aware that they had been joined in the bar by a number of other travellers watching the drama, he kept as calm as he could, but his voice trembled as he spoke.

"Mr Bell I made it perfectly clear to you that my son had nothing to do with this incident. Can you tell me why he has been arrested like this? This could all have been done at the police station without turning it into an entertainment for these people." He said gesticulating at the audience.

"Lord Telford I am grateful for your contribution to the investigation but we have spoken to a number of other people and whilst we are still at an early stage, and things may change later, a young man has been subjected to a savage beating and is seriously ill in hospital. His life remains at risk and I am sure that you can see in these circumstances we can take no chances with our inquiry."

The detective turned and walked towards the bar door and the exit ramp from the ferry. The three boys followed each one still in the firm grip of the arresting officers.

Tears cascaded down Lucinda's cheeks. She grabbed on to a chair to steady herself. "George you can't just let them take our son way. He's done nothing. Tell them. He's innocent. George for God's sake stop them"

Lord Telford reached out and put his hand on his wife's shoulder. "Lucinda there is nothing I can do. It will sort itself out and I just hope George has been truthful. Our lawyer is sending a criminal specialist up from Edinburgh – in fact he should be here by now. Let's find him."

Caroline and Kenny had watched the drama unfold and she had taken some comfort in seeing her son's attackers being led away. Kenny had drilled into her the importance of not getting involved, not saying anything, being dignified and concentrating on Andrew and that is just what she did. She stood in silence as Lord and Lady Telford walked past with Mrs Grant in close formation. Caroline took particular comfort from the anguished look on her former employers' faces.

The loudspeaker clicked on again. "Captain speaking again. Thank you for your patience ladies and gentlemen. You are now free to disembark the vessel from the car deck or via the gangplank on the starboard side."

At the top of the stairs leading down to the cars Caroline bumped into Brian Thompson. Tears welled in her eyes and she held onto the doctor. "Thank you for what you have done for my family. I am very grateful and they will be too, I know that." She managed to smile through the tears as she added: "I bet you lot won't be rushing back to the island any time soon."

She leant forward and gave a shocked Brian a kiss on the lips.

"Caroline don't worry about us – I'm sure we will be back before long. Please just you give our very best wishes to Jim and Andrew. I would have gone to see them myself but we have to get home – it's a long drive and I'm back at work tomorrow."

"I will Brian. Thank you again."

Chapter 12

"Your son is in the end room on the right, Mrs Edward," said the nursing supervisor after Caroline had explained who she was. "There will be a nurse in with him – it's standard in intensive care."

The shock and horror of what was happening to her family had magnified hugely when she arrived at the hospital, driven by Kenny, to find Andrew had been switched from the surgical ward to ICU – the implication being that he wasn't recovering as well as had been expected after his operation.

Her son was a mess. Caroline was shocked into silence as she entered the side room. There was a nurse sitting next to the bed, on the far side underneath the window. "Can I help you?" she asked. "Hello I'm Andrew's mother, Caroline."

"Oh – sorry Mrs Edward I did not know you were coming. Come in and sit down. I am afraid Andrew will not know you are here. He's been operated on and is now heavily sedated. The surgeon wants him to sleep for as long as possible."

"How is he – what was the operation for – has it worked?"

"It's best you speak to Mr Singh the surgeon yourself. Anything I say may be wrong. He's still on duty so I will find out where he is and see if he can speak to you just now."

Caroline was looking nearly as big a mess as her son. She had gone back to Kenny's after the big house confrontation and the drinking had kicked off again until almost dawn. When she had woken up on Kenny's sofa there was not time to go home and shower and change before the ferry departed. She looked as though she'd come straight from a party, which she had.

"If Andrew can't wake up I think I should go and see my husband – he's in here too. Ward 6 I believe. Is that near here?"

The nurse said she would get someone to show her where Jim was and she would call when Mr Singh was able to see them.

Caroline had gone over and over in her mind how she would react to Jim when eventually she saw him. Would she be cross because of the stupidity of being so drunk he fell into a ditch and couldn't get out? Should she tell them about her dismissal and their threatened eviction? What about whatever it was that they had found? Jim's cancer? Let alone Andrew. What a few days.

In the event despite all these thoughts swirling round her head all she could manage on seeing Jim was: "Hello Love – how are you?" It seemed a bit weak but no others words came.

Jim was momentarily speechless at the banality of the question.

It hurt too much to if he tried to sit up on the pillows and so it was from his horizontal position Jim gave a comprehensive summation of how he saw matters.

Very slowly and barely audible he answered his wife: "How am I? Well I'm in hospital, I've got what they are calling an advanced cancer, my son is in intensive care, I hear I am homeless, you are unemployed. So how am I?"

He seemed, to Caroline, completely broken. Three days without a drink would not have helped, she thought, but even so she was taken aback at such a dramatic change in her partner of over 20 years over such a short space of time.

She half walked and half fell into the chair next to the bed, pressed her eyes onto Jim's upper arm and sobbed quietly. He patted her head and fought back tears himself. He'd had a long time to reflect on his life and the conclusions he was coming to were not comfortable.

"God knows what we are going to do Caroline. But things are a mess. A fucking mess."

At this his head leant over to hers and rested gently on her unwashed hair.

Back at the port Lucinda had been shedding her fair share of tears too. She and George had booked into one of the few hotels open at this time of year. They had no idea how long they were going to be there.

Lord Telford had taken it upon himself to telephone the College headmaster to warn him that three of his pupils had been arrested on suspicion of attempted murder. Never the sort of call a head would want at New Year, or any other time come to that. He hadn't thought to get the home numbers of George's friends but the head said he would contact them to let them know of developments. "Tell them to phone me, if they want to," said

Lord Telford dreading the prospect of having to explain to parents how the kids he was looking after were currently in a police cell facing extremely serious criminal charges.

Three hours had passed since the islanders had left the ferry heading their separate ways. Lucinda told George she thought they ought to go to the police station. Surely it wouldn't take long for them to realise they had made a mistake in arresting George too and he would be released at any moment.

"I mean you told them exactly what happened on the night it happened. Won't they just have to get that confirmed and let George go?"

"Lucinda I haven't a clue. Funnily enough I don't have a lot of experience of these situations."

She could hear her husband's growing exasperation, and probably a desire for gin and tonic.

"Well I think we should go to the station now George. They are sure to appreciate the presence of concerned, responsible parents."

George agreed and they retrieved the Land Rover from the hotel car park and drove the short distance to where the three teenagers were being held. In the finest tradition of the Scottish police the public office was bare, cold and uninviting. No chairs just a counter with a frosted glass hatch above it and a bell push. After a while the window slid open.

The worried parents explained who they were and asked if they could see DI Bell who duly came out into the public office, every inch the professional with so sign of deference.

"Lord Telford. Your son will shortly be released on police bail into your custody. It will be a condition, a standard condition, of his bail that he lives at his home address with yourselves. For the purposes of the paperwork can you confirm which home address he will be living at."

"The island" "London". Two parents. Two answers.

"I'm not going back to the island with him Lucinda. We will have to go home. He needs to go back to school. London Mr Bell."

Another blow followed quickly on. The detective said that he was going to impound the Land Rover for evidential reasons.

Lord Telford exploded. "For God's sake man you can't do that. I've got to get to the airport. Why on earth do you need the bloody vehicle?"

The detective spoke quietly, to reinforce the seriousness of the situation.

"Lord Telford. I can tell you your son's friends have all admitted their parts in this very serious assault. They will shortly be charged with attempted murder. I have had an initial conversation with the procurator fiscal and she wants the Land Rover examined as part of this ongoing investigation. I am sure a man in your position would want to cooperate fully with us, even if it means the inconvenience of using public transport to get you to the airport."

Not trusting her husband Lucinda jumped in and confirmed they would, of course, be happy to hand over the Land Rover keys. As Lord Telford fumbled round his pockets looking for them the door to the inside of the police station opened once more and young George appeared, clutching a piece of paper and looking deathly white, which when added to his facial injuries was a shocking sight for his parents. He rushed across the outer office and flung himself into his mother's arms and cried quietly, his arms gripping her tightly.

His father appeared to ignore his son's anguish and asked what was happening to the other two.

"They have been interviewed in the presence of a social worker and the duty solicitor. The fiscal has instructed that they should be charged with attempted murder and they will be held in custody overnight before appearing in private at the sheriff court in the morning. As they have admitted their parts in the attack it is likely bail applications for them will not be opposed and so they should be released around lunchtime tomorrow. Their parents have been informed and I believe they are travelling up here now."

That was the last thing Lord Telford wanted. Angry parents. They'd probably be trying to blame him for the actions of their children.

"Right" he said, "Let's get out of here. Pull yourself together George. I take it you will let us know when George is no longer needed."

Mr Bell said that he would be in contact at some point but emphasised the need for George to read and understand the conditions of his bail.

Gracelessly Lord Telford led his wife and children out into the street without another word.

There he turned to George and made in perfectly clear that he wanted nothing to do with what had gone on.

"I am taking you at your word that you were in no way involved in this. God help you if you were. But on the basis that you were not then it really has nothing to do with us. Two people who were staying with us have committed a serious crime. That's the end of it. It was them. Their choice. We were not and are not involved. Simple as that."

Young George didn't think it was that simple but he did not have the courage or energy to argue with his father, a man who was difficult at the best of times – impossible would be the only way to describe him today. So, in silent procession, they began to trudge back to the hotel. It was nearly six o'clock and pitch dark. The town was obviously still in festive mood with the bars packed and restaurants doing a roaring trade. The bright lights and laughter from inside didn't get anywhere near lifting the spirits of the Telford family.

At the hospital Caroline had got hold of a wheel chair and pushed her husband along to Andrew's room where the nurse had told them he was showing signs of waking up. Suffering as she was from severe emotional overload Caroline was wishing she had left the big house last night and gone home to bed. She had enough to deal with, the hangover from hell should have been avoided. The anxious parents took position at either side of Andrew's bed. He was on a drip. His face was pretty smashed up. His arm was in plaster. The bed sheet had been folded back to reveal the boy's chest –bruised and bare save for the sticky pads with their wires leading back to the trolley mounted monitor that bleeped away to itself.

The nurse told them she had tracked down Mr Singh and he was going to speak to them shortly. She had just finished the sentence when the room door opened and in walked the man the Edward's took to be Mr Singh.

Tall, bearded and wearing a dark blue turban the most striking thing about the surgeon was his apparent youth.

He offered a reassuring smile as he introduced himself. Caroline stood up, Jim made to attempt the manoeuvre but seeing him struggle Mr Singh urged him to stay put.

"You might not think it to look at him just now but your son has been quite fortunate. He has obviously had a severe beating. There was quite a lot of internal injury including a badly ruptured spleen but I am completely confident none of it is life threatening.

"My colleagues and I decided not to remove the spleen as we are pretty sure it will repair. There are a couple of cracked ribs. Mercifully the break in his arm is clean and should heal itself.

"All in all your son has suffered a violent attack but he's been lucky this time."

Jim took exception to the implication that Andrew was some sort of street fighter. Lucky this time just jarred.

"Listen doctor my son is not a fighter. He was attacked by two cowards in the middle of the night. He didn't stand a chance. I don't like the way you are suggesting that he's some sort of no good kid."

"Leave it Jim I don't think that's what Dr Singh said at all, is it doctor?"

"Not at all. I'm sorry if I gave that impression. Obviously I know nothing about your son – I was just remarking that he has been fortunate in as much as the level of violence that he has obviously suffered could have resulted in far worse injuries. Anyway you must excuse me I have other patients to see.

"Andrew should be able to leave here in about a week or so. He'll need regular checks after that but we can discuss this nearer the time. I understand you live on an island Mr and Mrs Edward – that might make things difficult – I believe there is no doctor there and after his release he should be watched pretty carefully."

The parents told the surgeon they would stay with Andrew on the mainland until he was well enough to go back to school and only after that would they go back home.

When Mr Singh left them the nurse said she too would go for 20 minutes to let the parents have some peace. If anything changes, she said, pull the alarm. Anything at all.

Jim and Caroline did have a lot to talk about, of course. Not least the prognosis for Jim's illness and how it was going to affect them.

Jim's overriding view was "things are going to have to change" but quite how and in what manner was not specified.

Chapter 13

The girl behind the desk at the Telford's hotel called the family over as they trudged into the front hall. "There is a couple in the bar wanting to see you, Lord Telford".

It was the news the peer just did not want to hear. The visitors had to be one of the boys' parents and he just could not be bothered to face them at the moment. It was enough dealing with his own family difficulties without having someone else's forced upon him. Nevertheless he walked towards the bar followed by Lucinda and his son. The teenager instantly recognised Orlando's mum and dad sitting at the bar in front of glasses of what appeared to be water.

He took the lead. "Hello Mr and Mrs Russell, I'm George Emberton and this is my mum and dad."

Mr Russell stood up and shook young George's hand resisting the urge to comment on his face. The same with the father. For a first meeting it was odd to say the least. Father and son obviously battered and both with their noses taped up. Lord T took the initiative asking if they had heard the latest on their son. Mr Russell said he had spoken to the police station and they were not saying much other than the two juveniles had been charged in connection with an assault on the island. The police person had confirmed Orlando was one of them and said there would be no opportunity to see him before he appeared in court in the morning.

Telford asked if they knew what the charge was. "Assault I presume," said Mr Russell.

"I am afraid not – they have both been charged with the attempted murder of a boy whose parents work for me."

The news was met with a gasp and Mrs Russell bursting into tears.

Lucinda put her arm round the devastated mother and suggested sitting down together in the body of the room. So it was that Mr and Mrs Russell heard the troubled tale of how their son went off to an island in the expectation of having a traditional New Year in the Hebrides with an old English aristocratic family.

Reels they thought. Maybe some stalking. Long walks and log fires. Sandy beaches and friendly locals. Not attempted murder and jail.

Lord Telford suggested they would all be better for a drink. Mrs Russell rather pointedly suggested that drink may well have played a large part in the awful predicament they were in.

Her husband addressed the practicalities. "Is there any chance this kid is going to die, Lord Telford?"

"Please, George. And no I don't think there is. He underwent an operation shortly after arriving at the hospital and I gather he has some internal injuries, and a few broken bones but will make a full recovery. Your son and his friend must be pretty handy with their fists," he added the last part to underline his own son's innocence.

"Hang on Lord Telford," said Mrs Russell her face once more streaming with tears. "I think we are jumping to conclusions here. I am sure Orlando played no part in this. He's not that sort of boy. He would be horrified by any violence let alone what's gone on here. Our lawyers are arranging for a criminal specialist from Edinburgh to be here first thing in the morning and I am sure it will become clear that Orlando had nothing to do with this. Nothing."

As gently as he could Lord Telford laid it out to the disbelieving parents. "The officer in charge of the case, Detective Inspector Bell, told me not an hour ago that both boys, including your son, have been interviewed and have admitted carrying out the assault on the boy.

"You will not have failed to notice but my son and I have also been injured," pointing at his taped up nose, "and these injuries were caused by the boy who subsequently was attacked by your son and George's other friend."

"Listen Telford," said Mr Russell his face becoming red and contorted with anger. "The police have no right to question Orlando, he's 16 and there should have been an adult with him. Any so called confession he has made will not be admissible – I'm certain of that."

"You are right in one respect. However, there was an adult with him. A duty social worker, and a duty solicitor was also present so I think the police have acted properly. Your son should get bail and be released by lunchtime tomorrow and so you will be able to hear first-hand from him."

"We must go to the court, John," said Mrs Russell looking anxiously at her husband.

"That's not possible in Scotland," replied Lord Telford showing an unusual knowledge of Scots criminal procedure. "The hearing will be in front of a sheriff in private and is purely to establish the charges and arrange bail which I have been told will not be opposed."

Lord Telford called over the barmaid and ordered large gin and tonics. Young George stood up and mumbled something about going to his room and left the bar before anyone had a chance to comment.

George and Lucinda then began telling the story of Hogmanay at the big house and explaining to the horrified parents and how it had all gone so badly wrong.

Over at the hospital, as Caroline and Jim talked through their huge problems, they did not at first notice Andrew beginning to stir a little. Caroline had moved to the other side of the bed so she could talk quietly to her husband not really factoring in that their son wasn't able to hear details of the serious position his parents were in.

Jim had been given no prognosis but it was clear that the cancer was spreading and the oncologist was certain it was beyond surgery. He had been told a sustained period of chemotherapy and radiotherapy would delay its progress but certainly not halt it. Jim made it clear to Caroline that he thought treatment was pointless. It would just mean whatever time he had left would be months of extreme discomfort and poor quality of life.

"For God's sake Jim you are 41. That's no age. Surely there has to be a chance of beating this. You're just a young guy."

Jim just looked at his wife without speaking. He had gone through all the possibilities with the doctors and in his own mind. He'd had several days to reach conclusions. For his wife the magnitude of her problems was becoming clearer and more horrific by the moment. It had been merely unemployment and homelessness. Now widowhood seemed to be charging along behind.

The heavy silence brought about by the overwhelming crush of lives falling apart was broken by a cough from Andrew. Then another. Then they clearly saw his eyes flicker. Caroline jumped up and pulled the alarm cord that brought two nurses bustling into the room.

"I think he's coming round," she told them.

One of the nurses peered into his face, rubbing a cheek as the other looked at the printout from the monitor,

Jim and Caroline were told that Andrew was indeed beginning to wake up. "He'll be very drowsy and probably not have a clue what's going on, but don't worry that is perfectly normal. If he does wake it will just be for a short time and he'll go back to sleep. But it's a good indication things are heading tin the right direction."

Sure enough, as the parents watched on, Andrew's eyes did begin to open fully and he seemed to be trying to make himself more comfortable with little bodily movements that appeared to be taking great effort.

"Andrew. Andrew can you hear me?" Caroline's question went unanswered. She gripped his right hand, the one not plastered, and stared at his bruised face. The nurse kept up her reassurance and told Jim and Caroline not to expect too much. It would be at least tomorrow before Andrew was getting anywhere close to full consciousness, at best, and it could be longer.

At first no one in the room took any notice as the door began to slowly open, but when George Emberton put his head round it and peered in the disbelief and anger of Jim and Caroline was almost enough to unsettle the monitors that were still just quietly bleeping away to themselves.

Jim tried to get out of his wheelchair but slumped back. "What the fuck are you doing here. Come to see your handiwork. Fuck off – get out or I'm calling the police." He turned to the nurse and told her this was the young man that had put his son in hospital.

"I think you should leave now," said the nurse standing up and walking toward the teenager.

George for his part was flummoxed. He had got a taxi to the hospital to see his "friend" and explain that he had had nothing to do with what had happened to him. It seemed a straight forward thing to do, other than it was in direct breach of his bail conditions.

Now he was in the room and shocked by the full extent of Drew's injuries and the raw hostility of his parents he wasn't so sure.

Bugger it. He had thought about what he wanted to say and knew he had to say it, It was important to him.

"Hang on I'm going. I shouldn't be here anyway. But."

"But fuck all. Fuck off now," Jim reinforced his view.

"Jim let me say one thing. It's important. It's important for me to tell you and Drew that this has nothing to do with me at all."

"Of course it has to do with you. It was your fucking friends that did this to Andrew. Look at him. He could have died. Look at what those bastards have done." Jim's arm shook as he pointed at his son's battered face.

Again the nurse tried to calm things down. She turned to Jim and Caroline and suggested they hear George out. She could call the police but maybe they should listen to the teenager. Then taking their silence as acquiescence she turned to George and told him to say what he wanted to say very quickly and then go.

George was shaking. He looked more confused than anything else. His face had no colour at all and the taped-up nose added to the look of horror.

"I want you both to know that this had nothing to do with me at all. I did not know they were planning on having a go at Drew and if I had I would have stopped them.

"I was in the wrong on New Year's Eve and probably deserved this," pointing to his nose.

"You must believe me. Drew is my oldest friend. I haven't seen much of him but that will change. We have a lot in common and I hope we can stay friends despite what has happened," The tears returned. He was unable to say anything else but quietly turned and walked out of the room.

Caroline and Jim looked at each other. The nurse followed George out.

"He's just trying to cover himself," said Jim. "Give us a load of bullshit to keep himself out of trouble, bastard."

128

At this the nurse came back into the room. "I've told that young man not to come back, He asked me to say that he has asked his Auntie Ginny, I think, to speak to his father and sort things out. I don't know what that means but he was very keen for me to tell you."

Andrew's stirring had come to nothing and he was back in a state of unconsciousness but the bleeping continued to be reassuringly measured and regular. Caroline's phone quacked. It was her message tone.

There were two. The latest from George: "PLEASE BELIEVE ME CAROLINE. THIS HAD NOTHING TO DO WITH ME. DREW IS MY FRIEND AND I WILL MAKE IT UP TO HIM. GINNY IS GOING TO SPEAK TO MY FATHER. SHE WILL SORT THINGS OUT PLEASE.

The earlier one, which had gone unnoticed was from Kenny – still outside in the car park. WHAT DO YOU WANT ME TO DO. MY SISTER MIGHT PUT US UP IF YOU LIKE. Caroline felt guilty that it had taken her so long to get to her injured son's bedside, let alone that of her very sick husband and she wasn't going anywhere soon. She told Kenny to do whatever he wanted; she was staying at the hospital. George. She didn't bother replying to him.

Back at the hotel George and Lucinda were not having a very comfortable time with John and Isobel Russell. They had found it very hard to explain the events of the last few days in a way that made them appear to be sensible parents. John Russell had mentioned several times that he was the head of a large engineering company and George Telford sensed he was a chief executive used to getting his own way. There was no hint of deference or friendship as he questioned every aspect of the story of how his son had gone to Scotland for a traditional New Year but ended up in a police station cell facing a very serious criminal charge.

Tom Scott's parents arrived just as it looked as though Mr Russell had begun to exhaust his list of questions. After a brief introduction, and another round of G and T's it was off again with the tale of Hogmanay at the big house and all that followed.

Four parents were on hand outside the courtroom, part of the police station complex when the procurator fiscal emerged just after 12 the following day.

She walked up to them and after establishing who was who gave a brief outline of what had happened.

"The two juveniles made no pleas or declaration and in the circumstances I thought it unnecessary to oppose bail. Suffice to say there are strict conditions attached to the bail which will be explained to you. The two of them have been taken back to the police station and will be released into the public office shortly."

One of the parents asked what exactly the charges were and what was the plea or declaration bit.

"In Scots law there is an opportunity if desired for an accused person to give an early indication of their likely plea – however on the advice of their agents none was entered today. As to the charges, both are charged with the attempted murder of Andrew Edward and in addition Thomas Scott has been charged with taking a vehicle without the owners consent, driving without a licence or insurance and driving whilst over the alcohol limit."

The fiscal ushered the parents towards the door, turned and went off into the depths of the court.

Half an hour later the reunion was anything but joyous.

Young George had taken himself off to the hospital once again, but this time to the accident and emergency department to have someone look at his face. The department had been quite quiet and he was seen quickly. The doctors said exactly what his own parents had told him. There wasn't much that can be done. The doc did remove the tape saying it served no useful purpose. The swelling would go down, the black eyes would slowly disappear and within two weeks his face should be much less of a gargoyle and left to its own devices the nose would heal itself.

They gave him a box of ibuprofen saying to take no more than six a day and that was it.

As he walked back to the hotel George could not help himself thinking about Andrew – a mess, a real mess – and there was him needing only a couple of aspirin and some time to heal. He would never forgive his friends for what they had done. He didn't want to see them either here or back in London. Then he started worrying about school. He was on bail, could he go back? What about the other two? Surely they couldn't be allowed back with attempted murder charges hanging over them. What a mess, what an absolute mess.

As he walked into the hotel lobby he heard Orlando's laugh. What was there to laugh about. He didn't care and slid unseen across to the lift and up to his room. Minutes after arriving back there was a knock at the door. It was his mother.

"George, there is some good news in all this disaster. Mr Bell the detective phoned a little time ago and he has been told by the fiscal lady to cancel your bail. She has decided there is no evidence of your involvement and thought in the circumstances it was right to let us know sooner rather than later."

George was relieved but didn't express the sentiment, not wanting to give his mother any hint that he thought he might have ended up being prosecuted.

Things had progressed well at the hospital while the courtroom drama was going on. Andrew had stirred several times in the night and by morning had become fully awake. His mother had kept vigil right throughout, dozing fitfully in the bedside chair.

The nurse who had been on duty most of the night told Caroline she thought now Andrew was fully conscious it would not be long before he could be moved out of the ICU into a general ward. She said she would leave them alone for a while. Just pull the cord if anything changes.

So Caroline was able to talk to the son that for a few hours she feared she might have lost. Nothing of substance was exchanged, merely exhortations to lie still, constant questioning about comfort and long silences.

By lunchtime Andrew was able to sustain a conversation. The act of talking hurt a bit but not talking could hurt more he had realised and so he made the effort to assure his mother that he was ok. He tried to ask her about his dad and their island situation, job and house.

For her part Caroline felt too much truth was best avoided and met most of these questions with it'll be fine. It'll be fine. Inside she feared it would be far from fine.

Meanwhile George and Lucinda had decided to separate themselves from the accused and their families. Lord Telford had made it clear to the other parents that far from being in anyway to blame for what had happened he was as much a victim as Andrew. He had invited their sons to his home and his hospitality had been abused. He managed to work himself into a state of indignation. Heaven help anyone who tried in any way to suggest that he might bear some responsibility for what had happened. Ok the kids were nominally in his charge but he didn't know what they were up to and nor could he be expected to know.

In fact the more he thought about it the less sympathy he had for the other parents. He was delighted his own son had played no part in the attack and felt that effectively absolved him of any responsibility.

And so when he and Lucinda took their leave to head to the airport, by taxi, he felt no guilt at his leaving and gave not a fig for the plight of the other parents.

Caroline's phone quacked again. Jim had been wheeled along to his son's room again and the three of them were alone. "Can't you turn that thing off?" asked Jim.

Caroline ignored the request and opened the text message.

THE POLICE HAVE DECIDED I HAD NOTHING TO DO WITH THE ATTACK AND HAVE DROPPED MY BAIL. PLEASE TELL ANDREW. TELL HIM I WILL COME AND SEE HIM WHEN I COME BACK UP MAYBE HALF TERM.

Chapter 14

Five years later things have begun to change on the island. Not dramatically but slowly as is the way in Scotland's island communities.

Lord Telford felt a real sense of pride as he watched his son, tall, confident and handsome, welcome family and guests to a 21st birthday party, the likes of which had not been seen on the island for decades. The teenage acne had gone his dress sense had improved immeasurably – blazer and chinos – every inch the young gentleman. Even a casual glance round the marquee revealed how much times had changed. Local people. The neighbours and even some of the staff of the Telfords had been invited which had not happened during the current earl's entire tenure, until now.

Tonight, Lord Telford had been telling his guests, was going to be the start of a new beginning. He said when he looked at George, now universally known by the courtesy title derived nickname Embers, he saw his family's future and it looked good.

Coming of age for Embers had been met with the start of handing over of the family empire. Lucinda thought it was too much responsibility too soon, but her husband kept telling her it was a gradual process that would see their son grow into his responsibilities at a time he had the good fortune to have both his parents around for guidance.

"I just got this lot dumped on me when I was about his age" was his standard response to anyone questioning the switch of responsibility.

Unlike his favourite whisky Lord Telford had not been mellowed by the passing of the years and the prospect of getting his son running the place allowing him to live in the anonymity and peace of Clapham was all consuming. George, he thought, was a capable young man, he had worked hard at university, gaining an honours degree in rural land management, it was not beyond the bounds of possibility that he could turn round the fortunes of the island and with it the Telford family.

Telford dreamed of the time to come when he could remain in London permanently save for a few days stalking in the summer. Getting a regular income from the island estate and spending time, a lot of time, in his club. That's what earls should be doing, he thought.

He felt the concept of working for a living had something slightly vulgar about it and he had grown tired of trying to squeeze ever more cash out of his Hebridean assets to fund his London lifestyle. He resented being the first generation of Telford earls to be reliant on the relatively meagre income from the island – previous earls had actually had the resources to spend real money on the place far in excess of any income they might expect.

His years of under investment and over withdrawing were taking a toll on the fabric of the island – make do and mend was his motto. Previous earls had been able to pass their years in the House of Lords where his father had even got a foot into government at one point as a junior agriculture minister.

His grandfather had been the last of the Telfords with any real cash and the opportunity to lead an aristocratic lifestyle between Telford Hall, the island and London. Sadly it was a lifestyle that saw the family outgoings outstrip the incomings by a large factor. Hence today. Not skint but certainly far short of where he thought he ought to be, in the money stakes.

He really thought that his son might be the one that could turn things round. He was well liked on the island. The unfortunate incident with Andrew Edward all those years ago was behind them and people appreciated the effort George had put into rebuilding his friendship with the island boy to the extent that today they could be mistaken for brothers.

Five years ago when Andrew had been discharged from hospital his life was looking pretty bleak. A dying father, a homeless drunk for a mother. The prospect of being charged with serious assault. Fate, and young George, had stepped in to make things better. George first of all by persuading his father to do all he could to stop Andrew being prosecuted for the Hogmanay bash, as it had become known in the family by way of injecting amusement into a serious situation. Reluctantly Lord Telford had eventually agreed to speak to the police on Andrew's behalf and the matter had been quietly dropped.

Within 10 month's of Jim's death Caroline had moved in to the lighthouse cottage of Kenny Kelp. After her years of putting up with Jim no one begrudged her the obvious happiness she found in the new relationship, some of the more unkind people in the community suspected it might have been going on for a considerably longer time that was admitted, but never mind they were both very happy.

It had worked out well for Andrew too. Kenny had bought both of the lighthouse keepers' cottages when they were sold off after the light as automated. The smaller one had been used by him as a holiday let, now it provided a comfortable home for his partner's son. Andrew was also working in the seaweed businesses.

Tonight's inclusive guest list was one of the most striking signs of change by the incoming regime. Young George had insisted. Few of the island community had ever been to the big house, unless by way of employment. Certainly no one could remember any islander being invited to a social event, save for Andrew all those years ago and look what happened then.

Now the three hundred or so people crammed into the marquee to hear Embers speak were nearly 50/50 mainland friends to locals. The division was clear to see. It was the mainland friends in smart suits and long dresses. So it was with a feeling of change in the air that Lord Emberton stood up on the small stage at one end of the marquee, his sister Lady Alice right in front of him, as if for support.

George and Lucinda felt they had every right to be proud of themselves and their children that night. The boy had been focussed on assuming his role with as much knowledge and vision as he could. Unlike his father he actually loved the island and having spent his early years there knew and liked many of the people who his father held in little more than contempt. George had an understanding of human nature that had passed his father by altogether.

Embers had spoken often to Andrew of his desire to change the way things happened. Though careful never to be openly critical of his father he made it clear that he thought the future

135

was best served working with the community, especially the good people of whom there were many, rather than keeping going with his father's siege mentality, venturing out of the big house as little as possible and usually then only to try and extract some advantage from a grudging population.

Kenny was a case in point. Lord Telford resented Kenny's success in the seaweed business. The entrepreneur had seen an opportunity and worked very hard to make the most of it. His business grew each year as he diversified his product lines starting with near novelty food stuff's featuring a bit of seaweed but now with ambition to use the kelp as an energy source in anabolic digesters.

He had even started limited scale farming, growing seaweed on easily manoeuvred rope structures. The gulf stream and clarity of the sea combined to make ideal growing conditions. The arrival of Embers on the scene had transformed the prospects for the business. He needed to expand, physically, but his shed where a lot of the work was done was surrounded by land owned by the Telfords and every attempt Kenny had made to buy or lease space so vital to his expansion plans, had been met with unrealistic demands. Sums of cash that could only have been determined by Lord Telford's greed and ill will rather than any commercial equation.

Tonight it seemed things might be changing.

"First of all I would like to thank you all for coming. Its not the easiest place in the world to get to for a party, unless of course you live here, so thanks for making the effort it means a lot to me, and dare I say, to the whole of my family.

"Talking of them I need to thank mum and dad for putting on this great party for me. I think really it is a party for all of us – the whole Telford family, not just me." He sniggered as he added: "That's just in case dad decides to give me a bill for my share"

Whilst meant as a joke there were plenty in the tent who had experience of Lord Telford that would lead them to believe such a concept was not so far fetched.

The Island weather had put on its best for the party too. It was the sort of night that brought tourists back year after year and gave real joy to those residents who still had room in their hearts to love the place. There was a breeze, the most important ingredient to a comfortable island summer night because it kept the midges away. The warmth of the day had persisted into the evening. The marquee was standing on the lawn to the west side of the big house and the sky was beginning to glow with the setting sun. Looking out over the beach onto the breeze rippled sea the waves catching the gathering redness as the sun sank into the horizon, it was impossible not to be bowled over by the beauty of the place.

Embers continued his speech and his audience heard the sort of words that had been missing in the relationship between the big house and the rest of the island for so long. Words like investment, commitment, understanding and most significantly, thought many, cooperation.

Privileged education had removed all trace of the slight Scottish accent he had picked up at the island primary and George now spoke fluent public school. He smiled broadly as his peroration was reached: "Working closely with my father and our friends and neighbours I intend to devote my tenure here to improving the sustainability of this community and protecting the natural beauty of this exceptional island. We are all in this together, and together we can, and will, make this an even better place to live and bring up a family

"Now I have finished university I will be living here full time and working full time to do what I can to protect and grow my family's interests and with that the interests of everyone here. So never mind the birthday – please raise your glasses and drink a toast to 'The Island' and all of us who live here."

He could have been running for office. It was a beezer of a speech that would have inspired the off island guests and give hope to the local people that things were going to change.

Embers stepped down off the little stage to be embraced by Alice, then a hug from Andrew, and a firm handshake from his father. His mother had made off, she said, to deal with urgent business outside, but in truth she was having trouble controlling her tears. George's speech had been very emotional for her. After a married life of listening to her husband ranting on and on about how much he hated the place and all its inhabitants she found her son's obviously genuine and very public commitment to the future of the island quite moving. Most off all she was overcome with pride at her son's maturity and confidence and she hoped that it was well placed.

She just wished he could find himself a nice girlfriend. However any sadness at that deficiency was countered by a strong sense of relief that some of the horrors that he had appeared with from university and before were short term and in the past. She and George had warmed to none of them really. Not that there had been that many. Lucinda worried about her children's love lives. She was concerned that George had never really had a proper long term girlfriend and she fretted that living full time on the island was just going to make acquiring one even more difficult. There were also real concerns about Alice. She wasn't sure, there were no outwardly visible signs, but she had a mother's intuition and she thought, no she feared, that Alice was becoming very close to Drew.

As George had got down from the stage those close by heard Andrew congratulate him effusively. "For God's sake Drew all I said was let's all make a go of things."

"Yes but you said it in a way that no one could imagine your father speaking and there is a feeling here that things are changing – and changing for the better. Never mind. Let's get stuck into the Champagne."

"Sparkling wine" corrected Alice as she followed her brother and Drew through to the bar annexe of the tent. It was George's night and visitors and locals pressed to get a word, offer congratulations and share a drink.

That left Drew and Alice free to grab a bottle of wine and wander off over the lawn to the drawing room of the big house. Lucinda, by now back in charge of her emotions, asked where they were going.

"Just to chill out in the house for a while mum"

Lucinda and George were horrified at the prospect of a growing relationship between their daughter and Andrew. She was three years older than him and had spent less time than any of the family on the island. She had left the little school the year after George and Andrew started preferring to board at her English prep school aged just eight. At Chevering College a combination of brains beauty and breeding meant she was in the smart set and the holidays where often spent in wonderful places with exotic friends so it was a shock for her parents to now see her obvious interest in Andrew.

The young couple spent an hour or so in the drawing room, chatting quietly, holding hands and passing the time with others coming in to seek a bit of a rest from the party which was, in finest island tradition, turning into a rowdy ceilidh.

"Why don't we go and have a dance or two and then slip off to my place? No one will notice or care," suggested Andrew.

A bit squiffy and perfectly relaxed Alice agreed. She had thought for some time it was time to put their relationship onto a higher plane, though never in such candid terms. Andrew led her by the hand through the French windows and back to the marquee where the ceilidh band was giving it their all. Nearly everyone was up, the locals laughing good naturedly at the stressed attempts by many of the visitors from the South to get to grips with Scottish country dancing.

A postie's jig, well after midnight and fuelled by sparkling wine and whisky descended into little more than a farce with participants incapable through drink or laughter or a combination of both.

Andrew looked at Alice and nodded his head towards the entrance. Without a word she took his hand and headed for the outside. As they jumped into his ancient Land Rover Alice turned to Andrew and said she felt a little guilty. "It's my brother's big night Drew, we probably shouldn't be sloping off like this."

"No one will care or mind – or even notice."

As he drove towards the lighthouse and home Drew hoped that Alice thought she was involved in a spontaneous event. He would have been mortified if she ever found out how much planning had gone into tonight's planned seduction. He had spent hours tidying the house, nicked some candles from his mother's home next door, and even changed the bedsheets – ambition hurt no one. There were no clouds in the sky as he came to a stop at the high walls surrounding the lighthouse compound. The big metal gates were open but he always preferred to park outside.

As they walked through towards his flat roofed whitewashed cottage Alice could see a welcoming glow coming from inside, a contrast to the stark darkness of next door. It would be some hours before Kenny and Caroline returned from the party. Once inside Andrew lit three of the candles he had placed round the room. Alice laughed uproariously as she saw his obvious plan begin to unfold. No matter though, they were of one mind.

At the party things were still going strong. Some of the older guests had begun to drift off after midnight, a few of the more bibulous had nodded off but were still physically at the party, and it was becoming the preserve of the young. Embers university friends and some of the school chums he had kept in touch with.

Not, of course, the two that had nearly cost the life of his friend. He had not seen Tom or Orlando since the moment they were taken into the police station. They had been in separate cells and George certainly had no desire to speak to them again. The pair had been sent to the High Court in Edinburgh for trial on charges of attempted murder but the Crown accepted guilty pleas to the lesser crime of assault to severe injury and they were each given five years' youth custody for the assault with an extra 18 months for Tom's motoring offences. The judge called them thugs who ought to have known better given their life advantages. Young George agreed. He had heard they had managed to get transferred from a Young Offenders Institution in Scotland to a unit nearer their home counties families and served just under half their sentences before being released early with electronic tags. Simple as that. Didn't know and didn't care.

George never ceased to be amazed at how many of his friends on their first visit to the island were simply knocked out by its beauty and apparent tranquillity. If truth be told he was really only just coming to really love the place again. The innocent pleasures of his younger days on the island were somewhat clouded by the intervening years of listening to his father's continual moaning. He was a man who wore his prejudices with pride and went to great lengths to get back at those he deemed guilty of getting in his way or causing offence. He was not the sort of person who easily forgave trespasses.

But the son saw real hope for the island and his role in the next chapter of its development. University had taught him much and seeing the way Andrew had seized the opportunity given to him by Kenny in the seaweed business had opened his eyes too. He and Andrew had gone off to Indonesia together for a couple of weeks one summer to look at the alginate industry there and

Andrew had bought back lots of ideas, some of which Kenny was only too keen to follow up on.

So when his uni friends told him how lucky he as to be heir to the island estate he was very ready to agree with them. He had felt a real sense of responsibility when his father had told him of the plans for the gradual handover. It was a responsibility he was relishing.

The party went on an on –the ceilidh band packed in and people drifted off down to the beach. It wasn't long before a bonfire was blazing, it turned into a traditional island young person's event. A lot of booze, a fair bit of weed, sing songs, some skinny dipping and couples disappearing off into the dunes or back to the big house.

When Fiona Grant arrived for work at 6.30 am the following morning the scene was exactly what she expected. Devastation. Not that she cared. Lucinda had arranged a small army of people to come in later in the day and do the cleaning up. Mrs Grant was there to provide breakfast starting with the baking of scores of rolls. She had reckoned the first part of her service would be feeding the party survivors, the ones yet to get to bed, and she was right. The smell of fresh bread baking and then sausages and bacon frying away bought plenty of "customers" to the kitchen door. She was amazed at how well most of the guests seemed to have coped. They were obviously troopers. What she did not see were those that had fallen by the wayside. Sleeping where they had fallen in the house, in the marquee and even a couple on the beach. The sun was out already. It was going to be another beautiful day.

By 9 that morning George and his mother's small band of stalwarts had set off on an epic mission to begin the tidy up. Glasses and bottles were strewn round the house and at the beach and all places in between but the banter kept the team focussed – their labours punctuated by the sound of bottles crashing into the trailer parked up near the tent.

Over at the lighthouse the morning was having a decidedly slower start with neither Andrew or Alice in a hurry to get up. Andrew made some coffee, took it back to bed pausing only to set his laptop away playing a selection of pipe band performances. As he got back into bed Alice laughed and warned: "If anything is going to come of this relationship you are going to have to stop that – no one should have to wake up to a bloody pipe band for God's sake".

Andrew ignored the jibe at his musical taste and looked straight into Alice's eyes and said that he hoped something did come of their relationship. "I think we are made for each other in a strange kind of way. I love you." He was rather shocked by those three words, but pleased he had managed to utter them.

"Steady on Drew," said Alice, pulling him closer and making it obvious steady wasn't in her mind, despite what she said.

Lord and Lady Telford went out to watch the clean up crew and join in the post mortem on the events of the night before.

"Mum and Dad – thank you again for this party weekend. It is much better than I could have hoped for and everyone seems to be having a great time. No disasters as far as I am aware last night. Just a few sore heads today."

Lucinda was delighted her huge efforts had not been in vain. She and Mrs Grant had spent countless hours planning the food and drink, difficult for any party on this scale but extremely challenging faced with the remoteness of the island.

"I'm pleased you are enjoying it George – you have a nice bunch of friends and your father really wanted to mark your coming of age in much the same way as his had been.

"It looks as though its going to be kind for us tonight for the barbeque," she said waving her arm skywards where only the tiniest clouds were visible.

The finale of the weekend was to be a giant beach party – again the whole island was expected, not this time by formal invitation but by word of mouth and a poster on the community noticeboard by the harbour. The family was delighted that the party had coincided with Brian and Linda Thompson's annual summer holiday on the island, still with all three of their children in tow. Lord Telford felt a debt of gratitude to the doctor that had never really been paid off.

Lucinda asked young George if he'd seen his sister. "In her room I imagine."

"Hopefully on her own," grumped her father, the implication of the observation plain to understand.

142

Mrs Grant opened the dining room door that led out onto the lawn and shouted that breakfast was ready.

Inside she had excelled herself. Piles of fresh home made bread rolls, bacon and sausages in the warmer, and best of all a huge kedgeree sending wafts of curry smells out onto the stillness of the lawn, as if temptation was needed to bring in the mainly young guests.

For two hours people drifted into the dining room helping themselves to the feast which just never seemed to run out as Mrs Grant kept up a steady delivery of more and more dishes. By 12 the room was packed – brunch – and some hardy types had even started on the sparkling wine again, much to Lucinda's disgust but today was not the day to complain.

At first no one noticed Andrew and Alice appear in the midst of this. Andrew's carefully executed seduction plan had failed to include breakfast and they were both starving. Lucinda heard Alice's voice and turned to greet her daughter but was so overcome by shock the words stuck in her throat. Alice was wearing a pair of jeans, obviously far too big for her, and an Island Alginates tee shirt. All nicely finished off with a pair of black high heeled shoes. If she had wanted to make a statement she could not have done so with more force.

She watched as Alice loaded a plate with what was left of the kedgeree and went over to her daughter as she sat down on one of the window seats, her slim and neat outline framed beautifully by the heavy curtains with the view of the beach and sea behind.

Before Andrew had a chance to occupy the other half of the bench Lucinda sat down, smiled, leant into her daughter's ear and demanded to know where she had been.

"Morning mum," said Alice cheerily ignoring the threatening tone of her mother's question.

"Well – where have you been."

"Mum, not that its anything much to do with you I stayed at Andrew's last night. We just wanted to get some peace. OK?"

It wasn't ok, but her daughter was 24 and in the middle of this long planned much anticipated event an angry mother felt constrained.

Lucinda wanted to say "We will talk about this later" but she felt the words too clichéd and kept her mouth shut.

Andrew walked over carrying a plate of bacon rolls. "Morning Lady T – that was a great party – you must be delighted."

She could only manage something between a feeble smile and grimace before nodding her head and making way for Andrew to sit down.

Alice put her hand on Andrew's, in what might have been seen as a public confirmation of her mother's suspicions, and said simply: "It's started".

It would be fair to say that Andrew's apparent confidence of walking in the morning after in full view with Alice by his side, and his cheery greeting to Lady Telford was a near as he would ever get to acting. The butterflies in his stomach were unconnected to the excesses of the night before but created by the certain knowledge that whilst the Telfords had accepted him as a friend it would stop at that. He imagined they would be horrified to think of him romantically entwined with their daughter. He didn't need much imagination either. Lucinda's look just now said it all.

Scraping the last grains of rice off her plate Alice turned to Andrew and said she was going upstairs to shower and change. Maybe have a bit of a nap. That suited him, he had work to do at the seaweed shed that would fill the afternoon. Andrew was shocked to the core as Alice turned to face him, and leant forward to deliver a long lingering kiss. Right in front of everyone. "When you are finished come up to the house, I'll just be here," she said taking her leave.

Andrew stayed on the window seat unsure of what to do. He didn't really know many of the bruncher – mainly George's university friends and he felt too exposed just to get up and walk through them all and out of the house. As he chewed thoughtfully on his second bacon roll of the morning young George sat down and rather excitedly inquired: "Bloody hell Drew, did you sleep with my sister last night?"

"George – that is not the sort of question a brother should be asking," and couldn't stop the grin that spread across his face as he added "Alice just came over to my house to get some peace and quiet. It was too noisy here."

"Yeah – I bet she did. So, are you two going out?"

A non-committal shrug of the shoulders met that question.

"Listen George I have to go – there's a lot needing done. Can we speak later?"

With that Andrew jumped up and walked quickly towards the door and into the great hall of the big house. Instead of making for the front door he found himself drawn to the stairs and bounded up before anyone had a chance to see him and half ran, half tip toed along to Alice's bedroom.

Taping the door and walking straight in he was confronted with the object of his affections lying on the bed with a towel wrapped round.

She was surprised to see him, but maybe not that much.

"Alice, what are you going to tell you parents?"

"What about?"

"Us"

"Us. What do you mean by us?"

"Us, Alice, Us. I want us to be – us"

She patted the bed and Andrew sat down close to her.

She reached out for his hand, pulled it close to her and told him to calm down.

"Let's just take this slowly Drew. Let's have some fun and see what happens."

He had too many thoughts racing through his mind to offer a considered response to that suggestion. He leant forward and kissed her. Slowly retracted his head and muttered simply "OK".

As he left Alice's bedroom Andrew heard voices coming from the hall and so headed for the rear stairs that lead to the narrow passage between the kitchen and gun room. He and George had spent hours chasing each other round the house as children and he knew every inch of the property. No one saw as he slipped out of the back door and walked round onto the gravel at the front into his old Defender.

Lucinda, meanwhile, had gone off in search of her husband and found him, where else, but in the library, door shut, window open to the summer breeze quietly reading The Daily Telegraph on his iPad. He didn't seem all that concerned as she expressed her fear that their daughter had spent the night with Drew Edward.

"God George do take your nose out of the newspaper for just one minute. We are talking about our daughter potentially going out with Drew – Drew the piping seaweed cutter. I don't think that is what either of us want for Alice for heaven's sake."

"Lucinda, she's 24 and unattached. What do you want me to do about it. I'm sure it will be just a little fling, if it is anything at all that is. Anyway Drew is a better kid than some of the horrors she's bought home over the years."

Immediately the words left his mouth Lord T wished he hadn't spoken them.

"George our daughter is young and beautiful. She has wonderful friends, a good degree and an expensive education. I do not want her ending up here in some sort of relationship with Drew bloody Edward. Can you imagine Caroline's face when she finds out? It's enough to make me sick."

"Calm down Lucinda – it'll not last till next weekend – and if it does I'll have a word with her," though if pressed both would have admitted such power did not rest in the father's hands, or the hands of many fathers come to that.

"This needs stopped before it starts, George. Simple as that." With that Lucinda breezed out of the library leaving her husband with his paper and, she hoped, his thoughts on their daughter's future.

Drew was a bit of a state by the time he had finished turning the drying seaweed in Kenny's shed next to the lighthouse. He stopped off at home for a shower and to change. As he was about to leave, having carefully chosen his attire for the next part of the 21st celebrations his mother walked in.

"You look smart, love". Drew never failed to marvel at how his mother had changed since she started living with Kenny. She seemed years younger, her once unkempt hair now was always shining and nicely cut, and her lifestyle had improved immensely. Gone were the days on end of continual boozing. The morning snifters to steady her hand. These days it was everything in moderation.

Kenny had not only given her the support and confidence she needed but also a real job in the seaweed business where she had grown adept in maintaining stock levels and basic book keeping.

The remaining Edwards had a lot to be thankful to Kenny for. Both Drew and his mother also knew it worked both ways. Kenny's relationship with Caroline had created a life beyond work for him, one that had been absent before. Drew missed his dad in some ways, however, and he would never admit this to anyone but himself, life without Jim was actually more certain and stable, better for all, though he felt terrible even thinking that.

Caroline came straight to the point. What's all this she had been hearing about him and Alice.

"That's quick mum, its only five o'clock – are me and Alice right round the island?"

Yes, she said, and maybe even a bit of the mainland.

Years of self sufficiency at the school hostel had taught Andrew independence and he didn't feel the need to be too open with his mother.

With a grin he confirmed the story, at least in part. "Alice did stay here last night, Mum, but nothing happened. We are just friends and she wanted to get away from the noise of the party. It was a bit too much for her, just that.

"It's nothing to do with me Andrew. Just be careful. You know what the Telfords are like."

George's party was the first time Caroline had set foot in the big house since the confrontation after the attack on Andrew all those years ago.

When Jim died their service tenancy on Lighthouse View Cottage had passed with him and, despite the best efforts of Lady Virginia, Lord Telford had gone ahead with his threat and evicted them. In a damage limitation exercise he told people on the island hat he needed the house for Jim's replacement, though no one believed him. Their disbelief was well founded. In fact no full time worker moved into Light House View. A major renovation was carried out and the Edward's former family home became another holiday letting cottage.

Had it not been for the fact that Kenny had stepped forward and offered the homeless bereaved mother and son his letting lighthouse cottage on a permanent basis the callous eviction might have been a fatal blow to the little reputation Lord Telford had left. When Caroline and Andrew were settled in their new home the resentment at their treatment amongst the islanders simply faded away, as usual. It was just another grievance that no one would ever do anything about.

Andrew and his mother did rage at the sums of money that were subsequently poured into their former home to turn it into another upmarket holiday property. Whether the holidaymakers paying a premium price for their week's break in heaven would have cared anything about the family that used to live under the same roof in conditions of damp and squalor was a matter for speculation. Probably not.

"Mum a whole new chapter in both of our lives has opened – I'm just wanting us to make the most of it. I am delighted for you and Kenny and I love seeing you so well and so happy after all you had to put up with. I'm fine, just let things develop whatever way they do."

She smiled and left saying she and Kenny would not be at the barbecue until much later – they were meeting some folk in the bar first.

Andrew parked the Defender in front of the big house and walked quickly out onto the lawns is search of Alice. He bumped into George first. He was taking a half share in carrying a massive cool box to the beach. He asked Drew to take over from the young man who he did not recognise that was carrying the other half, which he duly did.

"Drew you had better be careful – my mother is fucking furious about you and Alice."

"George there's nothing to be furious about"

Neither believed that, of course.

They took a few more steps and Andrew stopped and looked at his friend.

"Did you mean the stuff you were saying last night – about building on your father's legacy and all that sort of shit."

"It wasn't shit Drew. If dad is as good as his word, and I think he is, then I am going to be free to make some fairly big changes round here."

"Like what?"

"I'm not sure yet but it's clear to me the whole island goes up and down together."

"Pardon"

"Put simply Drew if the island is fucked then my family is fucked. If the island is booming then we are booming."

The concept of the island reaching anywhere near being able to be described as booming was just too big to be grappled with just now.

"So for instance George – your father and Kenny have been at war over the seaweed for years now and the biggest threat to the business, the only thing that is stopping us growing is your father.

"Remember those seaweed places were saw in Indonesia. They were fantastic businesses getting bigger all the time, creating jobs and providing a really worthwhile product.

"That could be happening here if we had more space – space your father refuses to even talk about for some reason." Andrew was being charitable in his last assertion. Everyone knew Lord Telford didn't want to support the business because he would be getting a small rent for a business that could be making a fortune for it's owners. Simple jealousy.

"That's one of the things I have been thinking about Drew and I think there is a good solution. But first – we have another party to enjoy. Look sharp let's get this food down and the fires lit."

"Wow" thought Andrew. That's intriguing. He could not wait to tell Kenny.

"Anyway bugger that – what are you up to with my dear sister?" said George with a smile.

"Oh you know George – she's always had the hots for me. I'm always having to fight her off."

They chuckled and stumbled on over the soft sand to where the wonderful Mrs Grant was preparing to feed the crowds again.

As the twilight gathered that evening, with the second night of partying in full swing, George took pleasure from seeing so many familiar faces from the island community joining him for the informal bash.

There was even a smattering of holidaymakers, most of whom he'd never seen in his life, joining in the fun. There was only one real complaint from anyone. Well nearly everyone. The noise. A uni pal who fancied himself as a DJ had set up his decks in the dunes and the sound was overwhelming. Most were content to shout. The Telfords didn't care. It was their island and if they wanted loud music……..

Andrew and Alice had used the noise as an excuse to move away from the main party and had walked barefoot to the southern extremity of the beach where the sand gave way to a narrow grassy strip bounded by the highest cliffs on the island which in bad weather provided shelter from the prevailing winds.

They sat on a washed up log enjoying a bottle of sparkling wine, God knows how much her father had bought, thought Alice knocking back another glass.

It wasn't until Andrew was driving Alice back for a second night at his cottage that he realised quite how much he'd had to drink. Drunk driving is a skill that needs practice, and he'd certainly had enough of that over the years, and so the pair arrived safely.

Emboldened with the wine Andrew pulled Alice towards him on the uncomfortable front seat of the Land Rover and asked what for him was the most important question in his life just then.

"So Alice – are we going out? Are you my girlfriend?"

"Who knows Drew - who knows what we are. Why don't we say we are lovers. That'll give them something to think about in the bar."

"I'm more worried about your parents, to be honest"

"They'll be fine – come on"

And saying that she pulled free from Andrew and jumped out of the Land Rover and into the house, pausing only for him to catch up so she could grab his hand and lead him to the bedroom.

The night had been even warmer than the previous one and many of the non-resident party guests had failed to make it back to their accommodation in the big house and the various cottages that had been made available. Lots had spent the night on the beach and some were even having an early morning, if 9 am qualifies for such a description, dip in the sea.

Lady Telford had made it clear that Sunday morning was fend for yourself time. She wasn't going to ask Mrs Grant to do yet another massive catering operation and most of the guests would be leaving on the lunchtime ferry – they could hold out until then.

Peace would descend as the ferry disappeared into the distance –
then dinner, a special family only dinner, and then George's 21st
would be over, thank heavens, she thought.

Jock Ferguson the farm manager pulled up in his tractor just
before 12, as directed, and under the watchful eye of Lady
Telford slowly the guests began to file out of the house, throwing
their bags onto the trailer and climbing on board. It was pretty
packed by the time they set off for the ferry pier – a trailer load
of posh kids heading home in a rather more subdued mood than
the one evident in the boisterous expectation of their arrival.

George and Lucinda along with their son followed a short
time later – no sign of Alice – and the ferry was just docking
alongside the pier as they arrived. A festival of air kissing and
the guests began to file along the pier and onto he boat.

Ferry times always drew a good crowd of onlookers eager to
see who was coming and who was going. So it was today. Many
of the locals had made new acquaintance with the guests,
certainly not friendship – too big a divide for that.

The unmistakeable sound of Andrew's ancient defender could
be heard as he and Alice raced down to the pier to add their
goodbyes. It had been another lazy morning at the lighthouse
cottages. Within just a few minutes of the ferry casting off the
ropes and disappearing out to sea the watching folk drifted away
and peace returned to the island after a weekend that was
universally judged to have been a success. A great success.

George and his father wandered off together to inspect some
of the semi derelict fishermen's stores that stood between the
ferry pier and the harbour. Andrew and Alice went up to Lucinda
who seemed a little distant as she waited for her son and husband
to get back to the Land Rover.

"Morning mum"

"Morning darling. Thank heavens they are all away now – but
I think we gave your brother a birthday to remember."

"And its not over yet, Mum, dinner tonight. It will be OK for
Drew to come too, won't it?"

If the question came as a surprise to her mother it came as a
complete shock to Andrew, she had not mentioned this at all and
he felt deeply uncomfortable. He felt it was as though he was
trying to gate crash a family occasion.

"I don't think so Alice – it's just the family tonight – we've had enough of entertaining the masses, if you see what I mean Drew," she added hastily.

"Oh come on mum Drew is family, he's George's best friend, and mine too."

Stuck for a reply that would have been passing polite she deferred to Alice's father, now walking back from the old stores with George.

She got in first to set the tone. "George, Alice has suggested Drew here joins us for dinner tonight but I have said it's family only."

"Quite Lucinda. Sorry Alice family only."

The birthday boy joined in on his sister's side and that was enough to sway the decision. They couldn't argue with the guest of honour.

Great said Alice grabbing Andrew's hand and leading him off towards the harbour. Lucinda watched grimly as her daughter and Drew walked hand in hand along the seawall of the old pier to wave goodbye to the fast disappearing ferry.

She turned to her son and made it clear she had not wanted to have Drew, or indeed any other outsider, at the table that night. It was a special family occasion, the real party.

"I think you are going to have to get used to Drew, mum. From what I can see he and Alice seem to be a bit of an item."

Those words horrified Lucinda but she hoped that she had managed to hide her near disgust from her son.

"We will see George. You know what your sister is like."

"Watch this space mum, just you watch this space."

The Telfords, and Drew, gathered in the drawing room at 7 on the dot. The French windows out onto the lawn were open and there was a warm breeze blowing through the room. Lord Telford had given up on the modest sparkling wine of the weekend and pushed the boat out and was serving Krug Champagne to start the evening off with a bang.

It occurred to Andrew, and maybe to the others as well, that it would be the first time he had sat down for dinner in the big house dining room since that eventful Hogmanay years ago. He felt it not appropriate to mention that simple fact.

The guest list was quite similar. Lord Henry and Lady Ginny, without their spouses who had stayed at home in England as the children were back at school, Lord and Lady Telford, Alice, Drew and George.

The chat centred mainly on the wild weekend that had just past. Who had done what to who. Which locals had turned up, which locals had misbehaved, but all in all it was a jolly gathering at the end of a memorable weekend.

Despite her morning off Mrs Grant had spent a full shift back in the kitchen preparing dinner, all of the ingredients coming from the island. The first course of trout pate made with hill loch fish caught the day before by some of the guests who had managed to get away from partying long enough to sample other delights of the island. To follow, venison, a stag shot by George and cooked with wild juniper berries. Then plum crumble, with the fruit picked that morning from the big house orchard.

As they sat down in the dining room Lord T, well fortified by the Krug, tried to persuade his son to sit at the head of the table, in some sort of symbolic reference to the passing of control.

"Plenty of time for that dad. Don't think you are just buggering off and leaving me to run this place alone," his smile belied the fact that young George feared that that was exactly what his father was planning to do. He was up for a challenge but he wanted to assume the reigns rather more gradually that he suspected his father wanted to hand them over.

So the seven of them sat down with Alice at the bottom of the table, Drew directly opposite and George on Alice's right hand side.

Over the main course George leant over the table slightly towards Drew and dropped a bit of a bombshell. One that he did not seem to mind others hearing.

"Drew I know you and Kenny are a bit stuck for space with the alginates. I think I might have a bit of a solution for you.

"I was checking over the old fishermen's stores down at the habour and I reckon two of them could be brought back into use pretty easily."

Drew knew they could because he and Kenny had several times tried to persuade Lord Telford to let the rent them, or maybe even buy them. His lordship had always ruled that out saying he had plans for the buildings, plans which never seemed to come to anything.

"They could be ideal George."

"Yes I think so. Lets talk tomorrow but if you and Kenny undertake to fix the roofs then I think we could do a deal very easily."

Drew couldn't wait to tell Kenny. The shortage of space for processing the seaweed was a major factor holding back their business. This could be a game changer. Alice smiled at her brother and congratulated him on his perception. "When I listened to your speech the other night I did hope that you meant what you were saying. Seems you do."

His father pretended not to be listening. He was though and didn't much like what he was hearing.

Dinner that night certainly passed off a little more peacefully the Drew's last experience of dining at the big house. As port and cheese was circulating young George said quietly: "Shame you haven't got you pipes with you." The three youngsters found that hilarious. It was another sign of how far things had come, that they could laugh together looking back at what had been a very dark period in all their lives.

Monday morning dawned, Alice at the lighthouse cottages again, and it was back to work, for those who had any. After making Alice a cup of coffee Drew popped next door to tell Kenny and his mother about the happy news of the fishermen's stores.

"Bloody hell" said Caroline at the revelation. "Things are changing round here."

Drew assured Kenny that young George was serious and had even made the offer in front of his father.

"Well done Drew – lets strike while the iron's hot. Let's check them out this morning and you can get back to George and see how much he wants."

"That's the point Kenny. I don't think he wants very much. Mainly for us to fix the roofs."

The fishermen's stores were some of the more picturesque buildings on the island. They stood close to the old harbour and had originally been topped with turf roofs. At some point the grass had been replaced by sheets of red corrugated iron which were now rusting away. It shouldn't be that much of a job to rip off the old and hammer on the new, they reckoned. Maybe there would be a few roof beams to be replaced, but it would not be a big job.

Drew said he'd meet Kenny down at the harbour in half an hour after he had dropped Alice back at her house.

Caroline smiled. "Mmmm. Alice stayed over again, Andrew. Must be serious."

Andrew ignored the comment, save for his reddening face, and left his mother and Kenny to ponder over the developments. As they pulled up in front of the big house Alice suggested to Drew before he went any further he should find her brother and make sure the offer was serious, and still open.

"You know what my father's like Drew. He'll hand over to George but soon take things back if it isn't going the way he wants."

George came out of the front door aware of the deafening Defender heralding his sister's arrival.

"You need to get that thing sorted Drew – I'm sure I can hear you leaving your cottage in the mornings it makes such a racket."

"Morning George. I was about to try and find you. Can we talk about the store shed's you mentioned last night? Kenny and I are going to give them the once over just now. Do you want to join us?"

George declined the offer saying he had a good idea what they were like. "I'll have to check with our factors but I reckon if you fix the roofs that'll do for the first years rent. Then maybe two hundred pounds a month after that. A three year lease and take it from there."

Three years? I don't think that'll be enough George. I think the plan will be to develop a whole new product line which will mean buying a fair bit of new equipment."

"Whatever. I just suggested three years so as not to commit you if it turns out they are no good for whatever it is you want to do. Three years for a start and if it works for you then we'll just extend the lease, I can't imagine I will ever have a use for them."

Relieved the plan was still on course after some momentary jitters Drew gave Alice a lingering kiss, thanked George and jumped back into his Defender laughing as Alice and her brother made to cover their ears as they watched him drive off in a cloud of fumes.

Kenny was waiting for Drew at the harbour and was delighted to hear that he had seen George already this morning and received confirmation the offer was still on the table.

"God, things are changing round here. Long may it continue."

"I think it will Kenny. George loves this place and I honestly think he will do his best to make it better – for everyone that is, not just his family."

They gave the stores a good going over and concluded the tumble down buildings with the rickety roofs were just the job. When Drew and George had been in Indonesia they had been really impressed by one of the seaside places they visited where they were converting seaweed into a base material for the pharmacology business. All it would take to work here was space and investment, now that it looked as though they were close to getting the space the investment would come easily.

Kenny shook Drew's hand. He had pulled off a blinder that could transform Island Alginates and get them into the big time. News of this arrangement went quickly round the island because for most of the residents it was not a simple commercial transaction between landlord and tenant, it was an indication, and a powerful one, that things were changing. It was, in the minds of most, a change long overdue.

The local folk who had heard George speak at his party had been split on whether to believe his fine words but there was a real sense of optimism breaking out that things were indeed changing for the better on the island and with that a chance maybe a chance, that the relentless drain of young people leaving could be stemmed with the creation of real opportunities for them at home. Andrew had been the first of the island's children to come back full time after leaving for school in many years. Without exception over the past decade every single young person that left school had left home at the same time going on to higher education or employment on the mainland or further afield. Saga island some of the wags referred to it as and not in reference to the stories of Norsemen who bought terror to these parts centuries ago, merely an acknowledgement of the fast aging population.

The fishermen's stores were the last thing on Lucinda's mind as she bumped into her daughter in the kitchen. The only other person there was Ilonka, a Latvian woman who had taken Caroline's place as general skivvy. She spoke very little English so Lucinda felt no concern broaching a delicate subject with her daughter in front of the paid help.

"Your father and I are rather concerned about what is going on between you and Andrew."

"What's going on mum, and come to that, what's it got to do with you?"

"Well I don't know what's going on and it has to do with me because I am your mother. I think it would be very unfair of you to lead that boy on and it would be best if you made it clear to him, if you have not already, that the relationship is going nowhere and you are going back to London and finding a job, like we have been trying to get you to do for some time, you may have noticed."

Alice paused, thinking for a few moments then looking straight at her mother, speaking slowly and choosing her words carefully she made her position very clear.

"Mum. I have been thinking a lot about my future and this weekend has opened up a whole new range of possibilities for me. Not just Drew, but he may well be part of it, but by what's going on between Dad and George and the way things could be so different, so much better here. Better for us and better for everyone else.

"The first thing you need to understand is that I have no desire to go back to London. It's not for me and I won't be forced into a job I don't want or a career I'm not interested in.

"I think my future is here. George and I love this place in a way I don't think you and Daddy ever have and we see our future very much on the island. I think it is really good of Daddy to begin handing things over to George. Watching daddy grow increasingly unhappy here has been really quite sad. He seems to have got to the stage where he thinks he is at war with the place, and most of the people. George, and me, look at the island very

157

differently. I am very happy to stay here and give George some support and any help that he might need."

Then she confirmed her mother's worst fears. "And I am also very happy to stay here with Drew. I love Drew and I think he loves me. This feels so right. I think I have found my future."

"For God's sake Alice what are you thinking of. You are far too good to be thinking your future lies with some kid who makes half a living gathering seaweed – have some sense."

I am thinking of me, mum. Me and my happiness. Drew is not some kid who cuts seaweed. He is someone I have known for most of my life. He is a gentle and kind, hardworking young man with the prospect of building a real business and I love him."

Lucinda was staggered by her daughter's frankness and, she thought, stupidity. She also realised the conversation had gone as far as it could and so she left Alice in the kitchen with Ilonka and the very clear implication that further discussion was needed.

It wasn't long before the deafening Defender roar could be heard coming up the drive. Alice met Drew at the door. He was excited and smiling broadly. "Those sheds are going to be perfect Alice. Your brother is a hero."

Chapter 15

Kenny and Drew didn't wait for the lease to be drawn up and signed. Keen to progress as quickly as possible as possible they had sourced some second had seaweed processing equipment that would be good enough to get them started. By the time the paper work had been signed both of the store buildings had bright new red corrugated roofs. Kenny had spoken to couple of people about the possibility of working with them. They were going to need a lot more kelp if things developed the way he expected.

Alice didn't have an official role in Island Alginates but she was keen to help and had been making contacts amongst likely customers and speaking to some of the government grant agencies to see if there was any public support likely to be forthcoming. She had also been trying to persuade Drew to move in with her at the big house. She was virtually living full time at the lighthouse but her own home would be more comfortable for them. Her parents had headed south and there was no sign of them heading back to the island anytime soon. Drew was adamant it would be a step too far. He wanted to maintain his independence. He wasn't part of the family, and despite Alice's assurances he felt he never would be.

George meanwhile had hit the ground running. He had a confidence far outstripping his years and a clear idea of where he wanted to take things. He realised there was real money to be made from the main asset, the island. Unlike his father he was prepared to work hard and make the place more profitable. His father, he thought, had been far too dependent on tourism at the expense of developing other schemes. So it was George's first priority to examine the possibilities of renewable energy generation. His father had hated "pointless bloody windmills" but pointless windmills generated good profits for landowners, along with the electricity. He also decided to do what he could to improve the deer herd. For years the stalking had been left in the hands of the farm manager and nothing much had been done other than a bit of culling now and then. The quality of the herd had suffered as had the island forestry devastated by the marauding largely unchecked animals.

He had decided to recruit a knowledgeable stalker who would be charged with selective culling to improve the stock and then once they were in good shape they would start letting days on the hill to wealthy paying guests. It would be an all-round win.

George used to complain to Drew and his sister that at times his head hurt with all the ideas buzzing round. He had arranged the sale of the last remaining family owned properties in Shropshire and persuaded his father to allow him to put nearly all the proceeds into improving things on the island. It hadn't been hard. Lord Telford had a growing confidence he had done the right thing in handing over so much so soon. His public position was that George was a fresh young pair of eyes looking at things. Nearer the truth would have been an admission that his son had a vision and was obviously prepared to work, and work hard to achieve it, something he had never felt inclined to do.

Some nights supper time at the big house could seem more like a board meeting as George, Drew and Alice spent hours going through their options and thinking out new schemes. Supper usually was at the big house. Alice felt slightly sorry for her brother rattling round a 14 bedroom turreted pile all by himself. Of course there was also the not inconsiderable attraction of Ilonka to do the cooking and washing up.

If Andrew and Alice's blossoming romance was a matter of concern to her parents elsewhere on the island it was the subject of much speculation and comment. It was one of the main topics of conversation whenever islanders got together in the bar, or even in the shop. People's view of the relationship was coloured entirely by their relationship with the senior members of the Telford family.

At the shop the manager, Peter McGilvary obviously worked for them but that didn't mean to say he had to like them. His relationship with Lord Telford could really only be described as fragile and he was pretty pleased at the change of regime at the big house. He had been regularly derided for the way the shop was run. He could never get things the way the boss wanted. Stock was too old, too cheap, too expensive. The wages were too high – then the shop wasn't open long enough. What really made these criticisms hurt the more was the fact that Lord Telford himself hardly ever went into the shop. Most of his supplies had come from the mainland, the gardens and the farm.

So when Peter started referring to Andrew as "the young laird", every time he went into the shop, the sarcasm was so heavy it could have fallen straight through the bare floorboards. Andrew felt it and was annoyed more than embarrassed by the jibe. All Peter had achieved was cutting the takings. Andrew gave up on his daily habit of stopping off at least once and usually twice for a takeaway coffee. He didn't feel comfortable going into the shop that had been such a child's delight at one point in his life and had earned a place in his heart in later years thanks to Peter's very relaxed approach to enforcing age restrictions in the licensing laws.

It was his mother's friend Sandy that hurt him the most. Andrew just couldn't understand what the fuss was about. He was used to seeing tiny events take on an importance far in excess of their worth purely because the small community of the island very often had not too much to occupy their minds. However when Andrew found himself on the receiving end of a tirade from Sandy that really hurt.

Not long after George had agreed to hand over the fishermen's stores Andrew had been working by himself tidying up the years of rubbish that had been dumped inside when Sandy came past with his Border terrier, Angus.

The dog had run in to where Drew was clearing mounds of debris and fearful for its safety amongst the piles of rubbish he'd simply gently encouraged it back out and bumped into Sandy at the door.

"Hi Sandy – I was just a bit worried Angus might come to grief – there's so much junk piled up in there I just don't know what's going to come down next."

Without a trace of a smile or hint of the kindness he had always shown to Drew, Sandy said there was only one thing going to come to grief on this island. "That's you son. It'll be you that's coming down next."

Andrew was shocked – he'd never heard Sandy talk like that to anyone, he was always such a jovial happy go lucky sort of guy. He was about to walk away and go back inside but maybe taken to breaking point by the shopkeepers continual sniping he thought 'fuck it. I've done nothing wrong'.

Doing his best to smile and stay calm he asked Sandy exactly what he meant by that.

"What I mean Drew is that you have sold your soul to the devil."

"For God's sake not you as well – what have I done wrong, to you or to anyone else?"

He had a rush of anger adrenaline which made his hands start shaking. Sandy saw he was getting his message over and didn't want to stop.

"You have betrayed your father's memory and sold out on your mother. You need to have a hard look at yourself Drew. Your new friends up there are the people who treated you and your parents so badly and now for the sake of a quick shag you are happy to forget what those bastards did to your family and the rest of us and pretend you are in with them. The big shot at the big house.

"But I am telling you they don't care a damn for the likes of you, or anyone else on this island for that matter. You're just Alice's little plaything and when she's finished with you you'll be out on your neck."

Andrew was speechless with blinding rage. He wanted to argue, he really wanted to pick up one of the heavy poles he'd been clearing out of the store and batter Sandy over the head with it. A good job he might have done of it too.

Sense prevailed and he stood waiting for the wave of anger swirling through his mind to dissipate enough to allow him to respond.

As calmly as he could he took a couple of steps towards Sandy, his obvious anger enough to cause the little terrier to growl a gentle warning. "Sandy I didn't think you were like so many of the twats on this island who hate seeing people get on, who despise people trying to do something.

"My dad's only real enemy was the drink and that had bugger all to do with the Telfords. Kenny and I are going to make this business work and work bloody well for us and my mum. If you don't like that. If you can't stand seeing us getting on without being overcome with pathetic jealousy or something then fuck you.

"I would have thought you of all people would be happy to see things getting so much better for my mum. Or would you prefer it if she was still living in Lighthouse View cottage, in the cold and damp so you and Jean could patronise her to make yourselves feel good?"

"Listen to yourself Drew. You've been shagging the girl for a few weeks and already you've caught the arrogance of her family. You'll be coming round to put my rent up next. Well don't bother. And remember this when you are crawling out of the big house with your tail between your legs and those bastards are laughing at you: they despise you and are desperate to put an end to you and Alice and if you think you have any chance of beating them then you are more stupid than I thought." With that Sandy clicked his fingers at Angus and strode off to continue his walk uncaring of the devastation his harsh words had caused, with Angus trotting along next to him.

Andrew went back to work in the store but couldn't muster enough concentration for even the menial task of clearing rubbish as Sandy's words resonated round and round his head like the calls of the rutting stags echoing in the hills.

He didn't care what Sandy had said about Alice. He was certain they had a good relationship that would last. It was the pain of being accused of betraying his father that hurt, and hurt badly. And from Sandy. That made it so much worse. He wouldn't have taken a moment's notice of those words coming from half the population of the island. But not from Sandy Brydon.

He thought of all the hours he spent as a child at Sandy and Jean's house. The countless meals. The kindness. The encouragement of his piping, especially in the early days when the noise wasn't all that enjoyable. Was that really what he thought? Worse still was he be right? Was he being made a mug?

Drew gave up trying to clear out the store and instead headed home to the lighthouse cottages. He drove along arguing with himself as to whether he should tell his mother of his encounter with Sandy eventually concluding that he had to. She needed to know if that was what people were thinking and he also wanted to hear what she may have to say in response.

Kenny was at home too when Andrew got back and he went into their sitting room and recounted as much of the exchanges with Sandy as he could remember. When he finished there was a moment of silence broken by his mother dismissively saying that she wasn't surprised. "Andrew I am afraid this is the sort of place where a lot of people don't like to see folk getting on."

"Tell me about it," added Kenny. "You know the shit I've had to put up with Drew. They don't mind as long as you are one of them but if you try and do something different the knives come out. I've been amazed over the years since I started the business of how jealous a lot of people are and how desperate they are for you to fail."

"Never to your face. Well hardly never. But you can tell the way things change. People I've been friends with here for years just sopped talking to me. If I ever challenged them, and I probably wouldn't because I don't give a damn about people like that, they would say it's me. They would say I'm getting above myself or some crap like that."

"Kenny's right Andrew – there is a real unpleasant current running through this community and you just have to make sure you don't get involved, don't let it get to you.

"You are correct about your dad, I'm afraid. He was a good man and a good father but the drink got the better of him. It's an illness. If you have a broken leg they'll help you here, but if you are an alcoholic they won't. Maybe because so many of them are not that far behind. You know I was a bit of a mess, especially after your dad died."

Kenny told Drew he just had to make sure he didn't let people get to him. "Rise above it Drew. Let your success show people how wrong they have been. Even if you end up the bloody prime minister there will be still people here happy enough to put the boot in so don't let it get to you."

Caroline did take the opportunity of voicing more candidly than ever before concerns she had been afraid of airing with her son but could see this moment of frank discussion was her best chance.

"You do have to be careful with Alice, Andrew. I really don't want you getting hurt. She and George are a new generation I know but they are still Telfords with all that goes with the name. The way George's father treated me, and you as well don't forget, after your dad died was a disgrace and if I had been in a stronger state of mind I would have fought a lot harder than I did. The way things have turned out………." she left the sentence unfinished but the way she looked at Kenny left no doubt of his mother's meaning.

"I know mum. I love Alice, and I and sure she loves me." He was embarrassed by his honesty but continued through the blushes. "Alice and George are different. You should see it when we are having supper together. It's like a new world. A different place. We three can see a real future for this place and George is up for it in a way his father never was."

Caroline felt she had gone far enough with her words of warning. She didn't have a crystal ball and could not foretell how things would work out. She just hoped Andrew had found the happiness with Alice and the fulfilment with Kenny and the business that she thought he deserved.

The plan for tomorrow, said Kenny ever practical and concluding enough analysis of the island community had been done, was for both of them have a good go at the sheds and make sure they could be sorted out for what they needed. New machinery was required to move into the new products which would take a bigger investment than anything put into the business so far, but Kenny could see a whole new world of profitability opening up.

Andrew decided to walk over to the big house for supper that night as it was heading towards another beautiful evening and he wanted to clear his mind of all the negativity injected by Sandy. He was not sure whether or not to tell George and Alice about the encounter. There had been so much bad feeling and feuding in the place over the past few years he did not want to jeopardise the good will being created by the new regime.

By the time he neared the gates and the long driveway up to Alice's real home he had concluded that he should tell them everything of Sandy's hurtful tirade. They were bound to hear about it sooner or later, distorted, exaggerated, embellished; he should give the true version, bad is it was.

The blatant dishonesty of so many people on the island in the way they misrepresented and twisted stories to suit their own agenda really angered him. The fact that often the agenda was simply to cause trouble made him furious.

So that evening over Ilonka's latest Latvian twist on Scottish cuisine Andrew gave another repeat of the confrontation with Sandy.

'Twat'. Was Alice's verdict. Plus a peck on the cheek and squeeze of the hand.

George's response was more considered. "Sandy's been at me to replace the windows in his cottage. Apparently they are falling to bits. Funnily enough I have just re-prioritised that job – to the bottom of the list." He laughed perhaps more than he ought to have done.

He also dismissed Andrew's plea to be bigger than that. "Listen Drew he's pretty useless at the best of times. Who does he think he is to have a go at you over my sister. To hell with him. He needs a lesson in manners. What goes on here has nothing at all to do with him and he'll have to learn that the hard way."

Andrew was almost as shocked at that response than he had been at Sandy's original outburst. He wanted to say that George was acting more like his father that the progressive landlord they had been seeing of late, but felt it wasn't' really his place to make such sweeping judgements. Anyway, Alice seemed relaxed and that was the main thing.

"Listen Drew. I'm a different person to my father but at the end of the day I have to make the island pay and I want to live here amongst decent people. If some folk think they can take me for a ride they'd better think again. Sandy's a good case. He's of little use to anyone, thinks he's a big shot who can have a go at whoever he pleases and then expects me to run round spending money to improve his house.

"He, and everyone else, will have to understand the economics here. We've not got huge sums to invest – so what I do spend will have to make a return.

"The one thing I don't want is my father to come crashing back into the scene saying I've messed up and can't be trusted. Drew I really want to work with these people, the decent ones, and we can turn this place round together and everyone will get something out of it. I've no time for passengers though, and smart arses like Sandy.

"Look at Ilonka and Andris. Lovely couple. They just want to come to a nice place, work hard, make some money and go home. Andris is worth half a dozen Sandys. He knows what he is doing and just gets on with it. People like Sandy need realise that."

Andrew was quite taken aback by that outburst. It was on the point of being like listening to Lord Telford after a glass or two of Bruichladdich. He agreed though. Sandy had no right to speak to him like that.

Alice lightened the mood. The three of them were careful never to drink during the week. In a revolution at the big house alcohol was absent Monday to Thursday without fail. Tonight, said Alice, let's have a bottle of wine.

So as they waited for the main course George wandered off and came back with two bottles of some of the better Burgundy that had been left by his father. Carefully he pulled the corks out of both and threw them at the fireplace, missing both times.

The water glasses laid for supper were pressed into more serious service and George proposed a toast – "To Ilonka and Andris, and whoever follows them, they are the future of the island."

Andrew felt a little uncomfortable but understood it to be offered light heartedly and took a long swig of the Pinot Noir. Sometimes this virtuous lifestyle sat heavily by Thursday night.

Seeing that Andrew had walked across that evening George said he's give him and his sister a lift back to the Lighthouse. "Let's stop off at the bar to break the journey," suggested Alice. The fact the bar was a lengthy diversion from the intended route was not mentioned.

"Why not, good idea" agreed her brother. Despite Andrew's protest that he had an early start, the bar it was to be.

A short time later, when the three of them walked into the public bar they got an instantly uncomfortable feeling. There were still a few tourists about chatting happily. Also Sandy and

167

Peter were there with some of the more committed island drinkers. The tourists didn't recognise the youngsters walking in, and nor should they have, and the locals hardly acknowledged them. Sandy offered little more than a grunt and nod as the trio walked right past him and up to the bar.

Alice, walking last, turned directly to Sandy and almost provocatively said: "God you lot look happy tonight. Has someone died?"

Her inquiry was met with only a few unintelligible mutterings.

After throwing three glasses of much less desirable red down pretty quickly George led the way out back to his Land Rover and on to the lighthouse.

"It's quite sad, isn't it? There we are. Me, in my family's hotel, sharing the bar with some of my family's tenants, and it's as though we are strangers. Them in their corner, us in ours and the tourists oblivious to the undercurrent eating away at the community which from their outsiders point of view, must appear to be all sweetness and light. Well I'm trying very hard. But I'm not some sort of welfare state."

That night as he lay in bed Andrew could not stop going over the events of the day and what they could mean for his future. His future on the island, with Alice. It was one of those night trauma's that simply refused to go away.

How could Sandy be so vile? What on earth could his motivation be? Andrew had done nothing to harm him - ever. They were friends. Certainly his mother was a friend. Why would a friend attack you like that over nothing? No real answer came, and so he turned to the business. His friendship with George would allow them to take Island Alginates on to a new level. Who extra could they get to work for them? Two, maybe three people. People committed to being part of a successful dynamic enterprise. Not people who would turn up hungover and bugger off when it suited them.

He listened in the darkness to Alice's breathing slowing and deepening as she found the sleep that was eluding him. She was the most important thing to him. Alice, he knew, was his life. It wasn't the glamour and prestige of the big house, the island toe rag winning over the heart of the daughter of one of the great families of Britain. No. They were in love for love's sake. They loved each other. They loved the island and they had spoken endlessly of plans for their life together and what the future could hold, and it was exciting. As he lay that night with all these thoughts racing round his head there was one certainty that Andrew felt above everything else. He wasn't going to let the petty, the jealous, the sad, the drunken, the fucking idiots of the island spoil it for him. If, for whatever reason, they didn't like what Andrew was doing that was fine. Up to them. For Andrew it was everything. Life couldn't really be that much better.

God help anyone that tried to get in his way.

CHAPTER 16

By the time two years had passed from that encounter with Sandy life for Andrew, Alice and her brother had changed in a way no one could have predicted. George had got a real handle on his island and was working hard to create lasting businesses that had the possibility of reversing his family's declining fortunes. Alice had taken over running the hotel following the enforced departure of the previous incumbent who had been devoid of either imagination or work ethic, preferring the customers side of the bar. As for Andrew – Island Alginates had really taken off. The sheds had been the missing link in creating a vibrant business. They had even persuaded George to let them have the remaining two former fishermen's stores on the same terms and this had allowed much bigger investment in processing equipment meaning instead of semi drying bulk seaweed and taking it off the island they were able to begin the process of refining it into new products on the island .

Kenny and Andrew were a natural fit. A team with Kenny managing sales and Andrew looking after harvesting and processing. Managing a team of five full time employees with occasional extra help in the summer months when the warm waters of the gulf stream increased the rate of weed growth allowing even more to be cut. Much to Andrew's relief he wasn't the centre of island gossip much these days. People had been excited in the early days of his relationship with Alice giving rise to the crass behaviour of some of the locals. Now, alongside the change in management style of the island estate the transfer between the Telford generations had brought, there was a real feeling of optimism for the future.

Even the grim days of winter battered by the Atlantic gales and their endless rain seemed more bearable. The change hadn't just bought benefit to the three youngsters. George's investment in the hotel and his sister's inspired management was slowly turning it from a dowdy houf, as they say on the west coast, a bit of a dump, into a modern vibrant business that was attracting

170

upmarket guests drawn not least by a new chef working his magic with island produce.

Within these two years the new stalker had begun the all important task of turning the rather scruffy island deer herd into something attractive to the lucrative stalking market. Wild venison was a major feature of the menu. Island sheep and cattle, in Lord Telford's day, just went off to market. The new team on the block were getting some slaughtered and brought back for sale in the shop and hotel dining room

From early on in his tenure George had decided what was missing in his family's various island businesses was a sense of joint enterprise. They are all working for the same team. Team Telford. To reinforce this he instituted a weekly meeting for the people running the various parts of the empire. Jock Ferguson the farm manager, Peter McGilvry, from the shop, his sister Alice from the hotel, the new stalker, Euan Fernie, were all required to attend the big house every Monday morning at 8.30 am sharp. George had been amazed, and not a little bit angered, by the resistance to such a "revolutionary" business concept. Eventually the message had got through and the foundations of a joined up enterprise were being laid.

In mid August of that year George had some interesting news to impart. His father was coming to the island in two weeks time, with friends, to go stalking. It would be Lord Telford's first visit in well over twelve months. The younger generation had been obliged to go to London for Christmas and New Year with the family. That was a story in itself. Alice had tried to persuade Andrew to invite his mother and Kenny for Christmas in Clapham with the Telfords but her boyfriend had dug his feet in saying it was out of the question. He felt a little awkward himself turning up at Lord and Lady Telford's for Christmas and new year without trying to bring along his mother and Kenny Kelp.

Anyway news of the imminent arrival of Lord Telford and a stalking party spread round the island quicker than most rumours. There was intense speculation as to whether he would approve of the changes young George had been bringing about. Most comment centred on the eight wind turbines that had been erected on the top of one of the highest hills. Lord Telford had made known his intense dislike of "bloody windmills" what would he say when he saw eight dominating the skyline and visible from most parts. George found this speculation, and its implications, frustrating beyond belief. It was as though the locals believed he was not really in charge and that his father would arrive and treat him like a naughty boy and order the destruction of the turbines.

Nothing could be further from the reality of the relationship between father and son. It would be unfair to say that Lord Telford had washed his hands of the island, but he was content with the way his son was running things. His opposition to turbines had been greatly assuaged by the income the eight whirring giants were generating for his family.

Meall Odhar, the round brown hill in Gaelic, was nothing more than just peat and heather feeding a few sheep, quite nice for a summers walk. Now it was a cash cow bringing in as much money as just about all the other island enterprises that required real work. The Telford eight just stood there pumping out pounds so he was not going to complain. They were also, he would often remark with as close to a chuckle as he ever got, quite hard to see from Clapham.

So that Monday George said that he wanted to make sure that when his mother and father arrived things were looking as good as possible. It was going to be his chance to shine and show what a good job he was doing in turning things round. Not an expression he would use to his parents of course with its heavy implication that Lord Telford had left things in need of turning round.

That night at the usual big house supper even Andrew came in for a bit of "encouragement" to make sure all was looking good for his father's arrival.

"It would be great if you and Kenny could tidy up round the sheds. It's going to be the first thing he sees after getting off the ferry and you know he's still not very keen on Kenny and I really don't want him moaning on about the mess I've allowed you to create. You know what I mean, you can just hear him, can't you?"

Andrew could indeed. You didn't have to spend long with Lord Telford to get a good handle on the sort of things that he would moan on about. Pretty much everything to do with anyone on the island that he did not like, and that was pretty much everyone. Yes, Andrew would have the place looking immaculate. As they sat here enjoying Ilonka's much improved and less Latvian cooking Andrew saw another opportunity opening up for him.

These big house suppers always gave Andrew such a lift. The simple act of walking through the front door of the Telford's island home, as though he owned the place, maybe popping into the kitchen to get a beer from the fridge, only at weekends of course, and sitting down with George and Alice to chew over the events of the day, discuss plans for the future or just recount whatever laugh had been had that day. It was a hard to imagine the effect of the transformation for the boy brought up in the damp and smelly cottage by drunken parents, but a transformation at which he felt completely at ease especially with the beautiful Alice by his side. He thought the forthcoming visit by George and Alice's parents might be a chance to put his changed circumstances onto a more secure footing.

"What are you prioritising to keep your old man happy?" he asked of George.

Alice jumped in before her brother had a chance to speak. "Daddy will be bowled over by what's been done to the hotel. Each time we've tried to get money from him to do the basic maintenance work that he should have carried out years ago, let alone decorating and equipping the place properly, he's complained saying we'd never get a return.

"Now look at the place. It's thriving and I can't wait for him to admit he was wrong and we were right."

The consensus of the other two was that Alice might be in for a long wait.

By the time the ferry carrying Lord and Lady Telford and their friends docked Andrew had been as good as his word and he and Kenny had carried out a massive clean up round the sheds. No more were they covered in the detritus of a thriving aligate business, but they looked neat and tidy, a picturesque Hebridean scene to welcome visitor and owner alike. Almost that is - nothing ever gets properly finished in these parts.

The stalking guests were a couple who were as close to being good friends of the Telford's as it got. For years it was the friends of the children and their parents that were the basis of entertainment on the island. Today's arrivals were frequent visitors in the old days, but hadn't been for a very long time.

Spending most of the time in London had allowed George and Lucinda to rekindle their friendship with the Earl and Countess of Deal. Deal had been one of Telford's cronies before the hereditaries were kicked out of the house of Lords but since the Blair reforms they had drifted apart somewhat.

In truth George had not been looking forward to his father's visit with the cronies in tow, but was vowing to make the best of it. He was scared his father would want to show his friends that despite how it may appear he was really still in charge and George felt there was a risk that his father could do real damage to the changes that had been made already and those that were still underway.

Even the old Land Rover had been replaced with a newer model. George was waiting for them at the ferry terminal, they were arriving as foot passengers without a car. Andrew had wheeled a small hand barrow along the pier to help with the luggage. The guests piled into George's Defender, the luggage went into Andrew's and off they set for the big house, and the prospect of what was feared might be a very long week.

Alice met her parents at the front door with her customary warm exuberance, kisses and hugs all-round and then the Deals were dispatched to their "usual room" with firm instructions to meet shortly in the drawing room for afternoon tea.

Ilonka had pulled the stops out. Sandwiches and scones, a massive chocolate cake, laid out on a sideboard, crisp white napkins and all the best china. By the time Andrew had delivered the luggage and attended to a couple of small jobs George had asked him to carry out the four visitors were assembled in the drawing room, bathed in sunlight and the view over the bay as good as it could be. The lawns round the house were as close to immaculate as they had been for years.

Andrew breezed into the room unfazed by assembled aristocracy smiling at Alice as he did. Lord Telford caught him out of the corner of his eye and turned full on. The conversation paused. He gave Andrew a formal introduction to make it clear he was not just the pier porter. "Now everyone. This is Alice's, eh, friend Andrew. Andrew Edward. He lives on the island and he is a seaweed tycoon."

The guests laughed at the thought of being in the presence of a seaweed tycoon. Andrew was slightly concerned by his description as Alice's "eh, friend." He should have been.

George encouraged them all to tuck into Ilonka's afternoon tea, and after their long journey little encouragement was needed. It was a convivial gathering as the Deals caught up with the latest news from the island, a place they had come to know quite well over the years.

Euan Fernie the stalker knocked at the door and was ushered in by George. "I thought it would be a good idea to get Euan to talk you through tomorrow. There is already a big improvement in the deer stock and hopefully Euan will arrange a couple of good stags for us."

He was a little surprised when his father told him they had decided not to go out on the hill straight away. He wanted a day to look round the place, catch up on the news and generally reacclimatise to the island ways.

"That's fine, sir," said the stalker, "the deer haven't been moving much of late and so we should have little difficulty finding them. Anyway tomorrow's forecast isn't all that good."

Young George was finding the visit all a bit difficult even after even just a few hours. He had grown into his proprietorial role and was loving it, and by common consent, doing ok. He didn't want his father coming in moaning about things and sticking his nose in where it was not needed. His plan had been to get the visitors up the hills for a couple of tough days sport and then resting after their exertions. Eating, drinking enjoying gentle strolls and then off home again. Back to London He had gone as far as to tell Euan to keep his parents and their guests on the move when out on the hill to make sure a quiet end to their week's stay would be appreciated.

Just to make his position clear the young man sought to take control of the social arrangements. "Seeing it's looking like a lovely evening let's all meet up at seven for drinks on the lawn before dinner." That was greeted as a splendid idea and the guests drifted off. Before Lord Telford had a chance to leave the room Andrew buttonholed him. "George – can I have a word with you, tomorrow maybe before you all go off for the day." The use of the Christian name by Andrew rather shocked both parties. Andrew hadn't really meant to, it just kind of slipped out and Lord Telford was appalled. Not because of any perceived right to deference from his social inferiors, but by the implication of this young man feeling comfortable addressing him by his first name. No one on the island did that. He was obviously getting above himself and potentially posing a danger.

"What about, Andrew?"

"If you don't mind George could we leave it to the morning. Would it be ok if I called in after dropping Alice off at the hotel say about 9?"

Lord Telford's shock was turning to anger. George. Who the hell did he think he was calling him George. Even the concept of dropping Alice at the hotel was infuriating. This young man, this seaweed cutter, was living with his daughter and seemed to think that gave him some sort of right to participation in his family. It bloody well didn't.

Managing to hold back on what he really wanted to say Lord Telford was able only to half growl: "Nine o'clock it is then. Perhaps George will let me use my library." The sarcasm wasn't lost on Andrew who muttered something about being sure it would be fine.

On reflection, as Andrew kissed Alice goodbye the following morning at the gate to the hotel, he thought that he should have arranged his meeting with Lord Telford later in the day. There had been a real big house blow out. Mrs Grant had prepared a dinner fit for the important guests, doing her usual trick of using nearly all island grown ingredients. The evening hadn't ended until well after 1am and not before Lords Telford and Deal had given the Bruichladdich whisky a good going over. Despite he and Alice leaving before the drams came out Andrew felt decidedly rough as he set off from the hotel to the big house. There Lord Telford was sitting in the morning room trying to lift a bone china cup of coffee but shaking slightly spilling his over-filled cup. He put the shakes down to age, nothing to do with the fact the earls had kept going on the whiskies long after their wives and the young had left for their beds.

Andrew paused for a moment at the front door to gather his thoughts, the main one of which was that simple wish that he had asked for the meeting to be in the evening. Lord Telford after a good G and T would have been easier to deal with than Lord Telford with a hangover. But the die was cast, there was no going back now.

On his way to the library Andrew put his head round the morning room door and found Lord Telford still grappling with his coffee. This would do. The sunshine was streaming in through the windows and it was a much more convivial space than the gloomy library. Hopefully the brightness of the day would make things better.

"Good morning George, beautiful day again isn't it? The forecast was wrong, again"

"Yes." Agreed Lord Telford without a hint of warmth towards the long standing boyfriend of his only daughter. "How can I help you?"

Andrew turned and closed the door behind him. He turned back to face Lord Telford and was immediately overcome with another dilemma. Stand or sit. He towered over the seated peer, but was it impertinent to sit next to him? He compromised and walked to the other side of the room, a move designed to lessen the height discrepancy, but instead only left Lord Telford screwing his eyes up to see against the sunshine pouring in. It was a bad start. Mumble. Move. He settled on leaning against the far end of the mantelpiece.

It was already going wrong. Andrew had thought through exactly what he was going to say and where it was going to be said but the room switch changed that and knocked him off course. He felt his nerves taking over and his confidence falling away. So much so he lost the ability to use that first name again.

"Lord Telford," he began. The switch from informal to formal threw him further. Oh fuck. He actually felt his legs beginning to shake and so he half sat and half slid into an armchair opposite. Andrew could only stare at Lord Telford as he tried to get his plan back on track.

Sensing the young man's acute discomfort Lord Telford did nothing to help ease the situation as he snapped unhelpfully.

"Andrew, can you get on with whatever it is you want, I have guests waiting for breakfast."

The was an overlong silence before Andrew carefully, and slowly, took up the challenge.

"Lord Telford....I'm sorry this isn't easy. Lord Telford, as you know Alice and I have been living together now for almost two years. We are extremely happy. Happy with each other and happy with our lives here on the island."

Go for it, Drew, just go for it, he thought to himself. "I am committed to our business and Alice is completely committed to running the hotel and doing what she can to help her brother. I hope you can see what great progress Alice and George are making. I would like to think that if you asked them they would both say that I have played a significant role in what's been happening. I like to think of us as something of a team."

Telford could see where this was going. An unwanted destination. He could see Andrew had put a lot of thought into these words, but they were words that left him shocked. Last night when the meeting was set up he had presumed Andrew would be after land or buildings. Maybe even money for some joint enterprise with Alice. He now saw what was coming and didn't like it one bit.

He thought it best to wait to have his fears confirmed and just nodded offering no comment.

"And so I feel the time is now right for me to demonstrate my commitment to Alice. I very much hope that you will give me your blessing to seek her hand in marriage." He felt a bit of a prat using such formal language but despite hours of thought and not inconsiderable internet research he had not come up with anything more appropriate.

Lord Telford was nonplussed. He was clear in his own mind the response that he wanted to give, but for once was trying not to let his gut reaction rule but think things though.

He managed a weak smile. "I was wondering what this was all about, well now I know.

"To be honest I am rather surprised by your request. For a number of reasons however, in short, I have to say this is a request that I could not countenance."

He paused, hoping the sentiment would sink in and also to give himself a chance to weigh up the best way of ending this nonsense sensitively. Even with his head still puggled by the whisky of the night before the best course of action became clear. Honesty. Tell it like it is. Nip it in the bud. Shoot it down and quickly.

"Lucinda and I are, of course, only too well aware of your relationship with Alice...."

"Your relationship with Alice," Andrew could hear the distain loud, clear and unmistakeable.

"And whilst we are delighted to see her happy and working so hard in the family interests we have to consider the long term. You are a.........nice...guy Andrew. You have done very well getting to where you are today despite....." the rest trailed away unsaid but understood.

"However Alice is a bright girl with a bright future away from this place. We very much hope that she will use the experience gained here to create a worthwhile career for herself elsewhere.

"To be frank this is not a suggestion I could give any support or encouragement to. In fact I would urge you not to suggest marriage to Alice herself, if you have not already, as it can only end in disappointment."

Andrew had known it wasn't going to be easy but he didn't expect Lord Telford to be so brutal. So negative. So fucking rude. He went back at him, perhaps a little harder than was wise.

"George - Alice and I love each other and I very much hope we will be getting married. I have not asked her yet but I am certain when I do she will accept. We have spoken about the future, our future, together on the island. I really hope you will take some time to think this through. Talk to Lucinda. I might be the kid with the drunks for parents, the kid who smashed you up a bit a long time ago, the kid who didn't get much of a start in life. That's not my fault though. Now I'm the kid with a future, with a share in a great business. With a beautiful girlfriend who I love and I'm not going to give her up.

"Please can you think about it. I am sure it would mean so much to Alice to know that she had her parents, her dad's, blessing." He left the implication hanging. To suggest they would get married without his consent might just inflame a delicate situation to the point of conflagration.

"Andrew – there is little point in dragging this out. I will not give my blessing to you and Alice getting married. Not now, not next week or ever. We like you and can see how much you have done for George – but I know that Alice could not be happy being married to some one like you and spending the rest of her days on the island. She is capable of much more than this and if she is somehow forced to accept a life here it can only be as second best it will not last."

He sat motionless fixing Andrew in his stare. Andrew stared back trying as hard as he could to control his now raging anger. He looked at Lord Telford's nose. How he would love to give him another good go right now. Better than last time. Hurt the bastard. Really hurt him.

The stand off lasted an age. Andrew could think of no response, other than the violence he had already, quite sensibly, ruled out. As he sat there he could feel tears welling up. His lungs were agony. He was frightened to try and speak certain as he was the words would not come out.

He thought he may have said thank you, but could not be sure. He just got up and lunged at the door and out into the hall. He made no acknowledgement as he strode past the Deals and the woman that he had thought might have become his mother in law – out into the bright morning sunshine. Instead of going for his Defender he strode out over the lawn and over the low drystone wall that separated the manicured policies of the big house from the natural beauty of the machair, still with a good covering of the brightly coloured wild flowers that this Hebridean environment is famed for.

Not that he was interested in the flora. He just kept walking down onto the beach and off to the far end – climbing up onto the headland which gave a distant view of the hotel further down the coast. He threw himself down into a flat patch and lay perfectly still listening to the breeze singing through the long grass and the accompanying sound of waves breaking on the rocks below.

He wanted to speak to Alice. To tell her of his disastrous meeting with her father. He couldn't though. He had not told her of his intentions, obviously, and now thought he couldn't discuss the outcome without asking the question and couldn't ask the question with her father's clear injunction fresh in his mind. He was in turmoil. He couldn't just go back to work and have a normal day at the office. This was, he feared, the 15 minutes that was to shape his life more than any other event before, or likely, after.

There is a certain serenity in these Hebridean islands on days like this with the gentle breeze and Atlantic ocean, pacified by the summer, washing the shore. They say close to the ground you can hear bells ringing as the grass sways. These powerful natural forces slowly calmed Andrew and helped him begin to formulate a plan of what to do in the face of this parental opposition.

He discounted talking to Alice about it. He wanted her to accept his proposal, not have her mind filled full of doubts by her father's callous dismissal of the idea. He needed, he thought, an ally. George was the obvious one. Surely George would be able to persuade his father to accept Andrew into their family. After all they were the team. The three working together to change the fortunes of the Telford family.

Then he thought perhaps it should be Alice's mother he spoke to first. Maybe she more than anyone else would want to see her daughter happily married. Could she be his best ally? No, not a chance he concluded, she usually deferred to her husband on even minor things, she wouldn't stand up to him on this, even if she wanted to. It would have to be George.

It must have been nearly an hour that Andrew lay there with all these conflicting plans running round his head. He may have lain there for a time longer had it not been for the sound of people approaching. The beach in front of the big house was one of the most beautiful on the island but also one of the least used. People tended not to like visiting it because of the proximity of the house. There was an implication visitors would not be welcomed by the Telfords.

Andrew sat up to see who was walking his way and he saw Telford and Deal down by the tideline with their wives following on behind. Anxious to avoid meeting them he jumped up and walked quickly up the sheep path that led to the rough track along the back of the beach that was created decades earlier to cart logs from the far-off woodland. In the hollow of the track he wasn't seen and managed back to the house apparently without being spotted.

He couldn't make up his mind whether to go in and look for George and try and recruit him as an ally, or if he should go to work and continue to think it through. The beach walkers parted company as they reached the end of the sand with the Deals turning to head back to the house and George and Lucinda continuing up that same sheep track and on towards the woods. It was the first chance Lord Telford had to speak to his wife about his encounter with Andrew that morning

"I suspect we have a problem looming darling." Lucinda didn't respond just slowed her pace and looked at her husband.

"I forgot to tell you that Andrew had asked to see me this morning. I thought he must be wanting money or something but in fact he wanted to ask me to give my blessing to his marrying Alice."

"Oh my God, I've been waiting for that," said Lucinda. "What on earth did you say?"

"Well I'll tell you want I didn't say. Bugger off and don't be so bloody stupid. I rather wish I had though. I'm not sure exactly the words I used but I left him in no doubt that I, that we, would think such a union out of the question."

Lucinda stopped completely and turned fully to George. "Why George, would it really be such a bad thing. They seem very happy together and Andrew's turning into a pretty decent young man. Surely these days we shouldn't be getting hung up about class and background, if that's what you are worried about."

"Lucinda it's not just class. Ok so he's a decent enough kid. But he's a kid going nowhere with a drunk for a mother, no qualifications to his name. Suppose George never married and Alice had a child with Andrew. That child would eventually inherit all we own. If the bloody government changes primogeniture that child could even inherit the earldom. It's a non starter. I am not having a daughter of mine marrying a seaweed cutter. That's it. It is not going to happen."

"George I think you need to calm down and think it through. We don't know that Alice wants to marry him. She may turn him down. But if she does want to marry him how are you going to stop it? Those days are gone. Are you going to boycott the wedding? You'll just end up in the Daily Mail looking a prat.

"Are you prepared to let this come between us and Alice. Banish her or something. I really do wish you would think a little more before you start laying down the law. You need to get hold of Andrew quickly before something else happens and tell him you have changed your mind. You don't have to encourage it. You could say something like, well if Alice wants to marry you I will not stand in her way."

"Lucinda you just don't understand do you. Alice is the daughter of an Earl. She went to one of the best schools in the country. She has an honours degree from Exeter University. Her life is full of successful, interesting, decent people. I am not going to let her throw all that away on the back of a summer romance and set up married life in a lighthouse keeper's cottage with a manual labourer who has neither the education nor intelligence to be a lifelong companion to my beautiful and successful daughter."

"That's fine George. But what does she want? That's what you have to ask yourself. These days women, especially women like Alice, know what they want and if you try to get in her way all you will do is end up driving her apart from the family. If it comes to that what if George sides with her. Have you thought of that? You will become estranged from your daughter and son. Are you prepared to make that sort of sacrifice just for snobbery."?

"Oh God Lucinda its not snobbery. Its common sense. How could a marriage across such a vast divide ever last? Are we going to stand by and let Alice condemn herself to a dull life amongst these people? He'll not go to London to let her get on with a career, I can tell you that. Be a house husband, or park attendant or something. He'll want to stay here with his own kind and that will mean Alice spending her life with this collection of drunks and oddballs. God forbid, but what if they had children. Do you want your grandchildren to go to that ghastly mainland school with the local toerags. They will never be able to afford school fees – and I'm not paying to send Andrew Edward's offspring to a proper school."

"George they would be your offspring too, don't forget. But that's a long way down the road. I really think the only way to do this, to avoid a family split, is to give Andrew the go ahead and hope Alice turns him down. If she doesn't then I don't think it is for us to stand in her way. It's not the 19th century you know."

Without another word Lord Telford began to climb up onto the headland and off onto the old carter's road that Andrew had walked not half an hour earlier and head for home. Lucinda followed some distance behind, deeply worried.

Meanwhile at the big house Andrew had stuck his head into the kitchen to see where George was. Ilonka had no idea and so he decided to go back to work, to take his mind off things.

The kelp sheds, as they were now known, were as good a place for diversion on the island as any. Between the shop and the hotel next to the ferry pier and harbour there was always someone passing wanting a chat. Some days it was difficult to get any work done if there was a particularly good piece of island gossip to pass on, to speculate about or to exaggerate.

On summer days like this it was often tourists wanting to find out about the kelp business, see if there was anything to buy. There wasn't.

So once the work was done and the machinery turned off and cleaned down Andrew, as usual, drove up to the hotel to pick up Alice. Her 9-5 routine fitted with his. At weekends they might stay for a quick drink and a chat to whoever was in the bar. Unlike his father Andrew talked to the visitors out of interest not a desire to scrounge alcohol.

This night though he told Alice he just wanted to go home have a shower and change – they had the ordeal of another dinner with her parents and the Deals. Supper with just the three of them was always fun and now they had the guests it meant inevitably listening to Lord Telford and his crony moan on about just about everything, particularly the state of the country, their unfair removal from parliament and all else in between. Andrew in particular still found the pain of Telford's endless tirades against the community of the island which had not been diminished by the passing of years particularly hard to bear. These were his friends and neighbours. Now really Alice's friends and neighbours too and being written off as hopeless so-in-sos for whatever reason.

He had the first shower. A day manhandling the kelp left him in greatest need. Then as Alice took her turn Andrew sat in the living room of the little keeper's cottage wrapped only in a towel and listening to the powerful pibroch, the classical music of the pipes, The Lament for the Children. It's pathos suited the moment perfectly. Alice had suspected there was something wrong. When she emerged from the bathroom to find Andrew slumped and melancholy it confirmed her suspicions.

When asked he said nothing was up and remained immersed in the music. She sat beside him and gently took his hand. "Come on Drew – what's happened. I know something has?"

He couldn't decide whether to tell her of his morning encounter with her father. To do so, he thought, would be tantamount to admitting defeat in his quest to marry her, before that quest had even started properly. She gently badgered him until he felt he had no choice but to reveal all. So he slowly and, as accurately as he could remember, recounted the full conversation. He found it painful and struggled at times to hold back the tears of anger and sorrow for himself that rose inside.

Then as he got to the end of the sorry tale he surprised himself.

From nowhere and with no forethought came the words: "So Alice, will you marry me?" He slipped onto one knee, loosing the towel as he did.

In the event Andrew was more shocked by his asking than Alice was. She smiled the big broad smile that had electrified many young men, none more so than Drew, and gently said to him that of course she would.

"Nothing could make me more happy Drew. I love you so much, and I love our lives here together. I really do not care what my father thinks. If my life had gone the way he wanted then God knows where I would be but I know I could not be happier than I am now."

She leant forward and gave him a long and lingering kiss.

The big house guests were all seated at the dining table by the time Andrew and Alice walked in. Alice apologised for their late arrival explaining something had cropped up, adding hurriedly at the hotel, by way of further explanation. They had decided to keep the news of their betrothal to themselves for now. The island population was not good at keeping secrets so Andrew knew he couldn't tell his mother or Kenny, particularly Kenny, who would probably see it not so much as the proposed union of two young people in love but more like his team getting one over Lord Telford.

The talk was mainly of tomorrow's stalking. Lord Telford wondered if Andrew and Alice were planning on joining the rest of them on the hill. Andrew had little interest in shooting deer, and he doubted the invitation was well meant and so apologised saying he was too busy. Following suit Alice said she couldn't take the time away from the hotel. It was full, as usual, and she had to be there.

After dinner it was clear the Earls were off on their whisky tour again. Alice joined the wives in the drawing room leaving the men to it. George took his leave too saying he had things to check for the morning and asked Andrew to come and help. In truth neither had the stomach for another night's whisky fuelled whinging. On their way out the boys poured themselves two generous drams and once in the hall Andrew asked George to go into the library for a chat.

He was quite a wreck by now. Full of emotion, his anger at Lord Telford, his love for Alice confirmed by her declaration of love for him, the wine and now the whisky. It was a lot to cope with.

Emboldened by this heady mixture he sought the counsel of his oldest and best friend. He told George the full account of his conversation, perhaps confrontation, with Lord Telford that morning. He also confided in him that he had ignored Telford's stipulations and gone ahead and asked Alice to marry him and that she had agreed. George was sat on the same leather sofa as Andrew and looked a bit confused as he took in the momentous tale. Then he jumped up and offered Andrew his hand and used it to pull him up and into a great man hug.

Any doubts over support from George were immediately gone and Andrew couldn't stop smiling. George broke the handshake to reach for the whisky glasses. He gave one to Andrew and looked him straight in the eye.

"Drew that's the best thing I've heard for a long time. You and Alice are made for each other and I am sure you will be very happy together. Congratulations friend. Here's to you and Alice." The glasses were chinked and drained and they collapsed back onto the sofa.

Flushed by the moment and excited by his good fortune Andrew told George only the three of them knew of the engagement, for that is what it was, and he wanted to keep it that way. Did George think his father would come round?

"Fuck knows Drew. He's a dinosaur. Just listen to him and his pal tonight. You'd think it was his great grandfather talking. I wonder if he has told mum. I'm sure she would have a different view. She likes you, sort of, and she can see how happy Alice is."

Andrew took the qualification of Lady Telford's view of him as a bit of banter and ignored it.

"Seriously George. We've not talked about this yet but I think Alice wants to go through with it even without your father's blessing. To be honest he seems to have washed his hands of you two anyway I don't know why he should suddenly start caring about me and Alice."

"That's not fair Drew. He has left us to it here, but he is very much still on the case. I wonder if I should talk to him. It would probably be best if I talk to mum and let her try and change his mind."

So the conversation went on as they explored the various possibilities only ending when Alice walked into the library. George gave her a bit of a fright as he appeared to leap at her, only to give her the biggest brotherly hug.

"Congratulations sis. I'm really happy for you."

Alice turned to Andrew: "I thought we weren't telling anyone yet."

"Just George – we need him on our side."

George hugged her again and joked: "I'm surprised you've ended up with Drew. I always thought looks were important to you."

The laughter in the library was in stark contrast to the ever more serious tones coming from the dining room. The earls indulging their passion for complaint.

As the young drained more drams Alice and George concluded their mother was the route to sorting out this little family difficulty. She would not be the one to stand in the way of her daughter's happiness. In the meantime, they vowed, life will go on as normal.

Chapter 17

As usual Euan Fernie met the stalking party at the front of the house just before 9. Their weather blessing continued. It was a lovely day to take to the hills of the island. The earls were the only shooters, so that was easy. Deal was given a rifle and had a few practise shots over the lawns down to the sea to set the sights. Lord Telford was immensely proud of his stalking rifles. He had five in total, all Holland and Holland .375 bought by previous generations but treasured by this one. He remembered his first stag as though it was last week and could still bring himself to smile at the recollection of young George's first – shot at the same age – 13.

The guns went in the first Land Rover with Euan at the wheel as they set off for the interior of the island and it's complex maze of glens and ridges. The ladies followed on behind in the second Defender with George at the wheel. He wasn't going to shoot that day but would escort the ladies. Two of the estate workers had been sent on ahead with the ponies needed to bring deer carcases off the hill.

The interior of the island was, in many ways, its least attractive part. There were really only 5 big hills, each a little over 2000 feet, and whilst they gave good views from the tops they were not challenging or interesting. Three were largely covered in scree, and one in wind turbines.

Euan knew his market well and had learnt quickly since starting working for young George that Lord Telford didn't like messing about. He wasn't one for long walks with multiple ascents and descents in pursuit of their quarry. He liked, as far as possible, to get up the hill, find the herd, shoot a stag and get home. It was never quite as easy as that; however this was the favoured approach. The only thing that might delay the return to the big house would be if it was a lovely day and there was a picnic to be had, which was the case today.

So it was that the two Land Rovers bounced their way along the rugged hilly tracks towards the highest of the five hills. Euan had been watching the deer there yesterday and he reckoned they wouldn't be far. The road came to a halt about halfway up the hill and so the guns climbed out to walk the rest of the way up. Every few hundred yards of the drive-up Euan had been scoping the hillsides and seemed to know exactly where he was off to.

"Gentlemen the deer are very much in the area I saw them in yesterday, and the day before. There's two of you and one of me so we will go together but as we get onto them one of you will have to drop back. With luck we'll get a stag each for you – there are some old fellas that need to be culled out."

So with the thrill of the hunt and the expectation of the kill stalker and the earls set away up the hill. The ladies decided to keep to the lower levels and George offered to walk them into the glen where in the winter a waterfall crashed down off the tops, but at this time of year it was little more than a trickle.

The sheep tracks through the heather were well defined and in places there were signs of the starting of the late summer flowering, the purple just beginning to show. As the low ground party walked on three shots echoed round the hills over the space of about quarter of an hour. George hoped that each of those would have ended with a kill – the dying deer would lift his father's spirits immeasurably.

The warmth of the late summer day created a tangible dryness in the heather that hit the ladies' nostrils with a calming sensation. The trees in this area are few and far between but George had guided the little group to a pile of freshly cut wood, the trees being felled mainly for safety having given up their efforts to cling on to the shallow peat against the fury of winter gales.

The three of them sat on the logs and George produced coffee and some of Ilonka's home made shortbread from his rucksack. On the way up the chat had been inconsequential, mainly centred on Lucinda's joy at not having to visit the island too often these days, adding from time to time, of course, how much she missed her children.

Having his mother and Cicely Deal comfortably settled on the log with a cup of coffee and some shortbread had purpose. George wanted to see if he could recruit Cicely into his campaign for Drew and Alice's engagement to win family acceptance. "Has mum been telling you about our great Telford dilemma?" asked George of Cicely. "About Alice's unsavoury suitor."

"George" Lucinda jumped in rather more sternly than he would have expected, "I do not for a moment think that Andrew is unsavoury. Your father and I both like him. He has done well for himself, considering his bad start in life," she couldn't resist the qualification of her praise, "but it is clear that he and Alice have no long-term future together. How can they? Where is the common ground, and more importantly what about the future of our family, the next generation?"

Cicely appeared reluctant to add her contribution to this essentially private family matter. But Lucinda made it clear she was expecting her to join in, and on the parents side at that.

With a kindly smile Cicely encouraged George to take things slowly: "It's a very difficult situation George. You must understand your parents have to look at the individuals involved, of course, but they also need to take account of the wider interests of the family. As things stand if your sister married this chap and they had children it could be that if you were not blessed with offspring then one of the great families of England would have their future in......" she trailed off without finishing the sentence.

It was clear to George that, as he had suspected, Andrew's marriage intentions had been top of the ladies' agenda over the last 24 hours and he feared the support for the union that he thought might come from his mother and her friend was not going to be forthcoming.

Cicely went on: "George what you have to remember is that families like ours have," she hesitated as though weighing up the acceptability of what she wanted to say, "have a certain place in the order of things and these days now we are under virtual siege we have to be careful to protect what we have and ensure we are in the best shape for the future."

George was certain she was making some sort of genetic argument, seeking to ensure the blue blood stayed – blue. He wanted to ask her for clarification of exactly what she meant but knew that if it was as he feared he would be unlikely to be able to contain his temper.

"But mum surely you are not going to stand in the way of Alice's happiness. Andrew mightn't have a title but he's a thoroughly decent guy and just look at how the three of us, and it is the three of us, are actually beginning to transform this place. With all due respect we are the future and you guys are the past."

The sentiment might have been difficult to argue with but he should have found a more tactful way of putting it.

"George it's not just about Alice's happiness," said Lucinda getting visibly more cross with her son by the minute. "It's about what is right. I dare say Alice is very happy with Andrew at the minute but I very much doubt it will last the strain of life off the island, when she is back with her real friends. You also have to consider that what's right for Alice just now may not be in the interests of our family in the long term."

That was enough for George – before his mother had a chance to continue he made his own position perfectly clear. "God Almighty you should hear yourselves. This is the 21st century – you are not characters in some 18th century novel. Just in case you hadn't noticed our titles these days mean slightly less than bugger all. If I make a good job of running this place hopefully I will earn the respect of the community. If I muck it up then I won't and being a lord or an earl will make no difference at all to that.

"Do you honestly think Alice can't be happy unless she marries into another titled family? That's quite pathetic isn't it? If you find Andrew unacceptable then I rather think that is your problem, not his."

Lady Telford found he son's view shocking and his language in front of her guest unhelpful, but that was for later. She sought to calm the situation. "George, I think we need to discuss this a little more calmly later on, amongst ourselves. For now I think it would be sufficient for you to apologise to Cicely for that little outburst and perhaps go and get the picnic stuff I don't suppose your father will be that much longer."

It had been sometime since they heard the last rifle shot, the stalkers may well be on their way down. George rose from the log and without offering the suggested apology started to walk back towards the Land Rover leaving the ladies to their ruminations. A short time later the other Land Rover was first heard and then seen bumping along the heather. The stalking must have finished.

Lord Telford was in fine form as he got out at the log strewn picnic site. They'd had a splendid time. Euan had been as good as his word and had set the two of them up with a pair of fine stags, each shot clean and gralloched, loaded onto the ponies and away to the game larder at the big house. This was as good as it got for Lord Telford. The passage of time had left him a little bored of stalking but he felt obliged to entertain his guests to a stag. To get up onto the hill, down a beast or two and back by lunchtime was a perfect way to do it. Continuing in the afternoon was not on the agenda.

Everyone mucked in setting up the picnic – table, chairs crockery and cutlery all put out with Lucinda taking charge of Ilonka's boxes of food. Lobster, salmon, ham, salads, homemade bread, flasks of soup and an enormous chocolate cake. The perfect scene for a wealthy landowner. From their seats at the bottom of the glen every bit of land that could be seen belonged to them and the thought might well have been that they intended to keep it that way and not share it with some young random boy, even if he was a pleasant enough random.

That night before dinner George managed to get his mother on her own and in the quiet of the morning room set about a more measured attempt at winning her round. It soon became clear, however, that her mind was made up. She really annoyed him with constant references to history, family, just how important the Telfords were and how they needed to protect their heritage. It was clear he was getting nowhere and George concluded the only thing that may result from this conversation would be losing his temper and saying things that he may regret later. Andrew and Alice were not at dinner that night and so George was on his own with his parents and their friends. He wasn't in a mood for their chat, lightened though it was due to the fact that the lunchtime wine had merged into early evening G&T's and back to the Burgundy without pausing. After pudding, late summer raspberries from the gardens, as he left his father grabbed him gently by the arm and said they had to have a conversation, in the morning. No need to ask what that would be about.

Chapter 18

George was up and out long before his parents or their guests emerged the next day so it was nearly ten o'clock before he eventually caught up with his father, in the library. Sooner or later George would learn that important conversation with his father was best left until after lunch. It was, at that moment still a lesson unheeded. The library was about the only space in the big house that had been changed substantially to mark the passing of the generations. George had found it's dark panelling oppressive and the book laden shelves irrelevant to his life. So the whole room had been given a makeover with the fine wooden panels painted matt white, most of the books put into storage in the attics and he and Alice had spent days going through the estate papers and putting them in order. Box files filled one whole bookcase their contents neatly marked on the outside. Lord Telford had passed no comment whatsoever on the changes bought about to his former domain. George wasn't sure if the absence of a view being expressed was good or bad and in all honesty he didn't much care.

He was sitting at his desk going through some bills when his father came into the room shortly after half past ten. The absence of any salutation was not in any way unusual; however the grim countenance of his father's visage was a rather scary intimation that things were not going to go well. Over the past couple of years the biggest change in George's attitude towards his father was the growing feeling that his dad was useless and lazy. In the relatively short time he had been, nominally at least, in charge of things on the island he had come to realise that his father had discharged his responsibilities with immense ineptitude and idleness. George had largely kept these observations to himself but had spent hours wondering just how his father could be so relaxed about letting the place go to the dogs and being such a poor steward of the family's remaining assets.

He sensed his father may have reflected on these matters himself, but probably in a bad way - conjuring up negative reflections on his son's efforts as a cover for his own failures.

Before George had a chance to open up the conversation in the manner he had been mulling over for the previous 24 hours his father took the wind right out of his sails.

"George if this is about your sister and that boy I'm not interested. There is nothing to discuss. It is not happening."

Things had started much worse that George had feared.

"Hold on dad – you and mum need to be very careful about this. This is the sort of thing that tears families apart if people don't act in a grown up and sensible way."

"If by grown up and sensible you mean your mother and I should just stand by and let Alice throw her life away then I repeat: It is not going to happen if I have anything to do with it at all."

It was clear to George that his father was badly hungover and completely resolute in his opposition to Andrew. He sat still for an age looking at his father, who in turn gave a close examination to the new look library and its neat shelves and bright walls. George wasn't sure how to play it. Withdraw now risking giving the impression that the matter was settled in such short time, or take a chance of fighting on with the potential escalation of opposition.

It had to be the later, he concluded.

"Can you explain exactly what it is that you and mum have against Andrew? He is my friend, your daughter's boyfriend and a fantastic asset to this island and to this family. Since you" the uncomfortable pause at that point came as George struggled to find the right adjective to correctly characterise his father's retreat to London from the island. An adjective that might not inflame the already delicate situation.

"Since you" he started again "decided that you did not want to continue here Alice and Andrew have been every bit as vital to the development of our businesses here as me, more so as far as the hotel is concerned. Alice is transforming that place and you will have seen how the accounts show what she is doing is working.

"Surly the days of class barriers to marriage are gone? That can be the only thing that you have against Andrew. He's thoroughly decent, bloody hard working and most importantly loves Alice. Surely you and mum aren't such dinosaurs that you will let snobbery get in the way of her happiness?"

"You know George," Lord Telford's voice was a lot quieter than usual, slower too and more measured, "somethings I look at you and wonder where you came from. If I am honest with myself the things you are doing here now are the sort of things I should have done years ago, but didn't for whatever reason, and then you go and spoil it all with such, such naïve nonsense as this.

"You have to look at genes. That's the key. It is not what people appear to be, it is what they really are, what their DNA dictates. OK so Andrew appears to be a pleasant enough boy. But if he and Alice were to marry and have children what that might mean for our family terrifies me.

"You know the history. The Telfords have been at the monarch's side, we've produced statesmen and parliamentarians. We are at the centre of the networks that run this country and we want to stay there.

"Imagine this. Imagine Alice marries Andrew and they have children. It is entirely likely that succession laws are going to be changed to do away with primogeniture. So if you don't have children the Telford titles go to the child of the uneducated son of hippy drunks. You wouldn't want that now, would you?"

George struggled to come up with a response to that tirade that did not involve a lot of swearing. However he managed to hold his temper, if only for his sister's sake.

"Dad, live in the real world. Lets face it. You are not at any monarch's side, nor are you a statesman or a parliamentarian. Families need to be about the future, not the past. These days we are just like anyone else; struggling to make a living out of what we have got. There's no entitlement anymore. Jim and Caroline might have been a bit over keen on the old booze, but there is an argument that might suggest you too have fallen into that trap at times."

George's attempt at gently moving his father from his sense of entitlement to embracing the meritocracy we are slowly moving towards, failed rather spectacularly. He might have been better just swearing a lot.

"Don't you be so bloody rude. There is a difference between having a glass of Chablis with lunch and being pissed all day and every day which is what that unfortunate young man's genetic inheritance is.

"You need to realise who you are and what you have got and work hard to preserve it for yourself and future generations." George struggled not to laugh at that one.

"The bottom line is this," continued his father, "I want Andrew Edward out of Alice's life and preferably off this island and I expect you to support me and your mother in this. If you are not prepared to offer that support then I would be forced to the conclusion that your heart is not in your position here, that you cannot be trusted with the opportunity I have given you, and I will take it back. You are here as my agent and I can remove you if I think it is no longer in our family's interests for you to continue to act as such."

George was silenced by the ferocity of his father's onslaught. Surely he could not mean that he was prepared to turn everyone's lives on their heads just because he didn't approve of his daughter's boyfriend. Could he really force himself to give up the quiet and comfortable life in London to come back to the island for which he appeared to have nothing but contempt?

"Dad for God's sake this is a small family business not some dynastic inheritance. We'd be struggling to pay for decent Champagne for Alice's wedding let alone have something worth splitting the family over."

That was it as far as Lord Telford was concerned. The final insult. "George you are not hearing me. This is stopping now. Your mother will speak to Alice. You will speak to Andrew and make it plain he is not wanted in this family and not wanted on our island, do you understand?"

"That's up to you father, but I'm not having anything to do with it. You are talking about my sister and my best friend. If it comes to a fight, then I am with them." George emphasised the last phrase to leave his father certain that there was no doubt. As far as he was concerned Alice and Andrew were a great match and great for the Telford family's future.

"You are being stupid, George. It's all very well the three of you having a bit of fun here for a few months – but we have to think for the long term for future generations. I don't want us just to fade, forgotten into history. I want to make sure that you and those that come after you have the opportunity to serve the country like your forebears did. To continue their legacy. We are not going to do that with the likes of Andrew. Surely to God you can see that for yourself."

"You are wrong Dad. We are doing it already. This place is slowly being transformed. You've only been away two years but you must be able to see the difference I am making. Making with the enormous help I get from both Alice and Andrew. It's the modern world dad. We are going to make it here if we work hard and keep up with things, keep ahead of the competition. Alice has got the hotel buzzing. I'm slowly turning the deer into a real asset again. Not for us but for people who will pay to stalk in such a beautiful place. Just two of the things that I am afraid to say have been rather neglected. The estate is now making real money in a way it never did when you were here full time."

His father was prepared to hear no more. He walked round the back of the desk, momentarily looked out of the window at the gardens and distant hills. Turning to his son he said he was not for changing his mind. "Your mother and I are going to talk to Alice this afternoon. She's coming over for a cup of tea. As we do that I want you to see Andrew and tell him we need the sheds back as soon as possible."

Realising the full implication of this step immediately George started to raise a protest. "But Dad without those sheds Kenny and Andrew don't have a business."

He was stopped dead as his father chillingly observed: "Exactly. They have no business and so have no reason to stay here. I imagine that rather expensive machinery in our sheds is not paid for and so they will have to relocate right off this island and find somewhere else to gather their crop."

"If you think I am going to do that you are mad. You want me to ruin my best friend and devastate my sister – just to satisfy your misplaced sense of history, sense of importance. Dad you need to get into the right century. Do you think that driving

Andrew off this island you are going to break up his relationship with Alice, All that will happen is that she will go with him – God knows where. That'll leave me here alone. I can't do this all by myself. I think the expression is you are cutting your nose to spite your face."

"Well George I think you need to gather your thoughts and give proper consideration to our family's position." His father then stuck a knife right in to his son: "If you feel this is not something you want to be part of, saving our family, then Uncle Henry has said he would be very happy, very happy indeed, to come here and run things for us."

"You've discussed this with Henry already? Are you trying to get rid of Andrew, or get rid of all three of us? If you want rid of me just say so. I will go and get a job somewhere else. A job that pays better and lets me sleep at night and then Henry can come here and fuck the whole place up, if that's what you want."

Truth was that was exactly what his father did not want. He had rather a lesser opinion of his brother than most of the islanders did and he realised many years ago that Henry was incapable of doing anything sensible with his life.

Both Georges were, by this point, on the edge of loosing it. The father decided to try and calm things down a little.

"Think hard about what I have said, George. Then after your mother and I have spoken to Alice we will talk this over again. But I want you to fully understand that I want this relationship to end, for the good of all of us, and if you are not prepared to play your part then I will have to reassess your role in the family. Life's not about the easy choices, you know. We all have to take tough decisions and it's the ability to see the big picture and do what is right that separates out the people going paces and the rest of humanity."

That left George so cross, so angry, so enraged by his father's stark stupidity, snobbery, just plain wrongness that he felt unable to speak. Inside the pressure had built up enough to push the gauge well into the red sector. Something was going to blow and he needed to get out of the library, out of the house, before it did.

Without another word he stood up. Looked at his father, piercingly straight into his tired looking eyes, and made to speak but no words appeared. Instead he just walked out of the room leaving the door wide-open behind him. "Tonight" shouted Lord Telford after his disappearing son who offered no response.

George dropped his plans for that morning and instead drove straight to the hotel arriving just as the staff were beginning to set up the dining room for lunch. It was busy these days, both lunch and dinner, and a well practiced operation was underway.

The only thing George didn't like about his sister's changes to the hotel was the heavy carpet Alice had laid all over the ground floor. Combined with the stained oak panelling so beloved of his ancestors it gave the place a dark and gloomy feel. Traditional and upmarket were Alice's preferred adjectives. Old fashioned and staid were his. Today, however, was not a day for discussing décor. Ferdinand the Spanish manager was behind the reception desk, as usual. It always seemed to George that Alice did more hands on managing than the man paid to do the day to day work, but she was happy with him and who was he to interfere.

George cut short Ferdinand's attempts at conversation and asked where his sister was. On being told he continued to the stairs heading at speed to her first floor office.

"What brings you here Bro? Not like you to pop round. Mum and Dad doing your head in, are they?"

"It is about them that I've come sis, but not for me. For you."

"God he's not still going on about Andrew, is he. I thought he might just be getting used to the idea by now. Seeing a bit of sense, embracing the new century."

"Alice I really don't know what to do," said George slumping down into the only other chair in Alice's office. "He's basically told me to chuck Andrew off the island, or get off myself."

Alice's shock was evident. She knew there was a fight coming on but had not realised the stakes were so high. "Chuck Andrew off the island? He can't do that. Does he not realise those days went 100 years ago. To hell with him. There's nothing he can do." Her repetition of that phrase was a clear indication that she feared there might well be something he could do.

"He's told me I have to throw Andrew and Kenny out of the sheds and he knows that means the end of their business. Bankruptcy I bet. Drew's already worried about how much the

201

machinery is costing them. They couldn't afford to move, even if they could find somewhere else to go.

"I've told him I'm not doing it and he basically said well stuff you if you don't you can bugger off too and he'll get Uncle Henry to take over here. Uncle Henry for God's sake."

As he looked at his sister waiting for a response he could see she was struggling to contain her emotions. The colour had drained from her face.

She stared at him and he at her. Slowly he saw the tears form in her eyes and start running down her face. It was such an unusual sight. The past two years had not been plain sailing but the challenge had been practical, not emotional.

He wanted to put his arm round his sister but feared that would only make matters worse. "What am I going to do George?"

"That's wrong to start with sis. We are in this together. It is what are *we* going to do about it. I think we have no choice but to stand up to them, because mum's apparently in complete agreement, and make them see sense. If you are certain Andrew's the one for you then we can't let them get away with it. This is our lives. Our future and I am not going to stand by and let them screw things up for you, for all of us."

It took Alice an age to reply. In a barely audible voice she said they were going to have to come to some tough decisions. If they could not persuade their parents it might be that the only choice open for them would be for all three of them to go. "I'm sure we can all get jobs on the mainland. It might be good for us to break away and do something completely different. Not together, I mean, Andrew and I can get something sorted, I'm sure. You will easily get a job managing someone else's land. Between your degree and experience here you would be a great catch.. Maybe even someone we know – that would be embarrassing for dad if it came to that. It's not as though we don't have a bit of a cushion."

She was referring to the Telford Settlement Trust, established by their grandfather which gave them as the children of the earl a modest income and their cousins would get a lesser one after the age of 21.

"I'm not for leaving here Alice. I love this place and we have worked bloody hard to begin clearing up father's mess. This is my future and I am not going to give it up just to because our parents think they are still in the Victorian era. They are just going to have to see sense and realise that if they want the family to stick together then their prejudice will have to be parked.

"They are planning on speaking to you this afternoon. You just have to make it plain that you are not prepared to give up Andrew, as long as you are certain that is the way you want it, and I will back you up. Even they will be able to see there is no choice in it for them."

Alice listened and thought hard about her brother's words. It was what she wanted to hear. She stood up and walked over to where he was sitting and half reclined half jumped onto his knee throwing her arms round his neck and giving him a big kiss. As she lingered, their faces touching, George could feel her tears dampening his cheeks.

"George we can win this one easily. They are set in their ways but not that stupid. Even dad wouldn't throw this place to the mercy of Uncle Henry. My God can you imagine?"

George suggested a joint approach, they should see their parents together and show a united front but Alice said she could do much better alone. "Dad's always hopeless at saying no when I work at it. If you are there he'll go into alpha mode but if it's just me I'll make him see sense. Mum wouldn't stick by him for long. I bet she doesn't agree with this deep down. I bet her parents weren't over the moon when Dad asked for her hand in marriage." That observation returned a bit of levity. They were both smiling as the door opened and Andrew walked in.

"What's going on here then? Sales through the roof?"

Alice told her boyfriend they had serious things to discuss. George said they'd be better off without him and with a peck on his sister's cheek and a pat of his friends arm he left.

As the office door closed quietly Alice walked over to Andrew and he instinctively, gently put his arms round her shoulder. "I love you Andrew."

"I love you to."

They stood for ages, Andrew hoping the warmth of the embrace may calm things down and offer comfort, Alice struggling not to break down entirely, her emotions crashing round like an island storm leaving her unable to think let alone speak.

Some minutes passed before she was able to articulate her emotions. In a low voice carrying sounds of sorrow and anger she began to describe her feelings of helplessness in the face of her parents' ridiculous opposition to their union.

"If I can't get my father to change his mind I really have not got a clue what to do. These last two years have been the happiest of my life. We've done a great job here. I've loved watching you and Kenny really get hold of the business and start making something good and lasting out of it. George has done so well considering the mess that he took over and I have just adored playing my part.

"I can't stay here without you Andrew – that is the one thing I am certain of, but if you stay here with me you won't have a business, so if you are to have a business then I will have to go. Maybe that's what's going to be best for all of us. I can go, I can move back to London, maybe you can join me there later. I can live without this place but I don't want to live without you."

"Alice you are all that is important to me. The business is great and I love living here, but if we have to go and make our own way somewhere else we will manage. We can make a go of it I'm sure. But surely your parents will see eventually that your happiness is important, more important that your father's pathetic view of who he is. Let's face it the world will not be worse off without an Earl of Telford on the planet, and the island, with all due respect to George, will manage quite nicely without your family. It might be really liberating for all three of us to leave and do something else. As long as I am with you I will be happy – happy here or happy somewhere else. We could go abroad – I could get a job in alginates somewhere else. Canada – New Zealand – South America."

Andrew's voice trailed away as he contemplated the enormity of the possible changes that almost certainly lay ahead. For Alice it was less daunting. She'd travelled the world, gap year, university, boarding school, all had taught self-reliance and given confidence.

Apart from his one trip to the far east with George, Andrew's life had been the island, school, and pipe band competitions round Scotland and Northern Ireland. Fun though it was three days at the World Championships in Glasgow nearly ten years earlier did not prepare a young person for very much in the real world.

Suddenly Alice's whole demeanour changed. "Right," she said jumping up, stepping back and looking right into Andrew's eyes, "We are taking charge. We are the future, the future of this family, the future of the island and the future of the small parts of the Telford inheritance that my father hasn't frittered away. If he's worried about securing the future of his ancestor's legacy, then he needs to get real and work out that he's had his chance and squandered it and it's up to us now. George, me, and if it is to be me, you too.

"I'm not going begging when I see them tonight. I'm going to tell them straight and if he's stupid enough to chuck us out God help him. You and George are worth a hundred Uncle Henry's. Handing over to Henry – it's a joke, he may as well try and sell the place and forget being the bigshot landowner and go back to Clapham."

And so the strategy was agreed.

That afternoon Alice arrived in the drawing room at the prime time for sensible conversation with her father. Lunch had been drink free, last night's hangover was gone, refreshed only be tea it was the best chance for meaningful discussion.

She closed the door behind her and set off about delivering her message loud and clear, not asking, but telling.

It wasn't the Telford's way to air their differences in public so when George, sitting in the library with the door shut, heard his mother and sister ferociously shouting at each other he knew things weren't going smoothly. A short time later the violent slamming of the front door confirmed his fears.

He sat still waiting to hear what might happen next but there was only silence. His parents had not left the drawing room, he would have surely heard them, and the guests must have sensed something was afoot and stayed out of the way.

After ten minutes he decided to make inquiries. "What on earth was that all about Mum? I could hear you from the library."

His mother looked upset – his father was at the far side of the room, by the drinks trolley pouring a rather large looking

Bruichladdich – always a bad sign in this early part of the evening.

"George you are going to have to speak to your sister. Your father and I are not going to stand by and let her throw her life away on this totally unsuitable boy."

"Don't you mean, mother, this young man who has bought her much happiness and worked hard with her to help stabilise your family's main asset. You have to understand that without Andrew, Alice would not have spent the last two years on the island and without her I would have struggled to get things as far as I have.

"Are you and dad really so unimaginative that you are prepared to sacrifice Alice's happiness purely and simply out of snobbery? Nothing against who Andrew is, just what he is. A decent, intelligent, hard working guy who happens to be the love of your daughter's life."

Before the debate had a chance to move on any his father cut it dead: "George. This is the way it is going to be. If you don't like it then you can give up your role here and find a challenge somewhere else.

"We are going home on Sunday and by then I want you to have made perfectly clear to Kenny and Andrew that their lease on the sheds is terminated. You will get the lawyers to send them the appropriate letter as soon as possible.

"We have told Alice that if she continues to live with Andrew her role in the hotel is terminated, she is not welcome in this house, and her income from your grandfather's trust ends, and ends now.

"Nothing would make me happier than to see you and Alice continuing to work together to develop our estate here and make it ever more profitable. However, be certain that if you and she do not do as we say then there will be consequences. Henry says he can take over here at anytime so your services on the island can end as soon as you like. But let me emphasise I do not want it to come to that. But it will if you and Alice choose to defy your parents."

George could not believe what he was hearing. He had walked in to the room having thought through his various arguments and had been confident common sense could win through. Instead he had been given three full days to decide not only his future, but potentially the futures of his sister and his best friend – not to mention the entire population of the island that would be affected one way or another by a change in regime.

"You can't be serious Dad. You want me to screw over my sister and my best friend simply to satisfy your pathetic prejudices against Andrew. He can't help who his parents are. He can't help not going to public school and smart universities. These aren't choices he made as a teenager being brought up in the shitty cottage you rented them. A damp draughty dump that never got warm in the winter. Those were not his choices. Just because you were able to send me and Alice away to board to make up for your shit parenting doesn't make me a better person. Are you too stupid to understand that those days are over. It's not who you were, it's who you are and who you are going to be. Going to be through your own efforts and hard work, not because you went to some posh school and your ancestor was a chum of the king hundreds of years ago. The people on this island, I believe, have a respect for me and what I am trying to do here in a way they never have had for you.

"With me they can see I love this place and want it to work – and work for everyone. They saw through your disinterested approach. They could see someone who was a taker, not a giver."

His anger grew as the words scattered round the room. His mother's look of upset had turned to disbelief whilst his father looked as though he may explode. By the time the tirade had reached this crescendo the Bruichladdich glass had been drained and refilled in just a matter of a few minutes.

George stood staring at his parents, his hands visibly shaking such was the rage he had worked himself up into. It was clear to the three of them the discussion had come to an end. Too much had been said already and any attempt to continue would only make things worse. But how to disengage?

That came from George as he said simply and quietly: "Fuck you." Then louder and right from the back of the throat: "Fuck you." His parents had never seen such anger from George since the days of his teenage tantrums, but this was altogether more serious.

So there was nothing left to be said. George simply turned and walked out in as measured a manner as he could manage. He was most deliberate as he pulled the door quietly shut behind him determined to emphasise his words as a considered reaction to a senseless set of circumstances rather than emotional ill-considered rantings.

The cloud of the afternoon had turned into a steady drizzle by the time he left the front door and with the warmth of the day and stillness of the evening the midges had moved in and within seconds he could feel the intense burning like sensation of the insects attacking his skin. No matter how long people live in these parts few ever learn to cope with the midge plague.

He leapt into the Defender scrubbing away at his face. Switching on the engine and aimed the internal fan right at him hoping to blow away the remaining pests.

At the Lighthouse Cottage Alice and Andrew had been waiting, speculating on the possible outcome of the showdown. They were bitterly disappointed when George told them how bad it had been, much worse that he had feared.

They sat for fully an hour running over the various possibilities, each time coming back to the basic proposition that it would have to come to a bigger showdown. The parents were not for listening and the children were not for obeying.

George concluded the way forward was for the three of them to see his parents and show a united front and force them to accept reality. Andrew and Alice were an item and staying together, forever. He wasn't going to hand over the running of the island to Uncle Henry, he'd rather sell up given a choice, and mum and dad were going to have to learn to live with it.

Within 24 hours of that plan being agreed in the lighthouse cottage the hope and certainty of their argument had been transformed into the bitterness and resentment of an apparent defeat after a deeply unsatisfactory confrontation the following day during which their measured and cautious plans had exploded into a torrent of abuse and recrimination that reflected badly on all five of them. The conclusion of the "discussion" was to move Lord Telford's resolution from firm to resolutely unshakeable.

As the three upstarts left the big house Andrew told Alice and her brother to go on without him. He was heading to see his old teachers. Andrew's visits to Flora and Alastair had become less frequent as his needs declined. However when he did go over he tended to stay for a long time and this day was no exception. It took an age for him to unburden himself and the Mortons were greatly moved by the obvious pain he was in. They just let him talk for an age, it was clear that was what he needed to do.

The couple were not surprised as they realised that Andrew was as concerned for the others who may be affected by his actions as he was for himself. Faster than the other principals in this drama Andrew had realised the main consequence of his continuing relationship with Alice would be the ruination of Kenny. They were borrowed up to the hilt to finance the expensive machinery that was he core of their flourishing business. Losing the sheds could only mean losing the business and the jobs that it supported. He would never be able to look Kenny in the eye again. Kenny that had given him and his mother shelter and a much better life than they could have imagined.

The three of them sat as they had in days gone by in the chairs ranged round the living room window with its picturesque view. "Flora and I have nothing but admiration for you Andrew. I was always worried that awful day you left my office with your mother and father after being suspended would have a dire effect on your future but the way you managed to turn things round came as a great relief to us and all that has happened since has done nothing but cement our admiration for the way you conduct yourself.

"As for George – he has been the real surprise to me. I had just presumed that with the influence of his ghastly father and the arrogance bred with a public school education he would just be another useless drain on this place – maybe the one that would be forced to realise the shortcomings of the Telford family and have to sell up."

Andrew looked quite shocked to hear his old teacher speaking in such plain terms. He had never been given any reason to suspect the depth of contempt Alastair had for Lord Telford. When he asked outright for advice, a suggestion as to what his next move could the retired teacher could offer nothing sensible.

He seemed to be in an impossible situation which would mean whatever the outcome someone was going to be badly hurt.

Flora had been sitting listening intently and saying nothing. She eventually added that she felt incredibly sorry for both Andrew and Alice. She had taken a delight in seeing how the couple's relationship had gone. They had come to think of Andrew almost as the son they never had an it caused great pain to see the mess that his life had suddenly got into, a mess not of his making, which made it worse.

The following morning as George was sitting in the library his father poked his head round he door to remind his son that he and his mother and their friends were going the next day on the afternoon ferry and he needed George's willing acceptance of the plan to get rid of Andrew before then.

At the lighthouse that morning Alice was having yet another go through the options with Andrew. "I think what I need to do is to go away for a few days and think things through to myself. I'm going to stay with Kittty Graham for a bit."

"What?" demanded Andrew. "Where did this plan come from? You've not mentioned anything to me about this. Don't you think you should be staying here with me, and with George to show your parents we are serious. What good is going off to London going to do?"

Alice gently explained the good it would do would be to allow her to clear her head. Kitty and she had been friends since the first day at Chevening and whilst she spoke to her every few days on the phone she felt a face to face, heart to heart, could help.

Andrew agreed, his reluctance obvious, and they sat in silence at the kitchen table deep in their respective thoughts. George knew of the plan for Alice to go away for a little while before Andrew and he sought out his father to ask for a stay in execution.

He found him on the beach enjoying another marvellous sunny day with the Deals. One more week, George told his father, was all he needed. There were a lot of decisions to be made and more time was vital.

"That's fine with me George. We going tomorrow and then by next Sunday you will have to tell me one way or another. I want Andrew off this island with all speed possible and if you are not prepared to do it then you will have to stand aside and make way for someone who is.

That short encounter with his father for George was the clincher. He realised really for the first time since this business had started that he had no choice on the matter at all as far as protecting his sister was concerned. He could not maintain the status quo. If he refused to kick out Kenny and his alginate business, and in so doing smash the hopes and dreams of Alice and Andrew, all he would achieve is losing control of the family business, put a buffoon in charge of the place who would then kick out the alginates anyway. His was a lose/lose situation.

As he left the four aging aristocrats walking the white sands and made his way back to the house George came to the deeply unpleasant certainty that he was going to have to be the one who brought misery to his sister and his best friend. There was no alternative. Better two go down than all three of them and potentially the island too. Surely, he thought, they would realise that he had no choice in the matter and Alice and Andrew could only blame his father for their predicament.

After all, he reasoned with himself, even if the business was no more there was nothing to stop Andrew and Alice continuing to live at the lighthouse. He would do his best to help them get by. In time he could persuade his father to allow Alice once more to manage the hotel, there could be a role for Andrew too. Anyway with the amount his father drank it might not be all that long before he was out of the equation anyway.

George felt a lightening of his load as he drove off to the lighthouse to see the pair of them. He wasn't confident that Andrew and Alice would agree with his decision but, surely, he thought, they would be able to see that he had no choice.

Before the hour was out George discovered that Andrew and Alice most certainly did not understand his position – they felt betrayed by him and told him in no uncertain terms. Alice tried to persuade her brother that if they stuck together, they could call her father's bluff. He was a difficult old sod, certainly, but even he would not carry through with such a monstrous threat. Would he, she demanded of her brother, effectively throw his son and daughter off the island for good and install his useless brother to preside over the family fortunes.

"For heaven's sake George we have to stick together. This is what the old bastard wants. He wants us to be fighting – divided and he can get his way." Alice was by now screaming with anger and frustration. Inside she couldn't work out who she was more angry with her father, or her brother. Her brother – at least he could see how wrong the situation was – her father – well he was just as he always was, and would always be, unpleasant and unreasonable. He knew no better, she reasoned. It was her brother who was cutting their chance of continued happiness on the island out from under their feet.

Andrew tried to calm things down but he only made Alice even more angry. Eventually she ran through to the bedroom of the little cottage and slammed the door behind her. The silence sitting between Andrew and George was short in duration and rested against a background of Alice's anguished crying. Andrew didn't know what to do. Continue to confront George over his devastating decision or try and comfort Alice. He thought the latter the best course of action. Quietly he told George to go, a request made without anger – at the back of his mind he kind of half saw where his friend was coming from and almost agreed with him.

George left without saying another word – Andrew went through to the bedroom where he found Alice under the covers still sobbing, more quietly now, and sat down on the bed. "You know Alice when George puts it like that you can see he is maybe in a worse position than us."

His plea for understanding was met by an explosion of visceral rage. Alice's sobbing was almost uncontrollable but eventually she managed to get out what she wanted her boyfriend to understand.

"Do you not see what George has done. He is pretending he has no choice – we either all go or you and I go but he survives. I think he wants rid of us, God knows why. Well he's welcome to it. His sad lonely life – all by himself watching the water run down the walls of that ugly unhappy Victorian pile. I thought he was different from Dad – but he has just proved he is exactly the same. Selfish, greedy and hopelessly short sighted."

Andrew wanted to suggest she may be missing the point but truth was he wasn't brave enough to speak those words. Instead he lay down and embraced her gently hoping the silence of the room may calm things down.

Time was running out for George to meet his father's deadline. It was with a heavy heart and a feeling of guilt born out of betrayal that he drove back home anxious to arrive ahead of his parents and guests gathering for a last dinner before the next day's ferry. He found his dad by himself in the drawing room Bruichladdich in hand. As he walked in father offered son a dram and, unusually, George accepted. He was there to tell his father than he would comply with his wishes but he wanted to be certain he did so in such a manner as to leave his father in no doubt that he was doing so under extreme protest and he thought the plan wrong and just plain nasty and unwarranted.

"George, you will understand when it comes to your turn to think about these things that the most important duty the head of the family has is to do everything in his power to make sure the family continues in the way it should.

"For us that means we need to maintain our position in society, hold our heads up amongst our peers and make sure of the continuance of the Telford family in the position they have occupied for nearly 350 years."

George thought virtually everything his father had just said was utter crap but he was too tired of it all and too emotional to even begin pointing out the crass stupidity of it. There was no point. His father had made up his mind and throughout his short life George had understood that once his father's mind was made up there was nothing that would make him change it.

"One thing, though Dad. I am not prepared to actually instruct our lawyers to evict Kenny and Andrew from the sheds. I want you to do it. I am going to continue to live here and I don't want people spending the rest of my life saying I'm the guy that chucked his own sister and the love of her life off the island."

His father smiled, quite a rarity, leading George to think that he was about to agree to the plea. Then made it clear he was not.

"You are going to have to do it, and sign all the paperwork so it's clear the orders came from you.

"George there is a responsibility that comes with your position here that you are going to have to learn to discharge it in the best interests of the family. It's easy doing the popular things but you have to learn the necessary things are even more important, even if they are somewhat less popular.

"Don't worry about the people here. They'll think you are a bastard anyway no matter what you do. They think that of me and they thought that of your grandfather.

"It's just how people like this are. I don't give a damn what they think, my father didn't either and nor should you. Most of them aren't worth the time of day and are only out for what they can get. Don't give them another thought."

"What about Alice and my best friend. It's impossible for me to bring such misery to them. I don't want them thinking that I am the heartless tyrant who ended their dreams – because that's what is happening here and you know it.

"I want them to understand that, to be honest, there is a difference between you and me."

His father stopped him at that. "George there is no difference between you and me. We have to be the same person out for the same things. For us that is the best for ourselves. Everything else is disposable. We are what counts. Our family. That's why I am doing this."

"Making me do it," interrupted George.

"Helping you recognise your duty. What you have to do. The first thing you have to do is realise that what I am telling you to do is in Alice's best interests more than anything else. Do you not think that your mother and I love your sister? Of course we do, that's why we have to help her not throw her life away in this manner in pursuit of a hopeless dream. No good can come of her relationship with Andrew Edward. We have been against it from the start and kept our own counsel certain that it would fizzle out when Alice came to her senses. It's just taking a little longer for her to realise the hopelessness of her situation and so we, or rather you, need to hurry it along a bit."

George drained his whisky and his father refilled first his own then his son's glass. Just spirit no water.

As father and son stood looking out over the big house policies, each reflecting internally on their own positions the Deals arrived then the hostess last of all. Lucinda had made a real effort for their last dinner on the island for a while and appeared at the door dressed more for a smart Mayfair party than supper at the big house on a small island.

"Are you joining us tonight, George? Ilonka thought you were going to be out." George confirmed that he was in fact going to dine with them all that evening. He didn't feel much like eating but in reality, he had nowhere else to go. He thought he would just stay there and follow the example of his parents and their friends and get pissed.

Sunday dawned another bright and warm morning – the sort of day that bought joy to the hearts of the holidaymakers on the island taking a break from their mainland lives. Natural beauty and an apparent harmonious and friendly population striving together to beat the odds of the remoteness of their Hebridean home and the logistical challenges it posed.

Fortunately for the prospect of repeat bookings few of the holiday visitors ever saw beneath those seemingly tranquil community waters at the torrent that frothed and boiled, the jealousies and feuds that clouded the lives of so many of the people in the place leaving dark shadows across many relationships.

There was no Telford family unity to be seen as the ferry docked that afternoon. Lord and Lady Telford in a group with their friends. Young George watching by himself passing the time of day with visitors and locals as they walked by, and Andrew and Alice, tucked behind the terminal building. Just the two of them – Alice going off to see her oldest friend Kitty, Andrew trying to hide his inner turmoil as he saw his life changing for the worse with nothing he could do to stop it happening. At least he had Alice. She was the one certainty in his life. Away today, back the following Sunday to begin planning the next stage of their lives together. Different? Probably. But together they would cope and build something new. Andrew felt nothing but contempt for Lord Telford but had come to understand George's position, a bit.

After all the passengers had embarked the boat Andrew watched as George wandered off without waiting for the ferry to leave. He on the other hand walked to the end of the ro-ro pier waving to Alice as she waved back from the stern of the boat. It was the first time they had been apart in the two years of their relationship. Andrew felt an immediate sense of loss exacerbated by the fact that he couldn't think of where to go from his stance on the pier. Obviously not to the big house. Not to his mother's. He didn't want to go back to his own cottage at the lighthouse all alone, just yet. For no particular reason he decided to call in again on his old teachers.

Flora suggested tea in the subdued manner of someone offering comfort to the recently bereaved, and Andrew accepted. As she went off into the kitchen he and Alastair sat down in the usual seats in front of the window – the ferry was just visible on the horizon.

Now retired Alastair had dropped the caution of avoiding controversy and had several conversations with key figures on the island to try and gauge the mood of the community. He told Andrew that there was a real feeling of anger amongst the locals as they began to realise the implications for the wider population of what was a straight forward family dispute. There were now six other people working in the seaweed business and between them they had 5 children at the school, half the roll. The hotel was booming bringing people from far and wide and the number of locals employed there had shot up with that success. The thought of Lord Henry presiding over things had sent a shockwave through the place. He was largely unknown to most people here and those that did remember him had no hope or expectation that he had somehow gained the ability to run a complicated business like this. There was huge concern at the thought of him being responsible in any way for the future of the island.

"Even so Andrew I very much doubt that even the extreme consequences of what might happen will not be enough to shake out the complacency and fear that have held this place back for so long. There will be no uprising, I am afraid.

"There were only two people, just two out of everyone I spoke to, that were prepared to put up a fight and they were both pretty drunk in the bar when I spoke to them, and I'm sure once sober they would find an excuse and run.

Alastair shocked Andrew when he revealed the saddest thing was that the whole episode had made Flora and him question why they would want to remain on the island. There were quite a few people who say what Telford is doing is quite right. "You honestly would not believe the sort of things some say, and I'm not going to add to your burden by going into detail. There are, though, some very bitter and jealous people on this island who don't like seeing their neighbours getting on.

"It is almost as though one person's success is not a thing to be celebrated because the reality is that it rather highlights the lack of achievement of the others.

"It is a most destructive attitude and one that will hold this place, and many, many more other small communities like it, back by decades. I know things are tough for you and Alice at the moment but I can tell you this has been two of the most depressing days of my life. Long ago I realised that this was not a homogenous community, and I'm aware of all the feuds and fall outs. But I honestly thought that in the face of such wrongdoing, wrongdoing that will eventually affect everyone here, that our friends and neighbours might find the guts to stand up for what is right. Sadly they will not." It pained him to see the effect these truthful words were having on Andrew. When Flora came back with the tea there was a heavy silence in the room.

Andrew had seen the way the people behaved for long enough to realise that if there was a call for self-sacrifice, even modest self-sacrifice in the name of a greater good then most of the people amongst whom he had grown up were not going to rise to the cause.

The Edward family, he had come to realise, were everybody's friends when it was represented by his father drunk in the pub. You could have a laugh with, and at, Jim Edward and feel better about yourself. But when his son had the audacity to make a go of things, to work hard, make money and create a business that looked successful, well that was a different thing. Getting above himself. Who does he think he is? Living with the laird's daughter. He'd heard it all before, usually overheard to be accurate, snide comments from the rag tag assortment of hippies, losers and idlers that sought out peaceful backwaters like this in which to hide their failure.

"Alastair I understand completely what you are saying. I'm really grateful that you tried to get some support going for us but I'm not at all surprised that there is none to speak of. It's the nature of here, isn't it. Everyone loves everyone else, everyone loves the island, but if anyone has to do something difficult to protect our futures, well 'fuck it' they say."

He was mortified as the f word left his lips. Andrew still felt pretty uncomfortable being on first name terms with his former teachers even all these years later, swearing like that in their sitting room was unforgiveable.

He jumped up and apologised to Flora who claimed not to have heard anything amiss. She told him to sit and laid the tray on the table between the two chairs and stood upright looking out of the window as the sun continued its westward journey sending shimmering lights across the near still waters of the ocean. The ferry had now completely disappeared over the horizon.

"What I have never been able to understand, Andrew," said Flora beginning to pour out the tea, "is the way many of the people that have come to live here over the years that Alistair and I have been here, no most of them, say they have been drawn here by the beauty of the place. It is, to hear some of them speak, almost a spiritual pull that has made them give up their mainland lives and face the challenges of living in this remote community.

"But within sometimes just a matter of weeks, you never see them out. Their children that came here to run free on the hills and the beaches, end up sitting in the house virtually all summer long watching television and playing video games.

"Then the very same parents will be in the bar complaining that there's nothing here for children. They soon forget the reasons that they claim bought them here and go back to an attitude of entitlement and dependence. You know as well as we do don't you? You hear it all the time: "Someone has to do something. We want this, we want that, and we want someone else to do it for us.""

"It is tragic. We've seen it happen to so many people. Your family is rather the exception but you will forgive me if I say that you got off to a bad start here. Nothing to do with you, but your mum and dad came here for an easy time, and it was an easy time that cut your father's life short."

Tea was taken quickly and Andrew left. As they heard the Land Rover drive away Alastair and Flora concluded with a heavy heart what to them seemed blindingly obvious: The least painful way to end this trauma would be for Andrew to sacrifice his happiness and leave here, by himself. Surrender to the wishes of Alice's parents' demands. He would get over Alice in time – but that was a conclusion neither of them would have ever voiced in public. How could it be in the 21st century that such unhappiness should be visited on two such decent hard working young people out of what? They could not agree the word should be.

That night, for the first time in two years, Andrew was at home at the lighthouse, by himself. He couldn't settle. With his life in such turmoil there could be no rest. As the various difficulties he faced kept running through his mind he could find no acceptable solutions. Each thought seemed to bring a new problem. He tried a whisky and when that didn't work he tried another. The television went on, then off, then the world pipe band championships – then his old pipe tutor's recording of Lament for the Children. That and the dram had a calming influence.

The tune was composed to mark the deaths of seven of the author's eight sons and though it dates from the mid 17th century Andrew always found it moving, especially the way it was played by his old teacher Patrick Young.

The following morning he arrived at the sheds at the usual time to find Kenny was already there setting up for the day's processing. Though as soon as Andrew arrived he stopped what he was doing and the pair of them began urgently going over their predicament. Where they were and what might happen. One thing was clear. They agreed that if the Telfords wanted to play dirty they could say that Island Alginates was in breach of its lease on the sheds. They had done lots of work to the building with only young George's verbal approval. "Do what you want guys, I'm never going to want them back. Just keep it tidy." had been his standard response to any request for permission to alter this or that, add or take away.

It was clear to Andrew that the Telfords were going to play dirty. Kenny wasn't so sure, but he was one removed from the centre of things.

"Surely they can see what I've created here, Drew – well me and you. There's a real business with real jobs bringing money onto their fucking island. Do they hate you so much that they will kill us dead – what the hell have you done to them?"

That was an oft heard question from Kenny. He simply found Lord Telford's class based hatred of Drew literally incomprehensible. Kenny was a simple straightforward man who saw people for what they are, not where they came from or which school they went to. He found it extremely hard to understand how anyone could do it any other way.

"Kenny I like to think that they don't hate me, for being me, they hate me because I didn't go to a posh school, dad drank too much and mum used to clean for them. They don't want Lady Alice marrying the cleaner's laddie – that's it in a nutshell."

"Well that may be the case Drew – but I'm not going to go without a fight. They better be ready for me. I've put too much into this, worked too hard for some fucking old snob, fucking greedy old snob, to take it away for no good fucking reason."

The opening sentence of the solicitor's letter from the Telford's Edinburgh lawyers, sent by email for speed, infuriated Kenny and devastated Andrew.

"We are instructed by Lord Emberton to require immediate vacant possession of the harbour sheds leased by Island Alginates Ltd, the terms of which the company is in basic and fundamental breach of."

Kenny's fury was on a scale Andrew had never seen before. "Cunts. They are just lying fucking cunts."

Andrew's devastation was caused by the fact the lease termination had been sent in the name of Lord Emberton. Their friendship was over. What would this mean for his relationship with Alice. Was she going to have to choose between Andrew and her own family? Did it have to be one of the other? He supposed it did. Andrew could see no other way. If their relationship was going to survive Alice would have to cut her ties with her family. Could he expect that of her, even if it was what she wanted.

Tuesday saw no work done at the Alginates. Kenny spent the day at home constantly talking to lawyers or Caroline or business advisors or the bank or anyone that might be able to help.

Andrew tried over and over again to call Alice but there can have been no reception at Kitty's house because her phone just went straight to voicemail, not even one ring.

He felt the only people he could talk to were Flora and Alastair and so for a third time in just those few days he went round again. Tea and chat. Lots of both. He eventually left their house with confirmation of the conclusion he had come to during his evening of whisky and pibroch the night before. The only solution to everyone's problems was for Andrew to leave the island. Quit his job and go somewhere else where the skills he had built up in the seaweed business might be appreciated. His only nagging doubt was whether Alice would come with him. Surely she would. He wanted to find out for certain but still her phone was just dead. He tried messaging her, he phoned a couple of her friends but they hadn't heard from her and didn't have Kitty's numbers.

As he left the Morton's house to head home he decided to stop off at the shop, buy something for tea and a bottle of whisky. He'd get his mother and Kenny round and tell them what he had decided. He was going to go, and go soon.

There were a couple of tourists ahead of him at the till so Andrew waited patiently as their groceries were rung through. Peter McGilvaray's behind the counter chat was painful, but the tourists loved it. He was a real island "character".

When it came to Andrew's turn the shopkeepers face became serious. "Hi Andrew. Is this it?" pointing to the pile of groceries and whisky. "Aye"

"Is it true the Telfords are chucking you and Kenny out of the harbour sheds? They say it's because Lord Telford doesn't like you going out with Alice. Is that right?"

"Aye Peter, something like that."

"That's terrible Drew, really terrible. This place needs to hang on to its young people. You guys are the future. There's no future for an island full of old folk like me. Something ought to be done about this, it really should."

Andrew looked at him in silence. "Bastard" he thought. "Fucking bastard".

Chapter 19

In those last few seconds in the island store Andrew's plan changed dramatically. McGilvaray's two faced hypocrisy sent him into another blinding rage. He resolved as he walked out of the shop clutching his purchases so show McGilvaray, Telford, George, the world exactly what he was made of and that he would not be driven from his business, his home, his island by an aristocratic throwback with an overblown sense of his own importance. He was going to fight it head on and win. That fight, he concluded, started right now.

There was, for Andrew, no choice. He had been forced to fight hard for most of his life for the causes that mattered. Mastering the pipes, coping with his dysfunctional parents and the premature death of his father. Nearly dying in that savage attack and the long haul back to full health. The sheer bloody hard work with Kenny to build a business and, with it, a life for himself. Then Alice. She meant more to him than any of it, or all of it put together. He could cope with loosing most of what he had – but not Alice.

Instead of heading back to the lighthouse Andrew went the other way towards the big house. He was by now so angry he couldn't think straight. He knew he wanted to see George, to confront him, to get him to man up to his father. Just how that was going to be done was not a clearly formed plan even by the time he arrived at his destination some 20 minutes later. His drive along the single track road had been interrupted by oncoming tourists, but for once the island politeness towards the all important visitors was not on show. He simply stared ahead and forced whatever was in his way to creep gingerly onto the verge no doubt hoping to avoid bogs and ditches that may be lurking in the long grass.

So it was the Andrew's Land Rover crunched to a halt right at the front door. He left it in such a hurry the driver's door was left open as he ran up the steps and into the hall.

George looked physically shocked as Andrew burst into the library where he was deeply engaged in his never ending task of trying to sort out the estate papers.

As Andrew stared at him he struggled to find the words. To be honest he wasn't all that sure why he had gone there. There was nothing all that new to discuss, other than the new resolve engendered by McGilvaray's dishonesty.

George's inability to speak was mainly brought about by the raw anger he recognised in Drew's face. He could immediately sense a looming conflict.

After a pause of a few seconds Drew broke the silence. Speaking unusually quietly he said simply: "George. This has got out of hand you are going to have to put a stop to this for everyone's sake. Particularly yours. If you don't you're going to end up looking like a bigger arse than your father – and that will be some achievement. At least he just fucked up the common people he didn't care about. You are fucking up your friends and your sister and it's pathetic.

"You are going to have to man up and tell your father to keep out of it. He can't win. Alice and I are together for good. Either here running a successful business and working with you – or somewhere else. Anywhere else. If he makes her choose between the Telfords and me it'll be him that is the biggest looser. And what are you going to do if that happens and Alice and I move off and start a new life somewhere else. Just live here in this house all by yourself with everyone around you thinking you are a spineless jerk who was too frightened of his father to do what is right.

"When Alice gets back on Sunday you need to tell her that you are on her side, tell the lawyers to forget the eviction and tell your father to move into the 21st century." Drew left those instructions hanging and stared intently at George to reinforce the seriousness of the situation.

"Drew – How many times to I have to tell you. I can't do anything about it. I have no say. It's not up to me. I have nothing to win and everything to loose. If I go against the old man then I'm out of here and Uncle Henry takes over and the whole place is screwed."

Without hesitation Drew told him just how wrong he was. "You have to call his bluff. He's surely not so stupid that he will risk ruining this place out of pure spite. Risk putting Henry in charge when he knows full well the guy's a complete fucking idiot. Are you seriously telling me that your father is so stupid and spiteful that he would risk everything you people have here just to stop me and Alice being happy? Are you? Are you really?

"Get some balls George and stand up for your friend and your sister. Stand up for the people that will loose their jobs if this eviction goes ahead. Stand up for the future of the island – your fucking island. Do you honestly care so little for the people you've grown up with that you will see this disaster happen.

"It's not just me and Kenny --- its everyone – a lot of people. Six guys with young families. You're not going to give them a job are you so they'll have to go. Five kids lost from the school. Who's left?"

By this point Andrew was so angry he was beginning to loose control. He also realised, though, that this was likely to be the very last chance he had of making George listen and stand up not only for his sister and his friend but for the whole island community that he had grown up amongst.

He paused his onslaught to try and ascertain if it was getting him anywhere. To see if the power of his argument was even beginning to make George understand the dire consequence of blindly following his father's instructions.

It had not. In fact George's response confirmed in Andrew's mind that whatever his future held it would not be on the island. It was a response so crass, so pompous and so lacking in comprehension of the position he was in as to leave Andrew in no doubt, no doubt at all, that the person he had thought of as his friend for so many years, for so much of his life, was a complete and utter spineless idiot. God help the future of the people of this community.

"Drew for the purpose of this conversation, this issue we are dealing with, it would be helpful if you were to understand that in me you are dealing with two people. Of course first and foremost I'm George, your friend. I hope your best friend considering all we have shared.

"But at the same time you have to realise that I am also Lord Emberton – the person who increasingly has to shoulder the responsibility of ensuring my family maintains its position in the world and the value of our holdings.

"George is, and always will be your friend. Lord Emberton has wider responsibilities and those are what have to take priority at the moment.

Andrew's rage dissipated as those asinine words revealed George to be the shallow witless prat he always feared he might be. Quietly he laid it on the line: "Remember all those years ago on the beach – and that Polish kid. You were gutless then and I carried the can and now its happening all over again. You are disgusting." He couldn't bring himself to continue the confrontation a moment longer. Without another word he spun round and walked out of the library and out of the big house for the last time.

Getting back to the lighthouse in near record time Andrew went straight into his mum and Kenny's cottage and recounted the conversation he had just had as best as he could remember through the clouds of rage. He felt acutely embarrassed, though he should not have, telling the bit about having to regard George as two people.

Caroline was less than helpful with her response. "I've told you for years that you're dancing with the devil thinking you are friends with these people."

Kenny had a little more to say. He had been giving it a lot of thought, of course, and come to the conclusion that they could not reply on help from the locals so they would have to turn to the wider world for support to save their business.

"You know that guy who comes here a lot with his family, Raymond Douglas – nice guy. He's head of a big public relations agency in Glasgow and in the past he's told me he'd be happy to help with the business. I phoned him yesterday and told him what was going on here and how we face losing the business and the island faces losing so many young people as a result. He reckoned a story like that with you and Alice in the middle of it would be great for the Daily Mail. He reckoned other papers would pick it up – maybe the tv too and that could force Telford to see sense and back off. What do you think? Are you up for that? Would Alice be?"

"I don't know, Kenny," said Drew thoughtfully. "I'm certainly willing to give it a go, but I don't know about Alice – it's her family after all. I know the one thing she is not prepared to do in all of this is have a complete fallout with her parents and her brother. She seems to think there is a way through this for us.

"She's going back to London today from her friends house and I'll be able to speak to her tonight and see what she thinks. When do you need to let Raymond know?"

"He seemed keen to get the ball rolling as soon as. You speak to Alice and you'll have to tell her it's the only way this can work for everyone. For her, for you and for me and your mum.

"Make sure she understands how important this could be."

"I know Kenny but I'm not sure she would be all that keen to end up in the Daily Mail slagging off her family, even though it is her favourite paper," he added with a chuckle – a rare sight these days.

"Drew this is about the future of all of us. A bit of a stir in the papers will soon be forgotten. What might happen here will affect some of us for ever."

At that Andrew took his leave and wandered out of the cottage, not to go home but to walk round the outside of the lighthouse enclosure to the North side and the view of the open sea. There he sat down with his back against the whitewashed tower staring out at the waves crashing onto the rocky shore. He could hear the deep rumble of the bigger waves as they broke on the approach to the rocks shifting boulders many feet below the surface with their force. It was a noise he had listened to for hours lying in bed in the cottage. It made him think of Alice and what he had to lose.

It was at that point that he realised his dream was over. He could never win this fight. He knew that he did not have what it would take to beat the Telfords. The talk of newspaper headlines confirmed his worst hears. He would have to beat the Telfords and turn Alice against her own family. Force her into the sort of feud that tears families apart and might never be ended. He couldn't ask her to do that. He wouldn't. He loved her too much. Somehow, watching the waves had brought a clarity of mind to

Andrew that had been missing these past few weeks since the trouble began. He even, for a moment, contemplated entering those waves to allow them to end his pain. That was just stupid.

Andrew closed his eyes and listened to the sea and the birds as he came to the inevitable conclusion that he was the problem. He had overstepped the mark. His mum and dad, God rest him, were right all along. A kid like him had no business being friends with the likes of George and his aristocratic Telford family. Maybe if they had met somewhere else, at university or in a job, things might have been different. Then they would have been equals. But here, on the island where the Telfords had everything and everyone else had virtually nothing it could never work.

Andrew rolled over as if overwhelmed by the force of his realisation and buried his eyes into his arm. The noise of the gulls and the sea was replaced with his gentle sobbing. The pain he was feeling was almost as bad as the agony he was suffering as he came round on the island road all those years ago after being beaten senseless by George's cowardly pals.

It took Andrew nearly an hour to summon up sufficient interest in his future to stand up and walk the few steps home. As he did he realised when he spoke to Alice shortly he would have to tell her what he had decided. He was clear that it had to be his decision. He could not, he would not, expect her to give up the certainty of her life and future and all the comfort and privilege that came with it, to take a gamble on him. He walked round the lighthouse walls again and into his own home and was about to pick up the phone when Kenny came into the room.

"Drew, more bad news I'm afraid. Raymond phoned me a while ago and he says the Daily Mail aren't all that interested in the story. He says they think what is happening is disgusting but because we have seriously breached our lease of the sheds they reckon it means the story isn't worth doing. Something about it looking like we are just trying to get out of using the sheds badly, some crap like that. He reckons it's not worth pushing."

"Don't worry Kenny I've been doing a lot of thinking." Andrew tried to keep the tears of the previous hour private, but he could not. "I'm the one who has made a mess of everything. Mum and Dad were right. Even fucking Sandy and McGilvaray. I've got carried away. I really believed Alice and I had a future together, here on the island. But I'm not going to ask her to give up her family for me. I love her too much for that."

Andrew was shocked by his honesty in front of Kenny. For his part Kenny was shocked by Drew's tears. He didn't think he was the crying kind.

"Drew I know what you are saying but you can't let these bastards fuck up your life. You've got to look to the future, your future. Telford may be a big shot here – but in real life he's nothing. No one. This is about the future – not the past of some English arse who thinks he's God."

"You are right Kenny. It is about the future. It's the future of a lot more people than me. George is as bad as his father. His mind is made up and I'm not going to change it. So it's up to me. I can keep going. Keep fighting them. But I'm not the one who loses. That's you, and mum, and the guys who work with us, and their families. What if you all have to leave. It's the future of the school, the future of this whole island. I'm not going to risk that, just for me."

"Drew its not like that. It's them that's at fault, not you," but Andrew stopped him dead in his tracks. "Kenny I am the only one who can save this. I'm the only one that can make sure that you and mum have a future here, a future you've both worked hard for, do you honestly think I should keep going the way I am and see everything you have achieved thrown out the door. I wouldn't do it to you and I couldn't do it to my mum. You saved her Kenny. She would have ended up like Dad if it hadn't been for you. I owe you.

"And what about everyone else." By now the tears were flooding down Andrew's face and his voice was shaking. Faced with such emotion Kenny gave up. Drew was right and Kenny knew it.

That evening Andrew finally managed to get through to Alice. She was back in London and heading home to the island on Sunday's ferry. Gently Andrew explained to her the conclusion he had come to. It was the only conclusion he could arrive at, for everyone's sake.

He spoke slowly because of a need to avoid the phrases he knew would start his tears flowing again. For nearly four hours the pair talked round and round in circles until finally, exhausted,

Alice said leave it. "Leave it for now Drew, I'm home the day after tomorrow, nothing's going to happen before then. I'm too tired to keep going right now. I'm sure that together you and I will make my brother face up to reality and see that he is in danger of killing the whole island if he doesn't get some balls."

With that they said lingering good nights and hung up.

Despite the turmoil of the day Drew quickly fell asleep and when he woke the next morning he found his resolve to end the whole thing on his terms had not lessened at all. He phoned Alastair Morton and said his mind was made up and recounted the whole story of how he had reached that conclusion. He was the problem and he was going to solve it by leaving the island for good. It was blindly obvious he was in total turmoil.

After a cup of coffee Andrew walked back to the spot by the lighthouse where just the day before he had found the answers he had been looking for over the preceding weeks. This time he had his laptop with him and set about writing a long email letter to Alice bearing his soul and explaining his departure. For that was what he had decided. He was going to leave the island – tomorrow on the ferry that will just have bought Alice home to him, or so she would have thought.

He had a plan in his head. He would send her his email of explanation and farewell as the ferry approached as there was no signal for her to receive the news. News was how he thought of it. Not a devastating conclusion to a long affair, just news. For he kind of thought that she may well be coming to the same conclusion as him.

Then he would be waiting on the pier as she came down the gangway. They would have just a matter of minutes to talk before he had to go, the gangway would be raised and the ferry would sail out carrying him to a new life, a future very different from the one he had planned. Once home she would get the email and life could get back to normal. Hopefully.

It was at times like this Andrew wished he had spent less time on the pipes and more time studying at school. Writing didn't come naturally to him and dealing with such emotional matters took him an age to get the words right. He read and reread his email agonising over every word. Eventually he was as sure as he could be that he had said everything he wanted to say and said

230

it in a manner that would do least damage. He was grown up enough to understand that if this was not what Alice wanted, as he thought it might not be, then he had better not remove himself from her life leaving her with a sense of bitterness towards her family. That would simply negate his sacrifice.

So that was it. The email saved to drafts. He went back into the house found the biggest holdall he had and set about packing some essentials into it. He spent ages working out if he should take his pipes, and concluded he should. They could help him find somewhere to go. Plug back into the piping network. Find one of the many bands that his old friends had joined. It shouldn't take him all that long to get back playing to a decent level again. Friends – band – job – new life. Simple as that he thought.

First though to get through the next day. He decided to tell no one of his plan. He would just drive down to the Sunday ferry. People would think he was there to pick up Alice. Then at the last minute he'd go up the pier with his bag, say his carefully planned farewell at the foot of the gangway and he'd be off. The island could get on with its miserable life without him. He didn't even feel the need to tell his mum and Kenny. Once back in the world of the mobile phone signal he would phone his mother and tell her he had left, but maybe not reveal the finality of this departure.

He didn't keep his promise to visit his old teachers before the departure but did phone to say goodbye. Alastair said he would see him at the ferry terminal, maybe with Flora. The next day when the time came to walk down to the pier Flora said she couldn't face it. Alastair told her she had to go, they had been a big part of Andrew's life so far and if this was going to be the last chance they had to see him she would regret not being there. But Flora was resolute and once her mind was made up there is nothing that he can do to change it. She said being at the pier would just overwhelm her and make the going all that more difficult for Andrew and risk making a complete spectacle of herself. So Alastair set off alone for the ten minute walk down to the ferry worried that he too may have difficulty controlling his emotions. This whole episode had really crystalised his view of the island population. The people that in the past had earned at worst indifference were now carrying the burden of Alastair Morton's contempt for their two faced pathetic self interested response to a tragedy not just for two young people but for the whole island community.

Andrew was sitting in his Land Rover. He had deliberately parked some little distance from where the usual crowd gathered to watch the comings and goings. He wasn't in the mood for chat. He was actually a little afraid of what he might say to some of them. The two faced bastards.

It took an age for the ferry to berth and Andrew watched carefully as the ropes tightened and the crew set about lowering the gangway. He reckoned now was the time. It would take only a couple of minutes to reach the gangway by which time the first of the foot passengers would be coming down onto the pier. He got out of the vehicle and Alastair could see the sadness hanging over him. He hugged him, the first time that had ever happened, and patted him on the back and offered no more than a murmured "good luck". The former teacher was beginning to feel as bad as Flora feared she might have been. Andrew grabbed his bag and sprinted off towards the gangway without looking back and completely ignored the people he passed, some of whom tried to speak to him, and all of whom were totally oblivious to the painful human drama they were witnessing. He was really excited to see Alice again, to hug her but he knew the welcome embrace would be his last. The kiss of welcome the devastating and final goodbye. The tears returned but didn't stop him pushing past those ahead to try and be the first at the gangway.

As he neared his destination cars started coming out of the ferry's innards and driving down the pier. He had no interest in seeing who was arriving, it made no difference to him; there was only one returnee that he wanted to see, and then only briefly.

Fuck, Fuck, Fuck. He couldn't believe his eyes. Through his tears he saw Alice sitting in the front passenger seat of an emerging car. Someone must have offered her a lift to save her carrying her bag down the pier.

He froze to the spot without a clue what to do. If he ran down the pier to meet the car carrying the love of his life and say what he needed to say he wouldn't have time to get back to the gangway before it was raised and the ferry departed. But he couldn't just go. No hug. No kiss. No goodbye.

"You ok Drew?" asked a passing voice. He ignored the question as he agonised over his next step. "Go – you have to go" was the order from his brain and with only the slightest hesitation go he did.

He ran up the gangway and told the ticket collector he'd come back and buy one in a minute. Chucking his bag into a corner he went out onto the deck and climbed to the viewing platform at the bow of the boat just beneath the bridge windows to see if he could catch a glimpse of Alice.

She hadn't a clue what was going on. She had seen the Land Rover as the boat was coming in and had wanted to signal that she was coming off in a car but there had been no sign of Drew. She leapt out at the ferry office and asked if anyone knew what Drew was doing.

A helpful bystander said he didn't have a clue but whatever it was involved departing on the boat just now because he'd seen him walking up the gangway carrying a bag with him.

Alice suddenly realised it was the end. She had returned with a heavy heart but buoyed by her and Drew's resolve formed in that lengthy phone call to win through. Now she felt instantly distraught. If Drew wasn't there to meet her it could only mean one thing. Their relationship must be over.

That realisation hit her like a punch in the stomach. Such a hard and winding punch that she was barely able to breathe as she tried to run up the pier to where the ferry was slowly beginning its backward manoeuvre to leave the berth. She saw Drew watching her from high up. She shouted his name and was shocked as the word emerged from her mouth as more of a scream.

As the ferry picked up speed and began to turn for its voyage back to the mainland Alice realised any attempt at communication was pointless. She was too much of a lady to allow her emotions to be played out in public. So she stopped running and watched quietly as Drew disappeared from view. He didn't move, if he had they would have had an extra few moments of eye contact.

Up on the boat Andrew found himself frozen to the spot. He'd seen Alice running up the pier and heard her agonised scream. But there was nothing he could do. The die was cast.

Instead of looking at the girl who had brought him so much joy and contentment over the past few years Andrew stared straight ahead as the ferry turned giving him a panorama of the island that had been home for his whole life certain in his own mind that this would be the last time he saw it.

The years of frequent travel on the ferry meant Andrew was known to most of the crew. As one of the longer serving members walked past he turned to the near distraught young man and bought him back to earth with a bump. "Drew you'd better go and buy your ticket now – they're getting a bit grumpy down below."

The end